One Bead of

GOLD

by

LORRAINE STANTON

Order this book online at www.trafford.com
or email orders@trafford.com

Most Trafford titles are also available at major online book retailers.

Printed in the United States of America.

ISBN: 978-1-4269-6664-4 (sc)
ISBN: 978-1-4269-6665-1 (hc)
ISBN: 978-1-4269-6663-7 (e)

Library of Congress Control Number: 2011906229

Trafford rev. 05/13/2011

 www.trafford.com

North America & international
toll-free: 1 888 232 4444 (USA & Canada)
phone: 250 383 6864 ✦ fax: 812 355 4082

One Bead of Gold

Contents

One Bead of Gold

by

Lorraine Stanton

Chapter One:

The Morning After

A strange noise woke Jacqueline. She opened her eyes, looked upwards and tensed.

Something was above her head.

Keeping a wary watch on it, not moving a muscle, barely breathing, she cast around in her mind for an explanation only to realise she didn't know where she was, how she got there or what that big thing over her head could possibly be.

'I'm trapped!' she thought in startled horror.

Lying stiffly in the bed, her fists clenched beside her, Jacqueline stared up at the thing in the gloom, straining her ears for any sound that would give her a hint of where she was or what had happened to her.

But the sounds made no sense either.

Instead of hearing the ordinary early morning bird-type noises and the first traffic mumbles of the day, the only scraps of sound Jacqueline could detect were things she simply could not identify.

Swallowing against the steadily swelling fear, Jacqueline scrunched her eyes tight shut to listen as hard as she could, shutting out the distraction of sight; even supressing her breathing so that its noise wouldn't hide any familiar sounds she might catch.

Just as she began to convince herself she could hear a bird, she distinctly heard something completely alien.

A sort of snort-thump.

Her eyes sprang wide open.

One gasp. No more – 'it' might hear her.

She quietened her breaths again, but couldn't stop her heart pounding so loudly she couldn't hear over it.

Oh, yes, she could! She jumped at a sudden, loud noise.

There! What's that? A man. Yelling. No - it's more like he's calling something. She relaxed slightly. The man didn't seem angry. He was just saying things loudly as if he wanted someone a long way away to hear him. He made no sense to Jacqueline. He'd call one word or two. Then again. Then he'd whistle. Then the call or the whistle again, but the whistles were not any sort of tune.

Although she didn't seem to be in any immediate danger, Jacqueline couldn't relax completely. Too many times she had heard her father speak loudly outside the house, then was beaten as soon as he saw her when he walked inside.

She looked around wildly. She didn't know where she was, where she could hide, how to get away. She still didn't know what that thing over her head could be. It trapped her.

A dog barked. That noise again - the snort-thump. Blowing. The footsteps of a wooden legged giant. And more and more of all that. Lots and lots of it. Closer, closer. The calls and whistles, too. Right beside the room she was in. She stared at the wall in terror. What was it? Would it get her?

Then there was a moo-sound – a moo? – 'It's a cow, then,' she thought.

Jacqueline let her breath out in a huge sigh of relief. 'That must be the noise cows make when they walk. It's only cows. Lots of cows. That man has a dog and cows. Cor, I'm in a sort of farm place. Hey! Bonzer! Real cows and a dog and maybe I'll can touch them!'

It wasn't until she had that thought that she was able to relax and curl cosily in the warm bed. Now the strangeness of the whistle puzzled her instead of frightening her. It wasn't a bit like a tune. In fact, it was more like the way the man called to his dog, which seemed really weird.

The noises moved like a parade past the house. When they were all gone they left behind the bird songs that Jacqueline had been unable to hear before, with the sound of someone else breathing.

Jacqueline cringed to realise there was breathing in the room. She looked cautiously about herself until she made out a cot in the gloom. Once she was sure it was a cot she could see against the opposite wall, she was instantly sure that the little bundled shape she could almost see was her baby sister sleeping in the cot.

'Aw, that's all it is. Hey! If Lucinda's here, maybe Jonathan is too. They didn't lock me up by myself. Righto!'

Heartened, Jacqueline clambered out of bed and discovered that the frightening thing that had been over her head was the underneath of another bed.

'Crikey! Two beds on top of each other!'

Fascinated, Jacqueline examined the bunks. There was a ladder up the foot boards to give easy access to the top bunk. They appeared to be sturdy enough, so with a feeling of tremendous risk, she slowly climbed the ladder. A wide smile showed her relief when she was sure she was safe up on the top bunk. 'Oh, boy. This is mighty!'

No one was in the top bunk, although it was unmade as if someone had just slept there. Since it was barely dawn as far as Jacqueline could tell, she thought whoever it was must rise in the middle of the night. She pondered peacefully, safe from intrusion for a little while.

'I could fancy sleeping way up high like this. I'd even be above people's heads, I bet. Jonathan would have loved this.'

The thought of her brother brought Jacqueline back to reality with a shock.

'Jonathan! That's who it was! He was here when I was asleep and now they've taken him and I'll never see him again.' In grief she punched the bedding. 'I knew it. I knew it. They'll never let us see each other again now that they've got us. Ma told us and told us we'd never see each other again if the police got us, but we went with them anyway. This time she didn't lie. We're locked up by ourselves so we can't help each other get away.'

Tears pricking her eyelids, Jacqueline slowly turned to climb down the ladder. The memories of what had happened were coming back to her.

The children had all been brought to this house in the middle of the night.

One more fight between her parents had woken her. Her mother shouting again in that terrible sergeant-major's voice of hers. Her father swearing at her mother. The mother threw things at the father. There was a scuffle, hitting, shouting, accusing, swearing, menacing. The mother phoned the police, threatening to tell about the stolen and smuggled goods hidden in the garage. The father yanked the big, black phone out of the living-room wall, wooden box and all, making a horrible tearing noise. Jacqueline and Jonathan hid in the dark dining room staring at the hole in the living room wall, horrified.

Lucinda stood up in her cot, howling, hanging on to the top of the rails in the dark. The children could make out the dim shape of her white nightie across the living room through the open door of the baby's room. Their father bellowed at her to shut up, scaring her into screaming twice as loudly. In two strides he was beside her, his fist raised. He knocked her right across the cot. She bashed into the bars on the other side and lay quietly, gasping.

Jacqueline and Jonathan crept under the dining room table where they could peek out from under the edge of the tablecloth but had a better chance of not being seen.

Their mother shrieked at their father. He punched her. She clawed back, calling him names. Blows were traded. Insults.

Palpable hatred.

Jonathan crept towards the kitchen, intending to get a knife and kill his father to save his mother. Lucinda recovered her breath and began to howl. Jacqueline sped in terror to her bedroom to hide. A blow from their mother turned their father's head. He caught sight of a movement past the living room door. "What are you bloody kids doing out of bed? I'll teach you!"

He was slowed down by their mother hauling on his arm, hitting at him, yelling at him, but still Jonathan was caught as he tried to get back to the bedroom.

More shouting. Beating. Swearing. The baby wailing on and on and on.

Some people came and found Jacqueline hiding under Jonathan's bed. They put her in a car with the other two and told her they'd all be alright now. No one would ever hit them again. She was too weary and sick to care.

They were driven to a strange building all stark and white inside that smelled like the dentist's. A man doctor looked at all three children. He even made them take their night clothes off and pressed on the sore spots, even the old sore spots from last time that didn't really hurt any more until he said, "Does this hurt?" and made it hurt with his fingers. He wasn't even their doctor. Jacqueline hated him.

She hated the nurse that made her do what he said. Worse yet, some rude people took photos of the bruises and marks and people like police asked really nosy questions about home. They were pretending they weren't police, but Jacqueline wasn't fooled. She knew who they were whether they wore uniforms or not and she despised them for thinking they could fool her. She hated them all. She wouldn't do or say anything they wanted. They couldn't make her tell on her parents.

After they were there for what seemed like forever, the doctor gave them something 'to make them feel better'. It made them feel dopey. The nosy people put them in another car with a man driving and a lady in the back with them.

Jacqueline wouldn't let the lady hold Lucinda. She fought to have the baby on her own lap. Lucinda clung to her, terrified of the strangers, so the lady had to give in. "They all exhibit this strong separation anxiety," the man said and Jacqueline hated him, too.

Turning Lucinda so that the icky lady couldn't make silly faces and make friends with her, Jacqueline hugged the baby to herself, ignoring how the weight hurt her legs. Through the thinness of her nightdress she could clearly feel the lumps on Lucinda's head from crashing into the bars of her cot when their father had hit her. The hard lumps against her chest made Jacqueline feel as if she had a knife twisting in her stomach.

She hated her father with a burning hot loathing and wished she had told the nosy people everything he did so that he would get into trouble. She wished the icky lady would shut up.

As the car hummed out of the lights of the city into the darkness of the countryside the children squeezed together as tightly as they could. They had fought hard to prevent the icky lady from sitting between them and now they tried just as hard to avoid any touch from her, shrinking away from her consoling pats and glaring balefully up at her when she tried to comfort them with kindly words, which she did constantly. The woman seemed too stupid to realise that they were too clever to be taken in by her. Their fear and loathing turned to contempt. If this was how smart the welfare workers were, Jacqueline was sure she and Jonathan would have no difficulty getting away from them.

Their parents had warned them over and over again that the police would take them away and lock them up where they would never see one another again. Then they would grow up behind bars, never knowing what had happened to the others or to their mummy and daddy. The children had lived in terror of that, but now that it was happening it looked like there was a chance they could escape and make their way home.

Yet as the car took them further and further from everything familiar they pressed tightly against one another, keeping their distance from the welfare worker and cuddling Lucinda as she dozed off. They wanted to be touching and holding her tightly forever. For all of her life. They felt that they would only survive as long as they were touching one another.

Just the same, Jacqueline couldn't bring herself to look at Jonathan. She knew he was all swollen and discoloured, that almost any touch anywhere on his body hurt him. Looking at him reminded her of the times she had looked like that and felt like that; when she had been kept home from school because of 'falls' or 'flu' or an 'illness in the family'. She had to always remember what excuse it was to keep her out of sight until any marks that showed had faded. It was one of the leaping horrors of her life that she would forget and say the wrong thing and a teacher would ask questions, which would end up with Jacqueline being locked up in one of those places for bad children.

Their mother was better than their father at making sure nothing showed. He would just get mad and hit out blindly, but their mother more often made sure anything she did to the children wouldn't cause awkward questions.

Thinking of how much some of her mother's punishments hurt, Jacqueline trembled, closed her eyes and leaned against Jonathan. She knew that her weight was causing him pain, but she needed the touch of him. Guilty about making it worse for him, she pulled back after a moment and looked away. She didn't dare speak to him where they might be heard and she couldn't bring herself to look at him. She could almost feel his pain as it was.

Their grogginess made her uneasy that they were being carted off somewhere and wouldn't be able to remember how to get back home. She wanted to warn him not to fall asleep so that they could both watch where they were going to try to make note of landmarks to help them find their way back home when they escaped, but the icky lady was still babbling at them about how they need never be afraid again. Jacqueline was afraid to say anything to Jonathan that the woman might hear and get her with later.

Despite his fear and pain, the thrumming of the car and the sedative lulled Jonathan to sleep, leaning heavily into Jacqueline which brought the hot, tight skin of his bruised eye into contact with her arm. She closed her eyes, but not being able to see him no longer helped her avoid the images of the times she had been beaten along with or instead of him.

She recalled one time her father had threatened to flail the hide right off her back when she hadn't done anything near as bad as driving off into the night with strangers.

Dread made her nauseous. She knew for sure they'd really get it this time. This time they might kill her.

Horror jerked Jacqueline back to the top bunk, back to her current problem of having lost Jonathan after all.

Recollecting that she didn't know where she was, Jacqueline began to search the room. She needed to find both hiding places and escape routes before anyone knew she was awake to stop her. She knew from many panic stricken dashes away from enraged parents that surprise was her first defense. Under other circumstances Jacqueline would have liked the room. It was spacious when compared with the pokey little square box she shared with Jonathan.

There was a sort of line of polished wood all the way around the room where ceilings usually joined walls, but in this room there was another stretch of wall above the moulding making the ceiling the highest one Jacqueline had ever seen. She turned on the spot, staring upwards in the faint light trying to imagine how high it really was and why anyone would build a house with such tall rooms. She liked the airy feeling it gave.

Obviously the rooms weren't built for giants because the door wasn't above ordinary height as far as she could tell.

The space between the top of the door and the moulding was filled with a window which was letting in the small amount of light in the room.

Jacqueline was entranced by the idea of having a window on the inside of the house. 'Cor, look at that. It wouldn't ever be real dark in here, even in the middle of the night, as long as there's light somewhere else in the house.' She looked to see if there was a way she could get up to the window above the door to look through it, but was nothing she could climb up that she could see. She might have been able to touch the line of wood from the top bunk, but it was on the wrong side of the room. The thought of the top bunk reminded her that she didn't know how to get to Jonathan so she dropped her gaze to ground level and looked all around from there. Almost at once she was distracted again.

At the head of the bunks was a heavily curtained window under which was a desk with a lamp on it, beside which was a bookshelf built into the adjoining wall. The bookshelf went all the way up to the moulding, full of books right to the topmost shelf.

Not believing her eyes, Jacqueline walked up to the bookshelf to have a closer look. "Cor, blimey, I'd have to climb up to get those high ones." In her amazement she spoke aloud, the sound of her voice startling her back to silence and making Lucinda snuffle in her sleep. Even while she held her breath afraid that someone would have heard her, Jacqueline couldn't take her eyes off the bookshelf. The idea of books in a bedroom, of being able to read any time she wanted to, struck her dumb with wonder. She couldn't tell what kind of books they were in the dim light and she was too afraid to touch them, but knowing they were there made her feel better in spite of herself. Reading was one of the few escapes she had.

She walked along the length of the bookshelf and found a chest of drawers where they ended. There were knick-knacks on the chest of drawers and pictures hanging over them, but it was too dark for her to be able to tell what the pictures were of.

Next was a wardrobe door standing open. Remembering her purpose she went into the pitch dark of the inside of the wardrobe to hunt for hiding places. She knew better than to turn on a light; that transom window would be sure to give her away.

The wardrobe was big enough to have clothes hanging on both sides instead of at the back. Awed, Jacqueline put out her hand to feel her way to the back, only to have it fall on drawers. "Gee," she breathed in disbelief. She had never heard of having a chest of drawers inside a wardrobe. She tested them for stability and climbed up into the musty darkness of clothes that had been hanging for years. Above the clothes she felt shelves. There were sure to be plenty of places to hide in there, if she could vanish in the tiny wardrobe in her own room.

Encouraged that she could get out of sight if ever she needed to, Jacqueline set about finding out whether or not she could escape. As well as the window at the head of the bunks there was a bigger one on the wall facing the foot of the bunks. She was impressed by the idea of having windows on two walls. The room she and Jonathan shared was a corner room, but it had only one window and that was not as big as the smaller one of these two.

She walked across the room to the bigger window. It had a sill wide enough to sit on. She had a fleeting picture of herself sitting on the windowsill reading on a summer evening and was sorry she didn't live in this place. The sill was low, at her mid-thigh, but the heavy dark curtains hung on brass rings from a stout wooden rod all the way up at the moulding.

'If the room isn't too high off the ground it should be real easy to climb out a window like this.'

She lifted one corner of the heavy curtain to peek out. Even though she moved cautiously in case 'they' were watching to catch her, the brightness outside took her by surprise and she jumped back, blinking. Moving carefully, giving her eyes a chance to adjust, she slid under the curtain and knelt on the sill.

In front of her was a wide, square lawn mowed short and neatly trimmed. The grass thinned out to the left side until it vanished altogether leaving only a carpet of brown pine needles under a row of tall pines that marched past the house in a straight line, a wire fence around their feet and the sunrise pinking their dark green heads. She could make out the outline of the house-roof in the sunlight against the trees.

'The sun rises in the east and sets in the west. It's rising behind me, so it'll set in front of me. That means that's west.' Being able to figure out which direction she was facing gave Jacqueline no thrill when she realised she had no idea in which direction her home lay.

To keep from giving in to the lost feeling that threatened to overwhelm her, she clenched her fists until her nails cut her palms and stared up at the trees. At first she was thinking about climbing up to see whether or not she could see where she was from the top. The trees were higher than the house, she was sure. Panic hovered beside her just waiting for a chance to take over. She didn't know how far she was from home. What if she was so far away she couldn't tell even from the tree tops where she was? What would she do? How could she get home, how could she find Jonathan? What would happen to them when they did get there?

She was only a little girl, seven years old and small for her age at that. How could she possibly take herself and her six year old brother who knew how far across the country? Not going back didn't occur to her.

Staring at the tree tops sparked one of her frequent day dreams; that she could fly. Slowly her fists unclenched as the mental pictures of flying to the tree tops out of her father's reach replaced the fear of being lost with defiant glee. She pictured how furious he would be if he could never get her. She watched the birds celebrate the dawn on topmost twigs and saw herself there with them, her father leaping about, yelling impotently far below.

Smiling to herself she looked around the lawn. It would be easy to jump from the window to the ground, and she was close enough to the side of the house that she could be between the house and the line of trees in no time flat.

The room was easy to get out of, easy to hide in and there were plenty of hiding places just outside the window. The window had no bars to keep her in. She didn't know how 'they' thought they could keep her in a place like that, but they had certainly made a mistake if they thought they could.

'This is too easy,' she thought as she climbed down and went back into the dark of the bedroom. 'Bet the windows're nailed shut and they think I'm too little to break the glass.'

She wandered, blind in the dark, to the window at the head of the bunks. It wasn't as dazzling there, since the trees blocked out a lot of the light. She could see the barbed wire nailed to the trees to make a fence, and between the trunks she could make out fields of grass. The cows must have walked past right under the trees to have sounded that close to her. She couldn't see the path they had walked along, but she could see there were no bars at that window, either. It would be even easier to vanish from that window right under the tree trunks.

The ease of escape puzzled her. She went over to the door and leaned on the wall beside it to listen and to think. All her life she had heard that she was going to end up behind bars. Now that she had been taken away, as she had been told she would if she was bad, she found herself in a place without bars. It occurred to her that her parents might have lied to her. They had before. It was also possible that she would be moved to the place with the bars once 'they' found out she was awake. That's what must have happened to Jonathan.

She could hear faint sounds of a radio through the crack in the door, which meant someone was awake. If 'they' hadn't taken Jonathan off she had to find him before they did, while it was still so easy to get away. No matter how afraid she was of what she would walk into when she opened the door, she had to find out what was on the other side if she wasn't locked in.

Grief and fear overcame her. She leaned her head against the wall, tears running down her cheeks. She rallied after a moment. 'I'll fix them! If that door's locked I can get out the window and if the windows're locked I can break the glass with something - a book, even.'

The defiance lent her the strength to make the effort to reach up on tip toe and turn the big, rattly, brass doorknob. The door squeaked, making her jump, but it did open.

Jacqueline cautiously peered around the door frame. Her heart was pounding, her palms sweating. This was the most dangerous part. To her right the passageway went off into the nether regions. No one there. She decided to hunt for Jonathan in the dark down there after she had found out what was in the lighted room in front of her. To her left the hallway ended at a closed door. She glanced over her shoulder repeatedly as she padded softly towards the light, her bare feet silent on the hall runner. She peeked carefully around the doorframe of the brightly lit room.

It was the huge kitchen-dining-living room of an old fashioned farm house. The first thing that caught her eye was a crackling wood-fire in the grate of a big grey stone fireplace on the south wall. On the same wall, in the corner closest to Jacqueline, a little, plump, white-haired lady stood with her back to Jacqueline, puttering at a sink under a window. The morning sunshine was beaming in the window, spotlighting the lady in between cheerful yellow gingham curtains and highlighting the eddies and swirls of fragrant steam rising from the pots and pans on the stove behind her.

Everything smelled of wood-smoke and perking coffee. The fire was crackling happily, the coffee was blurp, blurping, a canary was trilling contentedly out of sight somewhere, the old lady was humming and crooning quietly along with an old wireless set that sat on the windowsill in the sun.

Because the grandmother's back was to her and she seemed completely absorbed in her Les Paul and Mary Ford songs while she worked, Jacqueline felt secure enough to lean on the doorframe and soak up the dreamy contentedness of the scene.

Tense almost every waking moment of her life, Jacqueline took any chance she got to store up nice things inside herself against the times when all niceness stopped. The scents and sounds made such utter peacefulness that she couldn't resist them.

Suddenly a plump, dark-haired lady swooped on her from behind, chittering at her about how cold she must be without slippers and a dressing gown.

'Drat! Forgot to watch that other room!'

Scared senseless, Jacqueline stared around wildly for an escape but the lady caught her and carried her to a small wooden sofa in front of the kitchen fire where she was tucked under an old, homemade afghan. Then the older lady gave her a big mug full of hot cocoa.

Her fright dissolved as Jacqueline took the mug and blissfully drifted away from all harsh realities into the pleasures of the cocoa.

Ignoring the handle, she wrapped her hands right around the warm mug. She hadn't felt cold before, but now she noticed her fingers and toes were tingling as they thawed. She put her face right down over the wide mug mouth to thaw her nose tip, too. The mug smelled chocolatey and milky and it almost burned her fingers it was so toasty warm. The steam warmed her face while making a teeney chill as it drifted past the sides of her forehead into the cooler autumn morning air. There were spoonsful of top cream floating on the cocoa, slowly melting into buttery droplets.

Jacqueline's only thought was, 'They got live cows here.'

She touched the bit of cream with the tip of her tongue, gently so she wouldn't burn herself, then closed her eyes to allow the cream taste to trickle through her mouth. She raised her eyelids the merest slit to watch the cream island slowly swirl in its brown lake. She sipped a wee taste of the cocoa and gave a big sigh of utter contentment.

The soothing sounds, the homey smells, the warm fire, the cosiness - all worked together until her usual fear was replaced by total bliss.

'If I lived in a place like this I could have all that neat cow stuff all the time. Milk. Cream. Whipped cream. Butter.'

Jacqueline was drawn out of her trance by the realisation that the lady with the short dark hair had been talking to her, " . . . my mother. You didn't meet her last night because she was sleeping when you got here. Now, if you thought it would be nice to call her 'Grandma' . . ."

The child shot her a look of pure venom. She was not about to call any dumb old farm lady 'Grandma'!

The lady reeled from the look, startled. " . . . or, we can decide that later. It doesn't matter now. Um – breakfast will be ready in a minute. I'm just going to check on the other two, but don't you worry, I'll be right back. I'm sorry, uh, I didn't catch whether you were Lucy or Jackie in all that confusion last night?"

"Jacqueline!"

The lady blinked at her fierceness and bustled away into the passage leaving Jacqueline glowering after her.

'What do I care if a stupid farm woman never comes back? She didn't even say my name. I saw them look at each other. They can't trick me by pretending to be nice.'

"And it's Lucinda, too," she hissed under her breath.

"What's that, dearie?" The older woman turned to her with a gentle voice.

"Jacqueline. My name is Jacqueline. I'm not Lucinda, she's just a baby and she's not Lucy and I'm not Jackie!"

"And you're not a bairn, is that it? You're a big, brave girl, aren't ye, dearie?"

Jacqueline glared at her. 'The stupid woman. It's a trick. She thinks she can fool me by being soppy.'

"What is it, puddin? Dinna ye feel well? Och, I know what it is. You haven't had a chance to use the potty yet, have you, ye poor wee soul? Here, now, ye come with your Grandma Sally. I'll show ye where it is."

Jacqueline needed a bathroom too badly to express her fury at having it called a 'potty' as if she were a baby. Instead she silently set her cocoa down on the arm of the sofa and slid to the floor, privately sneering at Sally's prattle as she followed her.

"Oh, my, look at your poor wee toes on that cold floor. We do have to get slippers for you, don't we, now? Paddy said they brought you here in only your nightclothes. Shameful, shameful. My goodness me, who would credit such a thing? Let's see now, maybe one of Xantha's girls left something here ye could wear. Och, ye wouldna ken who she is, would you? Silly of me. Xantha is my eldest and she has three little girls about your age. Paddy out there is my baby. Xantha's left old Inch Brae now, married her young lad, moved to the city, got a family of her own. All girls so far. She was always a thin little thing like you. Not a tub of butter like our Paddy and me.

Och, ye wouldna ken Inch Brae, would you? That's this old house. My David, that's my husband, ye ken; his great grandfather built Inch Brae 100 years ago or so and he named his homestead after the place he'd left behind in Scotland. I like that, dinna ye?

Here, now, can you reach that light cord by yourself? That's a big lass. We can always tie a piece of wool to it so it hangs lower for the littler ones, eh? Used to do that when mine were small. Here you are, now, are you all right by yourself, dearie?"

Jacqueline glared up at her in total disgust.

Sally hastily amended her question. "Och, yea, well then, of course, you're a big lass now, aren't you? You'll have to forgive me, dear, it's so long since I had anyone your age around here. Paddy's quite grown up as you can see, and Xantha's girls aren't here often. There now, you can lock the door like this, all right? You call if you need anything, eh? I'll just be in the kitchen getting breakfast. All right, then? Yes, well, there you go, then." Sally finally left, gently closing the lavatory door behind her.

Gratefully settling herself the moment she had privacy, Jacqueline looked around the tiny room in. Lock the door! She'd been punished all her life for things like that. She looked around the lavatory, bewildered. It looked ordinary. A toilet, a sink and mirror over the sink. 'What happens if I do lock the door?'

Fearful of sudden wrath, she took a moment to get up enough courage to try it, then stood beside the door for a space afterwards to see if anything would happen. Too nervous to be caught with a locked door, she unlocked it before she washed her hands. 'I s'pose Paddy's the dark haired lady. I got to get another name for her mother. I'm not calling her Grandma Sally. She's not my grandmother.'

Jacqueline pulled a face, longing for her grandmother who was always kind and loving to the children. Granny never hit them, nor did their parents whenever Granny was around. Swallowing a sob over her fear that she would never see her

Granny again, Jacqueline scowled. 'They really are stupid. Fancy calling a grown-up a baby. That's so dumb.'

She thought she could almost remember Paddy from the night now that she thought about it, but her memory of their arrival was all fuzzy. By the time they had been driven to Inch Brae the children had all fallen asleep in the car. Jacqueline couldn't clearly recall being carried to the house and tucked into bed. They'd been handled so gently that they hadn't been roused.

As a matter of fact, what she could remember of that confusing tenderness made Jacqueline feel a bit better. She began to wonder why the two women she had met so far did things the way they did. Allowing her to lock herself in any room was the opposite from the way her parents were. They flew into rages if the children dared turn locks, even the lavatory or bathroom doors.

Not only that, but Sally talked about slippers for Jacqueline without any tirades about how she was a spoiled little girl who didn't deserve them. She looked down at her toes and wiggled them.

'Maybe I could stay here until I get slippers. But I still got to get out of here before 'they' put me in that foster home with the bars on the windows. Maybe I can find out when 'they' are going to take me and run away just before that. Bet I could find out just by listening in. I never met anyone who talks so much in my life. Got to find out what they're saying when they think I'm not there.'

She opened the door as quietly as she could and crept down the hall towards the kitchen, stopping as soon as she could clearly hear without being seen.

Sally was saying to Paddy, " . . . poor wee mites. We'll just fix each of them something to eat when they do wake up, then. Plenty of time to get them into routine. They must need their sleep after a night like that."

"I should say so. It doesn't look as if this was the first time for them, either."

"Oh, dear me. Such a terrible thing. Tsk, tsk, tsk. Hard to believe people would treat little ones so, isn't it? D'ye know if the bairns have been taken away before, then?"

"I don't think so, Mum. The welfare workers told me they've been trying to get these ones for years. Now they're going for a restraining order to give the kids six months to settle."

"Oh, my. Does seem wrong to keep little ones from their own Mummy, doesn't it?"

"Mum, you haven't seen these kids. When you look at those bruises it seems more wrong to have left them there so long."

"Their own parents, Paddy!"

"Monsters! The poor little things. I suppose they'll be lost and frightened when they wake up."

"Well, then, we'll just have to watch for them, dearie. Mind ye, the big one didn't seem too frightened, did she? Bit savage in fact."

"Mmm, did you catch some of those looks, Mum? Talk about your looking daggers!"

"P'raps that's how she is when she's nervous. On the attack, I mean. Must be so hard on her. She's so wee. Seems funny to call such a little bit of a thing 'the big one' doesn't it? D'ye know how old she is?"

"When they called last night to see if I'd take them, they said three children aged 7, 6 and 2."

"Och, the dear wee mites. My, she is small for her age, isn't she? And so thin. Well, now, we'll just have to feed her up, won't we, dearie? You know, Pats, when you talked about taking children in, I did worry. But now I've seen that wee lost lamb there . . . "

Jacqueline scowled to herself. 'The liars! They call me big and brave to my face and call me little behind my back - You can't trust grownups! The all try to trick you. I'll show them! I'll be nice to their face, too, and eat their stupid breakfast. Then I'll find where they hid Jonathan and run away from here. They can't keep me in no 'staining order for six months. I'll be eight then and big as anything.'

She slipped silently to the sofa and sipped her cooled cocoa. The smells of toast and bacon were making her stomach hurt with hunger, but she was not about to say anything.

Paddy turned to put something on the table and saw her. "Jackie!" she exclaimed in surprise. "Where did you come from? You are the quiet one, aren't you? Just pop up here, now, and we'll have something to eat."

"Jacqueline!" she snapped as she climbed onto a chair.

Paddy looked at the child for a moment, puzzled, then glanced at her mother, who explained, "She prefers to called Jacqueline."

Turning back to Jacqueline with raised eyebrows, Paddy asked, "You do? All the time? Isn't there a pet name you'd like us to use?"

Jacqueline hung her head in embarrassed confusion. She was disconcerted by being asked what she'd like instead of being ordered like the things imposed on her, but the idea of having a 'pet' name sounded nice and friendly. Her parents' fury if anything other than her full name was used left her too afraid to let Sally and Paddy call her by anything but 'Jacqueline'.

Bewildered and frightened, all she could do was whisper, "My name is Jacqueline," praying she wouldn't be punished for impertinence.

The two women looked at one another, then Paddy shrugged and said, "Well, that's alright, dear. Here, do you like porridge?"

Jacqueline felt as if she had just managed to get off the hook over her name. That success didn't give her the confidence to tell Sally and Paddy that she hated porridge. The mere thought of trying to swallow the sticky, mushy stuff nearly made her gag, but she had been through this grown-up game enough times to know the rules well. First they asked if you wanted a food you hated, then if you said no you were sent to your room with nothing to eat for talking back. And if you said yes you ended up being given so much of the stuff you hated you couldn't have eaten it all even if you had liked it, but if you didn't eat it all you got sent to your room for not appreciating the work they'd done to prepare the meal.

Too hungry to risk being denied breakfast, but unable to force herself to swallow porridge, she sat absolutely still, her head hanging, waiting for the cuff for not answering when she was spoken to.

After a moment or two Jacqueline realised that neither of the adults seemed to be noticing her. They sat across from her tucking in to the steaming dishes of porridge, toast, bacon, potatoes and scrambled eggs, chattering a mile a minute. She slowly raised her head and sat, silently watching them. As if they'd agreed not to notice her, they carried on like she wasn't there.

It looked as if neither woman was going to put food on her plate. Desperate with hunger, Jacqueline didn't know whether this was a new punishment or if she was expected to get things for herself the way they did. She had never seen a meal where her mother hadn't plunked a plate in front of her already loaded, expecting her to eat everything on it without a word. Timidly she reached for the toast rack, only to find that each dish was offered to her in turn without comment on whether she did or did not take anything and without a break in the flow of words.

Not knowing how to avoid taking too much and be punished for being greedy, or not enough and be punished for not being appreciative, Jacqueline remained stiff and tense, silently nibbling at this and that, hands shaking, palms sweating, frantically trying to detect some sort of clue about what she was supposed to do.

No matter how she fretted, the adults simply chattered away to each other, tried to chat with her and ate with gusto. Even without understanding what was happening, Jacqueline began to relax a bit. Little trickles of warmth and comfort began to percolate inside her, loosening the hard knot in her stomach. Maybe this is alright. Maybe they don't hit. Maybe this will be a nice place to wait until 'they' come for us.

The conversation didn't interest her because she couldn't understand most of it. The women talked about people she had never heard of and farm work she knew nothing about. Idly she looked around the room. Remembering where the sunrise had been, she figured she was facing west. Behind her would be east, where the hallway was with the lavatory off it. In the south east corner of the kitchen was a door to the outside with a window in the door. Further along the south wall was the fireplace, then just about even with the table was a sideboard separating the cooking area from the living area.

She looked over her shoulder to the north west corner. There was the hallway again, then a wall-papered wall with photos hung on it. Jacqueline assumed those would be photos of the family. A double door with window panes all the way down both sides was set in the wall between rows of photos. There were white lace curtains on the other sides of the doors. Jacqueline had never seen curtains on doors inside a house, but she thought it looked so pretty she determined to have doors like that in her own house when she grew up. She was sure the sound of the canary singing came from behind those curtained doors and wished she could see what was in there.

Whatever it was it would be special.

The photos on the wall after the curtained doors were close enough for Jacqueline to see the clothes and faces. She recognised both Paddy and Sally in one photo with a man in a soldier's uniform, two other men and another lady who looked like a taller, thinner Paddy. She supposed that would be Xantha and the men would likely be their brothers, but where was their father? The next photo was of the one in the soldier's uniform, alone. There was a poppy taped to the black picture frame. Beside that was an old yellowed photo of a young soldier that looked sort of like an old fashioned version if the other soldier. She didn't dare ask any questions.

Instead of asking about the photographs, Jacqueline looked straight ahead at the doorway to the passageway. On the other side of the passage she could see part of the door to the bedroom she'd been in. The door was standing open. Jacqueline stared at it in horror.

Paddy noticed the look on her face and asked, kindly, "What is it, dear?"

"That door's open."

Paddy turned to look behind herself. Puzzled by the child's anguish, she glanced at her mother, then answered, "Yes, dear, I left it open."

"Then where's Lucinda?"

"She's sleeping, dear."

Rising tones of hysteria coloured Jacqueline's voice. "Where? What did you do with her?"

Paddy answered wonderingly, "I left her right where she was, Jacqueline. She's still sleeping in the cot we put her in last night. Didn't you see her when you got up this morning? You may go and check on her, if you like, but be careful not to wake her. She's very little to have been up so much of the night."

"Then why's the door open?"

"I've left the doors open so that I can hear the little ones when they wake up, so they won't be any more lost and frightened than we can help. Don't worry, dear, we wouldn't put your baby sister anywhere that you couldn't find her."

Jacqueline hung her head again, overcome by confusion. 'What's the matter with these people? First they let me lock myself in the privy, then they just leave doors open like it doesn't make any difference if kids get out of bed whenever they feel like it.'

She dreaded what would happen to Lucinda if she got up by herself and started to toddle about without permission. She didn't know what to do. Some things in Inch Brae seemed nice enough, but others were so muddling they filled her with dread. She couldn't possibly stay in a place like this until she had her slippers. No matter what it took she had to escape the mixed up feelings. Jacqueline and Jonathan had never included Lucinda in any of their plans. Until that moment they hadn't thought of the baby as another child, but just 'the baby'; a harmless thing without feelings. Now that it had occurred to her Lucinda was just like they were, she couldn't ignore her any more. But what could she do? Lucinda couldn't run or climb or hide and she cried all the time. How could they possibly run away with her? Yet they couldn't simply leave her behind. Jacqueline had never before

22

planned an escape from any place but her own home and the new rules to this place unnerved her.

She thought about the way Paddy worried about Lucinda waking up frightened and the generally kind way the two women spoke about the baby. Would she be alright if they did leave her behind? Some things were kind of nice about the place. Maybe Lucinda would be alright for a little while. 'If they'll be nice to her and keep her until I get big, I'll come back and get her. That wouldn't be like just leaving her, would it?'

Grasping for all her courage at once, Jacqueline took a deep breath, jerked her head up and snapped, "Why can't you keep her here?"

"I beg your pardon, dear?" the women were startled.

"She shouldn't have to go to that foster home."

"What's that, dear?"

"She's just little, you know. It's not fair on her. She's too little to be in that place. They put the bars on the windows for people like me, but she's done nothing. She didn't even get away. She just cried 'cos she's so little. It's not her fault. It was Jonathan and me made them mad. We sneaked out of bed. We're always bad."

The women were staring, open mouthed. Feeling that she'd gone too far to back out of it, but terrified that she was getting nowhere, Jacqueline tried pulling every heart-string they'd so far exposed to her, as well as using the name she thought they wanted to hear. Fighting desperately for her sister with the only weapons she had, she switched to the sweetest voice she could dig up. "If you like, I'll give her to you. Then when she gets big and be's bad, I'll come back and get her, okay? Then it won't be so long since you had someone here my age, alright, Gramma?"

They were still just staring at her in astonishment.

As Jacqueline's eyes widened in alarm that she had failed, Sally came to life, hurrying around the table so suddenly she caused the child to shrink from her in fright. "Oh, my wee pet. Jackie - Jacqueline, sweetie, of course we'll keep Lucy-inda. D'ye no ken? We'll keep you, too. Oh, my goodness, gracious me! What a horrible thing! What have they been telling you? You come with me, now, and sit on your Grandma Sally's lap. There, there, now. Who said you were always bad? What a terrible thing to say to a child! Paddy, lovey, would you mind taking care of the breakfast dishes while we have a wee chat, please?"

"Right you are, Mum."

"Thank ye, dearie. Now, wee one, let me explain something to you."

Jacqueline never forgot how it felt to sit curled up in the soft, warm lap, the afghan snugged right up to her shoulders, rocking back and forth, back and forth on the little kitchen sofa in front of the big stone fireplace, the soft gentle voice crooning on and on, explaining away her fears.

No bars. No being taken away. That was the foster home. Right there at Inch Brae. They would all stay. All three of them, together.

The little girl closed her eyes and leaned back, her head against the soft chest, enjoying every sensation of pleasure she could glean before it all vanished. She hid her face to make sure no one could see how excited and happy she was so that no one could use it against her when it all turned out to be a hoax.

Chapter Two:

The New Family

Jacqueline was still cuddled in Sally's lap when they heard Lucinda starting to whimper. Keeping her face averted, Jacqueline slid to the floor and trotted behind Paddy to the bedroom, there to pause uncertainly at the doorway.

Her new-born hopes faltered as she watched Paddy soothe and change the baby. The memories of her mother's tenderness to Lucinda were only a day away. She knew that although a scene like that might be nice to watch, it did not mean safety for herself. Her father could be gentle with the baby when he wanted to, as well.

When her parents were squabbling one of them could be really nice to the children while the other one sulked. The attention felt so good that the children would seek it even though they knew it was dangerous. Eventually they would be alone with the sulker. Then they would deeply regret they had 'taken sides' with the one who had been nice to them.

It had never mattered what the argument was about, which parent it was, or how long it took the other one to get his or her chance, the type of cuddling and petting Jacqueline had just enjoyed was always followed by such distress that she swore every time that she would never get sucked in again.

But she needed the stroking too much to resist it. Besides, the one time she had dared refuse her father's hugs and lollies, not only did he switch from being soppy to shouting and strapping in the twinkling of an eye, but also she still got punished by her mother as soon as her father had left for work.

So there she was, stalled in the bedroom door watching Paddy lovingly dress Lucinda in oddments Jacqueline supposed had been left by 'Xantha's girls', cursing herself for being so stupid as to snuggle up to Paddy's mother right in front of Paddy. She was too scared to enter the room and get the inescapable scene started at the same time as being too scared to draw attention to herself by turning and running. All she could do was hover, shaking.

Unaware of Jacqueline's misery, Paddy stopped the baby's tears and muttered under her breath about the lack of clothing for the children. She put her hand on Jacqueline's shoulder and guided her to the mirror over the chest of drawers, then knelt behind her to brush out her long, dark hair. She started to say something about Jacqueline's edginess, but when she looked up at the mirror and saw the fear reflected there, she stopped talking. She brushed and plaited in puzzled silence.

The sisters had opposite colouring. Lucinda had fine, wispy white-blond hair, very dramatic with her big brown eyes and olive skin. Jacqueline, on the other hand, had thick, heavy, dark auburn hair which would have had a curl if it hadn't been so long. Her skin was very pale with a slight sallowness to it, relieved by freckles on her nose and cheekbones.

In contrast with Lucinda's round face and wide, round eyes, Jacqueline had a narrow face, high cheek bones and almond shaped green-blue eyes. When she grew up there was every chance she would be the beauty of the two, even though as small children it was the younger sister who was cuter by far.

Often when her parents were upset with her they took advantage of Jacqueline's slightly feline look, telling her she looked like a ferret or a weasel or a cat which ended up leaving her with a dislike of looking at herself in the mirror. She didn't care for herself at all, but submitted with more or less good grace to whatever toilette was inflicted on her.

The severe, parted in the middle, tight plaits that her mother kept Jacqueline's hair in only made her face look more pointed than ever. The stray whisps of hair that escaped from her plaits curled around her brow in a charming way, but they weren't enough to soften her sharp look.

The two girls couldn't have looked less like sisters. Even their builds were different. Where Jacqueline was fine boned, thin and small, giving her a fragile, bird-like appearance, Lucinda was sturdy, chubby and cute, like a little bunny. Her hair was cut in a fringe that hung into her eyes, giving her an endearing habit of peering up through the hair as if she were shy. She seemed much healthier than Jacqueline. Looking at them together Paddy got the feeling that if they were to fight, despite the age difference the baby could clean up on the older girl. They appeared to be about the same weight, Jacqueline was so thin and Lucinda was so robust.

When she looked into Jacqueline's eyes, however, Paddy got an impression of tremendous strength of will. She had an uncomfortable feeling that this thin little girl was formidable. Paddy could well see why parents as bent on total control as the Eastons appeared to be would have difficulty getting along with her.

Once Jacqueline's hair had been battled into two thick plaits, Paddy quickly made the beds. She straightened the top bunk last, by which time Jacqueline had scrounged enough courage to blurt out, "Who slept there?"

Paddy turned to her, disconcerted by the snappish tone, and answered softly, "I did."

"This your room?"

"It was when I was small. Now I sleep beside this one, in the room you can see when you go to the kitchen."

"Oh, yeah." Jacqueline remembered Paddy coming up behind her as she stood in the kitchen door. She glared up her. "Why'd you sleep here, then?"

"I thought perhaps one of you might have had bad dreams, or wake up and not know where you were. I thought someone should be with you."

Jacqueline was not fooled by her kindly tone. She knew she had been guarded. "Where's my brother?"

"Don't you remember, dear?"

"No. I don't."

"We put him in Pete's room for now, so he won't be alone, either."

"Who's Pete?"

"Pete is one of my brothers."

"Where's his room, then?"

"Right beside this one, on the other side from mine. Listen, you don't have to snap at me, you know. You're allowed to ask me anything. I'll tell you whatever you want to know if you ask me nicely."

Jacqueline's chin quivered. 'She hates me after all. I knew it all the time. You can't trust grownups.'

Paddy sighed, swooped the baby onto her hip, swished the heavy curtains back from the windows and turned off the light. The bright sun streamed into the room making them all blink.

As she turned to leave the room and so faced Jacqueline again, Paddy said softly, "I'm sorry, Jacqueline. I've scared you, haven't I? I didn't mean to. I forgot how strange everything must be for you. We'll be good friends after a while, you'll see. It's only at first while we're still trying to find our way around one another that everything is difficult for all of us. You're not the only one who's scared, you know, pet. I've never had a little girl of my own before, so this is a bit strange and scary for me, too. We can help each other through the strangeness if we trust one another. Come on, I'll show you where Jonathan is sleeping, then I really must give Lucinda her breakfast. She must be hungry."

Puzzled by it all, Jacqueline followed behind Paddy like a puppet. She looked into Pete's room without noting where it was. She couldn't believe an adult could be scared. She couldn't imagine helping an adult. Despite the fact that Sally had described Paddy as her baby, Jacqueline couldn't make head nor tail of the idea that adults might have feelings like she did.

'Why would a lady be sorry to a kid when the kid was bad? What happens when grown-ups want to be friends with kids? Then how do you know what's the thing to do? How do you know what's bad then? How can grown-ups and kids be friends anyway? Grown-ups don't ever climb trees or play tag or dolls or play chasey or dig in the sand or anything friend kids do. These people are weird.'

Jacqueline didn't feel safe. Her head started to throb.

She wandered back to the kitchen sofa and curled glumly under the afghan, staring into the fire until she lost all contact with the world around her.

She snapped out of the trance with a jerk. 'Damn! Now they know how to get me,' she cursed in her mind. She tried not to daydream when anyone could see her, or at least not to start with fright in front of anyone. She had been punished for that in school, in Sunday School and at home, as well as being teased by her friends, so now she was sure these people, also, would think she was a bad girl for her fantasies.

However, Paddy disconcerted her again by saying, "Gosh, I'm sorry, dear. It was clumsy of me to startle you like that. Did you hear what I said? No? My, you really were in a world of your own, weren't you? I think I heard your brother and I thought you might like to go to him yourself since you know your way around. It might scare him less to see a familiar face first, too. Here's some socks to keep his feet warm and a jersey of Pete's for him to wear. Just roll the sleeves up."

Relieved, Jacqueline jumped down from the sofa and ran from the room. She couldn't remember where Jonathan was, but she wanted to get away by herself for a moment.

Once she was in the passageway out of sight she leaned against the wall to think. Almost immediately she heard some small sounds coming from the open door just past her room.

She ran, overjoyed to be reunited with her one true ally in all the world.

Jonathan was sitting up in the dishevelled bed, his swollen, discoloured face streaked by tears. His black hair was mussed from sleeping and from his nervous habit of rubbing his hands up and down the sides of his head. The beating and the weeping had swollen his eyes too much for anyone to see that they were the same wide set, rounded, dark brown eyes as Lucinda's. He also had the same olive skin but in his case it matched his black hair better than her fair wisps. On the other hand, he had more of Jacqueline's slight frame than of Lucinda's sturdiness, though not to the same extent. Where Jacqueline was the size of a five-year-old at seven, Jonathan was just a bit small for his age. In fact, he was taller than his older sister.

Jacqueline scrambled up onto the bed using his secret name as she confided, "Joe, guess what? Guess what? We're in a farm place 'n Ma lied about the foster home. There's no bars and they say we can stay here. She tricked us. We don't got to be scared. 'They' don't put kids in places like that and it's not true we'll never see each other again. We can stay together here. We can. And they don't hit here. And they got real cows and a dog. Ohhhh . . . " she trailed off as the smell hit her. 'Now they'll thrash us for real. They won't be icky-weird about this.'

Jonathan had wet his bed.

Panicked, Jacqueline looked around for a way out. She shook Jonathan to stop his sniffling. Then looked around again. She saw a window on the other side of the room, over what was probably Pete's bed, got an idea and ran to shut the door so no one could see what she was doing. Quickly, quickly, she helped Jonathan out of his soaked, smelly pyjamas. He put on Pete's jersey, crying as it came into contact with his sore spots.

Jacqueline climbed up on Pete's bed, hurled the curtains back from the window and struggled to open it. Panting and whimpering she pushed and heaved, but it would not budge.

Finally defeated, she turned to look for another way.

"See, I knew it! They nailed the windows shut. We are so trapped in this place. It's all been a trick." Rage and terror boiled inside her. She thought she heard footsteps in the passageway. "You useless article!" she hissed at Jonathan in a whisper. "Now look what you've done! You've ruined everything! Trust you! You would!"

Realising she sounded exactly like her mother infuriated her. He cringed from her, letting out one helpless wail as she pushed him, hard. He stumbled two steps backward and fell with a thump. Too crushed to be able to not cry, too terrified to howl out loud, he returned to the hopeless, muted whining sound he'd been making when she came into the room.

In a wild frenzy Jacqueline managed to haul the bedding off the bed in one heap, pull the blankets and sheets apart, stuff the sheets and pyjamas under the bed and pile the blankets back on the mattress. She tried just as hard as she could to spread the blankets and smooth them out, but the extra strength the panic had lent her ran out.

Tears of exhaustion began to drip off her cheeks as she toiled. She needed to kneel on the blankets to reach the side of the bed against the wall, but that made it impossible for her to pull the blankets she was kneeling on to the wall.

Frustrated and frantic, she turned on Jonathan again. "Shut up and help me, dammit! You did it, you fix it!"

She kicked him. Painfully he got to his feet. He tried to do as she said, but he didn't really understand what she wanted. Besides, his father had left bruises on his arms, legs and back, so stretching across the bed or lifting the blanket hurt him. He hurt all over. He started to wail again.

Panicked, she ordered, "Stop it! Stop it! They'll hear us!"

So he reduced it with a gulp to sniffling again. That gave him the hiccoughs.

They ended up with a lumpy mass of blankets under the coverlet, scarcely covering the pile of sheets under the bed and the bare mattress on top.

Paddy tapped on the door. They grabbed for each other's hands and spun, wide eyed, to face the door. Their hearts stopped cold. Each of them had vivid memories of what happened to children who shut doors to hide what they were doing.

"Jacqueline? Is everything alright, dear? Do you need a hand?"

"I'm helping him," she lied desperately. "We're coming. I'm - uh - telling him all about Inch Brae."

"All right, love, but don't be too long. Remember, he hasn't had anything to eat yet." Paddy walked away.

They gaped at each other in disbelief. Both had abruptly stopped crying. Jonathan had been scared out of his hiccoughs. Jacqueline wiped her eyes with the backs of her hands, then tried to wipe her brother's with the dangling edge of one sleeve, but her touch hurt him and he pulled back. She whispered to him, "Now, don't start crying again. They'll catch us."

He nodded, knowing that as well as she did. Merely trying to roll the sleeves up made him wince. "They shouldn't of took us in just our pyjamas," Jacqueline complained. "They knew they were going to keep us. They could've got clothes from our cupboard."

"I had my dressing gown on," Jonathan remembered suddenly. "I was trying to get to the kitchen when he got me."

"Well, where is it?"

"Dunno."

Jacqueline shoved him in exasperation, climbed down off the bed and began to hunt through the room. She found a nail on the back of Pete's wardrobe door with Jonathan's dressing gown hanging from it. She jumped up and down, pulling on it to jerk it loose. When she had it she thrust it at him. "Here, stupid. Put it on."

She opened the door carefully and checked the passageway. No one. There was no one in sight.

Hand in hand they stole towards the kitchen, trying to regulate their breathing and stop shaking so no one would know they had been crying. At the doorway they stopped so that Jacqueline could see what was happening.

Lucinda was playing on the floor in front of the fire. Sally was at the sink with her back to them. Paddy was nowhere to be seen. "Got to watch that one," Jacqueline whispered. "She comes up behind you. I got an idea. Run!"

Pulling Jonathan after her, she dashed across the room to the lavatory, calling out to the startled woman, "Potty! He's got to go potty!"

They reached the haven of the little room, Jonathan protesting he wasn't a baby. "I don't say 'potty'," he sneered.

"They do. Shut up." Jacqueline jumped up and down to reach the light cord. Once the light was on she shut the door then showed Jonathan a wonderful thing. "Look, they let me lock it."

Jonathan nodded. "They didn't get mad when we shut the bedroom door, either."

Jacqueline looked at him, her eyes narrowed in thought. "Mmm, but they're pretty tricky, too. That one that talked through the door's called Paddy. She came up behind me."

"Did she hit you?"

"No, they haven't hit anyone yet. And there's another one - Sanda - Zanda - Zantha - some weird name, who's got kids about our age and they might let me have slippers they don't want any more."

Carefully they washed the signs of crying from their faces, taking turns to stand on the closed toilet seat so that they could see in the mirror over the sink. Jacqueline felt sick when she saw Jonathan's face under bright light. She couldn't bear to touch him or use the face cloth after it had touched him. It was as if the hurt would be transferred to her.

Only when they were satisfied no one would guess they had been crying and therefore demand to know what they had been doing did the children feel safe to leave the lavatory.

In the hallway they almost bumped into Paddy who was walking down the hall towards the kitchen. Frightened, both children jumped back.

'She always sneaks up on me!'

"Oh, did I startle you, dear? I'm sorry. Good morning, Jonathan, I'm Paddy. I expect Jacqueline has told you about me, has she?"

Jonathan was too shy to do anything more than look at Jacqueline, beseeching her to answer for him. Not having any idea of the proper response, or, in fact, the safe response, to an adult apologising to her, Jacqueline blurted out instead, "What's down there?"

"My father is down there. You'll meet him later. How do you feel this morning, Jonny? Are you hungry?"

He stared at her from the one eye that wasn't swollen shut, afraid of being punished if he answered the unfamiliar nickname, but afraid he'd be punished if he didn't answer when he was spoken to.

"Jonathan," Jacqueline corrected Paddy firmly as they turned to go into the kitchen.

Paddy sighed. "Him too? What is this fascination with big, long names? What, pray tell is wrong with Jonny? Aside from the fact that it's for him to say whether or not he wants his name shortened."

"His name is Jonathan," Jacqueline insisted, showing Jonathan to the table.

"Yes, dear, but there's no harm in being a little less formal, is there?"

Jacqueline wasn't sure what that meant, but she was sure there would be terrible trouble if her parents found out they weren't using their proper names. She had graphic memories of the reactions to seeing 'Good work, Jackie' written on some of her school work. She parroted her mother in a smug voice, "Use the name that was given to you as it was given to you. Have respect for your parents."

Paddy snorted. "My dear girl, my given name is Annabella Patricia McLean. It's nothing to do with respect that I'm known as Paddy. It's easier to say."

Jacqueline flushed with humiliation. Just as she was sure she had something right, she was wrong again. Jonathan glanced fearfully back and forth between his sister and Paddy, steeling himself for the explosion.

Sally stepped in. "Pats, never mind, lovey. There's plenty of time to settle it. This is their first day. If it means so much to them we can use their full names for now."

"I suppose you're right, Mum," was all Paddy said, much to the children's amazement. They kept their heads bowed, glancing at one another and peering around the kitchen. They had no idea how they'd been reprieved, but they didn't want to do anything to spoil it. Jacqueline sat silently beside Jonathan while he ate. Lucinda toddled peacefully around behind Sally McLean.

Somewhere down the hallway a little bell tinkled and clunked as if it had fallen on the floor. Swiftly, Paddy excused herself and left the room.

That left only Sally to watch the children. It was an easy matter for Jacqueline to wait until she had her back turned to slip back into the passageway unnoticed. She had to find a better way to dispose of the sheets and pyjamas.

At the end of the passageway she found a small corner room with dusty boxes of odds and ends stored in it. One window looked into the same row of trees that she had seen from her window and Pete's. The other looked into a back garden nearly hidden by a row of bushes that had once grown decoratively against the house, but were now so tall they covered the lower part of the window. Jacqueline had no trouble getting that window open.

She raced excitedly into Pete's room, managed to drag the sheets down the passageway, then in tremendous relief, stuffed them out of the window and behind the bushes. Danger over, she stood for a moment on the windowsill to look at the back garden and catch her breath.

The west fence was the same line of pines she'd seen from both her windows and Pete's. The south fence had an evergreen hedge growing all along it. The hedge had overgrown the gates through it so that each path going south from the back of the house went through a tunnel clipped into the overhanging branches. Jacqueline thought it looked like something out of a fairy-tale.

She could see a hen house with a run on either side of it and a kitchen garden that was almost finished for the approaching winter. 'There's lots of neat hiding places here,' she thought to herself, noting all the spaces under and in the overgrown shrubbery. 'I wonder if we'll ever be allowed out.'

As she closed the window and ran back to the kitchen, she invented an excuse for running off. Once the danger of being asked where she had gone was past, Jacqueline was able to put her fears aside and thoroughly enjoy exploring the house with Jonathan.

They found dozens of little books about Shirley Temple on the bookshelves in the girls' bedroom. Delighted, Jacqueline made a mental note of where they were placed on the shelf so that she could find them again.

They were told the dusty little room at the end of the passageway would be Jonathan's when he felt brave enough to sleep alone. Since he had never been in a room without Jacqueline that he could remember, the whole idea horrified him.

The children assumed that meant they were stay at Inch Brae. Perhaps until Jonathan's bruises had faded. No matter what they were told they didn't believe their parents wouldn't have the final say, and their parents had told them they would end up in a place with bars on the windows.

When the children were tired of that end of the house they racketed into the kitchen, looked at the pictures on the walls and peered through the glass in the double doors. Through the lace curtains they saw a front room. Piano. Flowers. Thick carpet.

Polished wood. Lace doilies. More glass doors to the outside. Canary cage in the window. Cut glass knick knacks. Vases. Lolly dishes. Jacqueline let out a sigh of pure bliss. 'It's beautiful. I'm going to have a room just like that when I grow up.'

She was interrupted by Jonathan calling, "Look! Look!" She turned around to see him standing on a stool looking through window in the kitchen door. Jacqueline ran across the kitchen and climbed up on the stool to stand beside him.

They were looking into a storm shelter built over the kitchen door. To the left there were wooden stairs to the path. To the right there was another door standing open. They could see straw on the floor inside the door and little kittens playing in the straw in the open doorway in the morning sun.

"Cor," they breathed to each other, eyes shining. The more they saw of Inch Brae the happier they were. Jonathan was laughing aloud, forgetting that it hurt his face to smile.

They heard the sound of the bell hitting the floor again and turned to watch Paddy run in response. "What's that?" Jacqueline asked Sally after Paddy was out of sight.

"Oh, um, it's Mr McLean, pet. He rings a bell when he wants something."

"Why?"

"Well, um, you see, he canna call for her and he canna come to get her."

"What happened to him?" Kittens forgotten, Jacqueline and Jonathan climbed down from the stool and walked over to Sally.

She sat at the table looking at them with such a strange expression that Jacqueline felt sorry for asking. She climbed up on a chair on the other side of the table and waited quietly.

She and Jonathan glanced at one another while Sally explained it to them. They didn't fully understand what she was saying, but her intensity struck them. "He was shell shocked in the war. He's an old man, now, sweetie. He can't get around too well and he might look a mite funny to you, but he's our Daddy and we love him. Here, now, I'll take you to him. Listen, now, you musna be too surprised when you see him. He got very hurt in the war, d'ye ken, lass? Hurt inside his head so he canna walk nor talk nae more, but he can still feel and think and know. He would like to meet you."

Solemnly the children all followed her down the hallway. They passed the lavatory, then a bathroom beside it, to stand in a disconcerted knot around the door across from that. Jacqueline and Jonathan hung back, peering around Sally's skirts at the strange old man wobbling back and forth in the wheel chair while Paddy wiped his chin. Lucinda was enchanted. She broke away from the others and ran to the old man, fingers in her mouth, to stand at his feet, her head on one side.

The old man seemed to get excited. He made mumbling noises and wobbled faster, waving his hands in the air. Paddy knelt to explain to him who the children were. Jacqueline and Jonathan huddled behind Sally, too disconcerted to come out in the open, but Lucinda giggled. She climbed up on the wheel chair, hugged David McLean and settled winningly on his lap. Jacqueline was horrified although Lucinda and her new friend seemed perfectly happy. Paddy and her mother were entranced.

They were interrupted by a knock on the back door. Nervous, Jacqueline didn't follow the McLean's all the way back to the kitchen with the other two. She was still in the hallway when Mrs McLean opened the door to admit the woman who had been in the car and a stranger.

Sure that the welfare workers were there to ship all of them off to the lock up her parents had so often threatened her with, Jacqueline ran up and down the hall looking for a way out of that part of the house. All the doors were closed except for the lavatory which had no window, the bathroom which had only louvers and Mr McLean's room. She was too afraid of him to go into his room alone. He kept grunting at her like a strangling dog, waving his hands and jerking back and forth.

Jacqueline ran again up and down the hall. She cursed herself for not escaping when she'd had the chance. If only she'd been on the other side of the kitchen she could have fled through the bedroom window, but she couldn't cross to her bedroom without being seen. Besides, she could see Jonathan, dumb with fright, staring right at her, giving away where she was.

She had to go through Mr McLean's room, she had to. She didn't dare open any of the closed doors, she had no way of knowing what was in any of the rooms or if she could get out of them. Back she went, nearly wetting herself with fear of the strange old man.

He kept grunting and mumbling at her, wobbling back and forth in his chair and drooling. She was terrified. He knocked the little bell off the arm of his wheelchair sending it tinkling to the floor. Then Jacqueline did wet herself, knowing the bell would bring Paddy on the run. Seeing the puddle spread on the floor around her feet and not able to do anything to stop it, Jacqueline was so overcome she couldn't even run to hide before Paddy was at the door.

"You dear little thing, you stayed to keep Daddy company, did you? What is it, Dad? We have guests, the children's welfare worker . . . what's the matter, Jacqueline? Don't worry about Daddy, he always gets excited when there's anything different." That was when she saw the puddle. "You've wet yourself? A big girl like you? Don't you remember where the lavatory is?"

Her voice was not unkind, throwing Jacqueline into confusion. She expected a thrashing for wetting herself and stood, shaking, rooted to the spot, the wet trails down the inside of her legs turning cold.

"Why, you're terrified, you poor little thing. Come on, we'll clean you up. There's no harm done."

Jacqueline was unable to move, even though she saw Paddy get out a mop and pail already filled with water and disinfectant. She was too overwrought to wonder why such a thing would be kept in a cupboard in Mr McLean's room.

"You have to move, puddin, or I can't mop the floor." Paddy looked into Jacqueline's eyes. "We don't spank people for puddles on the floor, sweetheart. You don't have to be afraid."

"But I'm seven."

"Even if you are seven, but you do have to move."

Jacqueline ran to the lavatory and locked herself in.

A few moments later there was a knock on the door. "Are you alright, Jacqueline?"

"Don't tell them I'm here."

"Who?"

"Tell them I ran away already. When they're gone I will and you won't get in any trouble."

"Tell who? The welfare ladies? But why?"

"They'll take me to that place. Don't let them take me. I'll never tell, I promise."

"If I promise not to let them take you, will you open the door so that I can see you? I have to tell you something."

"You can't trick me."

"Have I tried to trick you yet? If you trust me not to tell them where you are, can't you trust me to open the door?"

Jacqueline unlocked the door. The very idea of someone bargaining with her instead of threatening her made her give in out of confusion. Paddy opened the door a crack, slipped in and locked the door behind herself. She stood Jacqueline on the closed toilet seat while she washed her legs for her, explaining softly as she did so, "Mrs Philips has brought some of your clothes for you. Didn't you believe Mum when she told you you were to stay with us? You silly little thing, you wet yourself with fright, didn't you? I'm so sorry, pet, I would never have let you frighten yourself so much if I'd known. Mrs Philips brought Mrs Hone with her to meet you because she's going to be your worker from now on. Now, do you think they'd have bothered with your clothes or the local worker if you weren't going to stay here? I don't think they would. Now, feel brave enough to face everybody? We'll let what happened be our little secret, alright?"

She lifted Jacqueline down, but the little girl just stood there, too amazed to know what to think, say or do.

"Need a moment more? Here, give us a hug, then. Hugs sometimes help, don't they? Righto, shall we try this again?"

Jacqueline allowed herself to be led by the hand out to the kitchen, one part of her mind telling her it was probably a trick, but the other part wanting it to be true so desperately that she went along with it to will it to be true. She took her place sullenly beside the other two, refusing to look up or to answer when the welfare women spoke to her.

The welfare workers had brought with them the few of the children's clothes and toys that the parents could be persuaded to part with. For the pleased and excited children this was the proof that they could stay that all the talking had not given them. Jacqueline felt a great weight fall from her back when she stopped worrying about being locked up and about her parents punishing her for leaving.

Just the same, exclaiming over having their own things and happily getting out of night clothes and into warmer, more substantial pants and shirts did not stop Jacqueline watching for her chance to eavesdrop. She needed to know what was being said about all of them when it was assumed they couldn't hear. It was the only way she could be sure of what to expect.

After Paddy had helped all three into their play clothes she left them to play in the girls' bedroom and joined her mother and the two welfare women in the front room to have tea and talk. Jacqueline went to the lavatory so she could walk past the doors and see where everyone was sitting. When she walked back towards the bedroom she stopped just past the doors and positioned herself where she could hear without being seen yet get into the passageway without being caught if anyone moved.

Mrs Philips, who had ridden in the car with them to Inch Brae, was explaining about their names. " . . . their parents won't allow any abbreviation of their names. In fact Mrs Easton takes it as a deliberate criticism of their choice of names for the children. A direct insult."

"Then she shouldn't pick such cumbersome names!" Paddy protested.

"We have found that one of Mrs Easton's tendencies is to make it extremely difficult for people to do as she wishes they would. This leads to quite a bit of frustration on her part, which, unfortunately, has made things more difficult for the children. You might find that they are confused about seemingly simple directions since they are used to being unable to do their parent's bidding."

"Aye, I do see what ye mean, lass. The wee bairns are feared of most everything."

"Yes, Mrs McLean, they are, unfortunately, all suffering from anxiety. They cling together more than most siblings, although they also fight more than most siblings."

"All wee ones fight."

"Not the way these ones do. We had considered separating them for their own good . . . "

"Surely not!"

" . . . but we do find that siblings seem to do better if they can be placed together."

"Isn't that amazing," Paddy commented sourly.

"Yes, the study of human behaviour is one of the most fascinating sciences. I became a welfare worker because I loved the study of family dynamics in university. We do prefer to place family groups in one home if it can be done, but it's usually quite difficult to find a home willing to take or to keep all the children together. I am pleased that you're willing to give the Easton children a try, Miss McLean, but we do find that fatherless homes are not usually the best choice."

"What do you mean, Mrs Philips?"

"These are problem children, Miss McLean, and since you have never been married and have not before cared for children, the chances are you would not have been the first choice without the emergency last night. The fact that they have been left here does not necessarily mean that this will be the best situation for them in the long run."

"Well, we'll just do the best we can. You can't think of moving them again, for goodness sake! Think of what they've been through already."

"We have to do what's best for the children, Miss McLean. If we were to find a home with two parents, far enough from the natural parents to preclude aggression, willing to take all three for an extended period of time, experienced in handling difficult children, we naturally would need to consider that a viable alternative."

"For Heavens sake! You've never been homeless or beaten like those children, have you?"

"Neither have you, Miss McLean. That really isn't what's at stake here."

"Mrs Philips, I really don't think it could be 'best for the children' to not know if they're going to be in a strange place from one day to the next!"

Mrs Hone spoke up, "I can see you are genuinely concerned for the children's well-being, Miss McLean, and that's a good sign. I understand your father lives with you?"

"Yes, you see, the children aren't living only with me, by myself. My parents are both here, and my brother. Plus another brother of ours lives with his wife in the cottage right here. My sister has children just about the same ages as these, so I've had some experience. They'll be alright here. We'll manage."

"Miss McLean, isn't your father an invalid?" Mrs Philips asked. "For how long can you take care of him and the children too?"

Mrs McLean joined in the fray. "Why, we'll all work together, lass. Don't you think it's a sight more important for us to know more about how to help the bairns whilst we do have them than to squabble over why we aren't what you had in mind for them?"

"What would you like to know, Mrs McLean?"

"If these pour wee mites are so afeared of using the wrong names, how are we to know what they might call a body? And are we stuck for good and all with those lumbering great names they've got now?"

Mrs Philips answered, "You can choose anything you would like them to call you. As for the children, it could be in their best interests to break their obsession with formal names. If you can find something everyone is comfortable with there's a chance it will help them begin to overcome the ritualistic behaviour patterns characteristic of the offspring of compulsive parenting."

The little bell hit the floor, Jacqueline scuttled into the passageway, Paddy dashed down the hall.

Once Paddy returned the welfare workers took the children into town to get the rest of the clothes they needed. It would have felt like Christmas to the children, except that the welfare workers tried to use the excitement and the chance to be alone with each child to find out how they were doing in their new home.

They were met with a sulky silence from Jacqueline who knew better than to let herself be tricked into saying something that could get her into trouble with her parents if she said it one way, or ruin her chances in her new home if she said it the other way. They were met by a nervous silence from Jonathan who was too afraid of Jacqueline to say anything without her approval.

When the children were back on the farm and the women had left, the rest of the afternoon was a blissful, sunny time. Once they had the proper clothes for it, they were allowed to play outside in the chilly autumn sunshine until the dinner gong rang. As they raced around, yelling and exploring, for the first time they truly believed they were not locked in.

Chapter Three:
Allaying Fears

Paddy showed the children around the house yard for a few minutes. She told them that the area inside the fence around the house was called the home paddock, and the room they'd seen through the window in the back door was called the nursery, which they thought was very odd until she explained to them that in the springtime it was used for baby animals that needed special care. Jacqueline was delighted by that idea. She hoped she would still be on the farm in the spring.

There were three steps up from the back porch to the clothes line so that the clothes hung high above the garden. Hanging on the wall below the clothes line was a contraption Jacqueline and Jonathan had never seen before. They stared at it. It was pointing out towards the farm.

"That's the horn out of an old car that we've long since used for scrap," Paddy explained, seeing their stares. "I want you to pay close attention, now, this is quite important. We use this horn to call one another in from the farm. Pete's code is short long long short, for P." She tapped it out on the wood, explaining, "If I blew the horn to show you he would come rushing in, but I can blow mine."

Paddy blew a short blast on the horn followed by a longer blast, telling the children, "Because Pete and Pat both begin with P we use my other initial, A, to save confusion. We'll decide what letters to use for each of you and you'll have to learn them so that you know when you're being called. The one that you do have to know and get right right away is S.O.S., short short short long long long short short short. If ever anything awful happens you blow the horn an S.O.S. and not only will we all come, some of the neighbours will too. But you must never, ever, play with the car horn. It's only to be used when it's needed. It's not a toy."

They stared at it again, fascinated by the idea.

When Paddy left them to play weren't sure what they should do.

Too nervous to go far from familiar ground at first, the children played with the kittens right beside the back door. They didn't know what was expected of them or what the rules were, so they were especially careful to stay within bounds.

It took a few minutes for the need to let off pent up steam to overcome the need to stay out of trouble. At first they shoved one another, listening carefully for reactions from the other side of the back door. When there was only silence they tried going up and down the steps from the back door to the path, over and over again, even jumping down from step to step once or twice each.

Still there was no sound from Paddy or Sally. In a flash of daring, Jacqueline and Jonathan dashed down the stairs, chased one another round the side of the house and raced back again when Lucinda started to cry that they were out of sight.

Taking Lucinda with them, the older two set out for some serious exploring of nooks and crannies, corners, hideaways and places to play in the future. From force of habit they noted all the good places to hide.

A two-wheel track went from the steps at the back door to a wooden gate which was wide enough to let a tractor through.

Peering between the wooden planks of the gate, the children could see that the two-wheel track went all along the east side of the home paddock to the gate that led to the dirt road running past the farm. In the other direction the track carried on past the children over a grassy hill in the paddock beside the house. They wondered if they would ever be allowed to see what was on the other side of that hill.

The inside of the east fence was lined with tall, beautiful, colourful dahlias. Jacqueline stood beside them looking up at the full majesty of the pines marching along the west fence to protect the home from winter winds. Watching the tips wave in the breeze made her feel light headed and giddy. Clouds scudding by the waving tips made her feel she was moving, not the pines. She had to look down at the grass so she wouldn't get dizzy.

Just as she began to lose touch with her surroundings, imagining herself at the top of the trees with the birds, Jonathan came roaring around the corner of the house being a tiger. He stopped and snarled at her, ready to pounce. She bounded off, a startled horse, until he protested that he wasn't chasing horses.

She was a cave-man horse which he agreed to because he was then a sabre-toothed tiger. They chased around the house and garden, growling and snarling, jumping out from behind the hen house and bushes until they were too much for Lucinda who ran crying to the kitchen door. The tiger and the horse turned back into frightened children sure that they were in trouble for making the baby cry, but all Paddy did was stick her head out of the door warning them not to scare the hens.

With the baby safe inside the house and the ferocious beasts scared back to the caves, the two children became vehicles on the wheel-track highway from the gate to the steps. In a few moments the Jacqueline-ambulance had sped all the way to the top of the gate, sirens howling. The Jonathan-fire engine was not more than two steps behind, though he couldn't possibly be any louder. It was more fun to be a fire engine whooshing water all over the burning building on the other side of the gate, so Jacqueline became one, too.

"Hey!" Jonathan protested. "Ambulances don't that. You can't do that."

"Can so. I'm a fire-engine too."

"Are not."

"Am too."

"I'm the only fire-engine. You can't be one too, then there's no ambulance for the burned people. That's dumb."

"Is not!" In anger Jacqueline shook the gate, which swung and wobbled on its chain, making them both grab for balance. Jonathan made little 'ooo' sounds of fright, giving Jacqueline an idea.

A split second later the vehicles had disappeared leaving zoo apes swinging back and forth as far as the chain on the gate would allow, hooting and howling louder than any apes in any zoo ever has.

The apes swung on the gate, whooping, until the children burst out laughing. Then they tried singing as loudly as they could. Though they shouted and sang at the tops of their voices, no one yelled at them to stop it. In the freedom, the fresh air and sheer joy, the children risked using their secret names for one another.

On her way from the kitchen to the hen house, Paddy heard them. She detoured to the gate to ask, gently, "Joe? Is that what you like to be called?"

With wide, horrified eyes the children clung to the gate. This time Paddy expected them to be afraid. "It's alright," she soothed them. "It'll be our secret. Would you like to come with me while I get the late eggs and feed the hens? I loved to do it when I was your age."

Timidly, beginning to trust her a bit because each nice thing had so far been followed by another nice thing instead of an awful thing, the children allowed her to lead them. They didn't speak, look up or smile, but listened solemnly to her chatter while they walked.

"When my brothers and sister and I were growing up, collecting the eggs was the first outside job we were given. I was the baby and I was so proud when I was first allowed to do it without Pete's help. I was younger than you, then, but I still remember how grown up I felt to be trusted to carry the eggs all by myself. Dad told me when he was growing up it was his first job, too."

She showed them how to scatter wheat for the hens to scratch, how to clean the mash tins and refill them, how to mix the mash so it wasn't too dry for the hens, how to make sure the water trough was clear so the water would flow and not flood into the run making puddles that would get the stupid hens all wet, how to judge when the grass in the run was short enough to switch the hens over into one of the other runs.

The children were so interested in everything she showed them that they relaxed with Paddy in spite of themselves. Jacqueline dared to call Jonathan 'Joe' and he dared to call her 'Jay'. Pleased with herself over her minor victory, Paddy was careful to make no comment. From then on the children were known as Jay and Joe.

While the children were in the bathroom washing up for tea Pete stomped into the kitchen from the evening milking. In a trice they switched back from chattering, bouncing cherubs to solemn, silent, wide eyed waifs. They crept from the bathroom back to the kitchen and onto the sofa where they sat very still, holding on to one another, watching Pete take off his boots and hang his jacket up in the wardrobe behind the kitchen door.

They didn't answer when he greeted them, but just stared. "Struth!" he exclaimed, seeing Joe's face, but when all of the children jumped at the sudden, loud word, he shrugged, handed the milk bucket to his mother and went to wash up.

Despite the fact both Mrs McLean and Paddy told the children they didn't need to be afraid of Pete, they shrank from him and wouldn't speak when he was in the room. Since he ate tea with them, the whole evening meal was miserable.

Jay didn't lift her head once from the time she sat down to the time she was excused. She kept her eyes steadfastly on her plate and would answer no one. Joe whimpered that chewing hurt his bruised eye, then subsided to a muted, moaning snivel that didn't let up no matter what anyone did for him. Lucinda bore his grizzling for a few mouthsful, then her chin quivered and she began to howl for her mother and didn't stop until she had cried herself to sleep.

The entire family was relieved when Lucinda finally fell asleep for the night.

Jay sat staring at her plate listening to the other two and praying that the meal would be over so she could escape from the table and the pressure of not knowing what was expected of her or how to behave. Having the strange man at the table able to see every mistake she might make added to her fear until the fear froze her. Meals were awful enough in her own home, where parents sat one at the head and one at the foot of the table, the strap always within easy reach. The rules were simple. Full plates were placed in front of children expected to clean them without a word or else. At Inch Brae people talked and laughed, spoke to the children and helped themselves from serving dishes in the middle of the table. Jay found it utterly overwhelming.

While the women cleared the table, Pete took Joe to give him a bath, which was a huge relief to Jay, even if Joe did look frightened out of his mind. Her relief was so plain that Mrs McLean sat down with her on the sofa to talk to her about it.

First Jay was given a big mug of cocoa, then Mrs McLean told her, "You know, sweetie, Pete is my littlest lad. Ye dinna need to be afeared of him. He wouldna do a thing to hurt you, no more'n Paddy nor I would."

"Why did he have to have tea with us?"

"He lives here. That's his room Joe's in."

"Well, he didn't have breakfast or lunch here."

"Oh, my, well, ye see, dearie, his older brother, Bruce, lives in the cottage - did ye see the track that goes from the back gate over the hill? Well, the cottage is at the end of that, only ye can't see it because of the hill, but actually it's right close to Inch Brae, so our Pete ate with our Bruce and his Sharon today because of it being your first day. He thought Paddy and I would be so busy today that maybe it would be easier for us if we didna have him as well. You see, dear? He was only thinking of his old Mum. We didna know you'd be so - um - shy."

Jay hung her head in embarrassment. Before she could think of anything to say she was glad to have Mrs McLean distracted by Joe on his way from his bath to wish everyone goodnight.

Not too long after that Jay was curled contentedly in the top bunk beginning to drift into her favourite fantasy of being the only person in the world able to sprout big feathered wings from her shoulder blades.

No one could catch her. She could fly from her father to the house roof and laugh at him when he swore. Even if he climbed onto the roof, she could fly to a tree or another roof before he caught her.

The door opened quietly, letting in a stream of light from the kitchen and the cosy buzzing of adult voices around the front room fire place.

Jay's wings evaporated. She held her breath hoping Paddy wouldn't notice that she'd moved herself to the top bunk.

She wondered how Paddy could move easily through the room in the dark to Lucinda's cot, until she remembered the room had been Paddy's and Xantha's when they were small. Of course Paddy could close the door and glide through the room in only the dim light from the transom window. She'd had a lifetime of practice.

Much to Jay's horror, after Paddy tucked the baby in and patted her back, without a false move she went directly to the bunks, speaking to the top bunk as if she could see in the dark. Jay almost stopped breathing.

"Jay, I have to talk to you."

Jay stayed absolutely still, praying Paddy would believe she was asleep. Better yet, Paddy should believe there was no one there. Jay's being asleep had never stopped her from being beaten before.

"I'm sorry to bother you so late, but it took until now to get Joe to sleep. Normally I wouldn't disturb any of you after you were in bed, but there is something we must clear up now. It's too important to leave until morning."

Jay still couldn't move. She couldn't get used to an adult apologising to her. It unnerved her.

"Today when I went to make Joe's bed I thought you'd already done it for me, but tonight when Pete went to put him to bed there were no sheets and no pyjamas."

Jay's heart stopped pumping and sealed off the bottom of her throat.

"He was so frightened it took until now to get him settled enough he could sleep. He couldn't stop shaking. He thought the sheets were under the bed and it shook him up something awful to find they were gone."

'That tattle taler. I'll beat his brains out when I see him again.'

"Do you have any idea how much it scared Joe to find those sheets were gone?"

'So what? Who cares? Nasty old bat. Just like grown-ups - try to blame me when he did it.'

"Listen, dear. This is very important. You must never sneak. No matter how bad things are, or how scared you are, you must always tell me the truth. That's the only way I can help you. I can't do anything if I don't know what's wrong. Do you understand? You mustn't ever try to hide things; it always makes things worse. Don't you see? Then you have the problem and dishonesty too. That's two problems. If you come right to me then all you have is what's upsetting you and I can usually do something about that. You see, dear? You must always tell me the truth."

Jay lay in silent, rigid disbelief. 'I know when I'm being tricked!'

"Now, we'll start with the first problem. Why did you move the sheets?"

Jay remained dumb. She'd been through this part of it before. At last she knew what to expect. 'They can't beat it out of me. I'm no tattle tale like that stupid Jonathan.'

"Oh, I forgot to mention Pete saw something behind the shrubs under the window of Dave's old room when he went out to feed the dogs. While I was getting Joe to sleep he went to see what it was. He found the sheets and Joe's pyjamas. They'd been wet. Jay, tell me, were you afraid to let us find out Joe had wet his bed?"

Silence.

"You don't need to be afraid of that, dear."

Silence.

"Jay, I know you're not sleeping. Pretending is another form of dishonesty, you know. Now that you've nothing further to hide we can get on with sorting out this tangle. We can't make a happy family together if we don't trust one another, lovey. Come on, now, why don't you tell me why you hid the sheets?"

Jay was too stunned to answer. 'What happens if they know everything? What do they do if they don't hit for bad things like wetting your bed?'

Paddy sighed. "You like the top bunk, do you?"

Jay jumped.

"I know how you feel, I always liked it when I was your age. I fought with Xantha over it for years. I felt like my dreams were better up there, somehow."

"You're not mad at me for getting up here?"

"No, sweetheart, I'm not mad at you. If you want this bunk you're welcome to it. Do you see? You gave yourself a problem by trying to sneak up here. There's no problem you can't tell me about. It's not that I'm mad about the wet bed, it's that I want you to know there was no need to sneak."

Silence.

"That's the most important thing of all, Jay; that we trust one another. And that you respect yourself. If you try to mislead other people you'll damage your own trust in yourself. Did you know that? I don't need you to tell, what I do need from you is that we settle this with honour enough that we can each sleep in comfort."

Jay couldn't understand. "You said it's my fault Joe's scared."

"I want you to understand that trying to deceive hurts everyone around you and solves nothing. You should have seen him. Even his legs were shaking when he couldn't find those sheets."

"Serves him right."

"Oh, Jay. What a sad way to think. There is never any justification for a little boy to be that terrified. Never. Nothing he could possibly do is bad enough for him to be frightened like that. We will never hurt him the way he was hurt yesterday."

"You won't?"

"No. Not ever. Nor you, either."

"But he wet his bed. He's six."

"We don't hit people for wet beds. You weren't hit for wetting yourself this afternoon, were you?"

Silence.

"Wet beds are nothing to be afraid of at Inch Brae. All you do is let us know so that we can strip the bed quickly. We didn't know about the one last night so the mattress is smelly now."

"You won't hit us for the mattress?"

"No."

"Or rub my face in my pants?"

"Jacqueline! No one would do a disgusting thing like that!"

Silence.

"I'm sorry, sweetheart. I promise you, cross my heart, no matter what, I will never, ever do anything like that."

"Sometimes I wet my pants."

"I guessed that."

"Why do you keep a mop in Mr McLean's room?"

"He sometimes has accidents."

"I hid them so you wouldn't put us in that place with bars on the windows and give Joe a good thrashing."

"Didn't you believe us that you wouldn't be put in a place like that?"

"I did after you let us play outside."

Paddy patted Jay's arm awkwardly. She wasn't sure where the line lay between comforting Jay and scaring her. "Can you tell me why you moved them from underneath the bed?"

"The windows in Pete's room were nailed shut."

Paddy wasn't sure how the answer fit the question, but she decided against asking about that. "No window in this house is nailed shut. Why in the world would you think the windows were nailed shut?"

"Pa does it to stop me from climbing out the window when they lock me in my room."

"Good Heavens! What sort of . . . um - Jay, listen to me now. It doesn't matter what happens, we do not do that here. There's a little round catch at the top of the lower window sash. You turn it. Then the bottom window will slide up or the top window will slide down."

"Oh."

"You're a good, good girl. You were very brave to tell me when you were so afraid. If you want the top bunk I'll sleep in my own room next to this one, alright? If you or the baby need me just come and get me. Or, if you'd rather, I can stay in the bottom bunk until you're settled in."

"I'm alright, thanks."

"Well then get lots of sleep and have sweet dreams. We'll start from the beginning again in the morning." Paddy hugged Jay, kissed her goodnight, tucked her in and slipped quietly from the room.

Jay stuffed her head under her pillow and without quite knowing why, sobbed herself to sleep.

Chapter Four:

Settling In

The sound of Pete walking the cows past the house on the way to morning milking woke Jay. Curious, she climbed down from the top bunk, ran to the front window, carefully wriggled up under the curtain so that there would be no burst of light to wake the baby, climbed up on to the windowsill, stood with her eyes closed for a moment to give them a chance to accept the light, then looked at the top of the sash to see if Paddy had told the truth about the catch. It was there, though hard to turn. Once she had managed to wrestle it around to face the other way she found the window slid up easily.

Enjoying her own daring, Jay jumped down from the window sill onto the dewey grass and tip toed around the side of the house. She was not trying to be quiet; it was too cold to put her feet down flat. Her little pink bed-warmed toes were horrified that they were expected to walk on the early morning autumn dew, so they protested fiercely, moving from just cold to a shocked stinging as if they'd been burned. In her excitement the pain in her toes just added to Jay's thrill.

Beside the house, almost under Pete's window, Jay found a fallen log. Once upon a time it had been a huge branch high up in a pine tree, but over the years had become just part of the fence. Gleefully, Jay clambered onto the log to use it as a grandstand for the milking cow parade. Being neglected and offended, her toes went numb. Jay forgot about them. She was sitting on a moss covered, damp, cold log wearing only a thin cotton nightdress, so the discomfort of her seat distracted her from her toes. When the herd of cows passed in front of her they frightened and fascinated her so much she was unaware of anything else.

She hadn't known how huge cows were in the flesh; somehow pictures in books didn't show that they were up to a man's shoulder and too wide to go through a normal door. Their feet thudded on the ground with the snort-thump that had scared her the morning before. Their heads were nearly as big as Lucindas' whole body. Their eyes were bigger than Jay's fist.

Pete spotted the little white figure against the dark tree trunks and waved to her. Flattered, she waved back, startling several of the enormous brown beasts, who snorted and stomped, trying to shy away from her, but held in place by the press of the crowd. Their distress disrupted the orderly flow of the herd, making Pete yell and whistle at the cows and the dogs. That was the exact call and whistle that she had been unable to figure out. The strangeness of it delighted Jay. The whistle wasn't a tune at all. She'd been right when she'd thought it was the same as the way he called out. The whistles were instructions to the dogs. She could tell that by watching the dogs and cows react to each whistle, though she couldn't hear any difference between one whistle and another herself.

A big brown, black and white dog whipped around the herd to Jay's side of it in response to Pete's yell of, "Fleabag! Tuck in left!" emphasised with whistles and arm waves. All by himself the dog straightened the confusion out, moving the cows around the corner out of sight behind the ancient hedge. They returned to the slow, orderly walk while Pete yelled, "Shy!" and something Jay couldn't understand in the other direction.

Pete himself didn't once change from the sleepy amble behind the herd, one arm on the flank of the very last cow who didn't blink once at the yelling going on around her. She was chewing rhythmically, eyes were almost shut with contentment, as if she and Pete weren't part of the herd.

As they passed Jay, Pete's cow turned to look directly into Jay's eyes, giving her the creepy feeling that the huge animal could see her thoughts. A smaller, long haired, black and white dog trotted towards Pete and his cow, then off again in response to a gesture from Pete, who called to Jay, "Mornin' Shortie!"

Jay laughed out loud, making the pet cow flick her ears in disapproval. "Morning!" she called back, wishing she could think of a funny answer.

One of the cows already around the corner lowed, a scary, primeaval kind of noise.

Jay watched until they were all out of sight around the corner, then she ran back to the bedroom window.

'What a mighty place! Dogs with funny names, cows that let you walk with them, pet names for people. Cor, this is real mighty.'

Jay climbed in the window to find the baby grizzling about the cold draught from the open window. Laughing at her with sheer happiness Jay swished the curtains open which made the baby cover her eyes with her fat little hands, then she closed the window, dressed Lucinda and herself, after which they walked hand in hand to the kitchen.

Mrs McLean swooped the baby up high in the air and swung her around. Over the top of Lucinda's gurgling and squealing she called to Jay, "Morning, puddin, did you have a good sleep?"

Suddenly realising she had to be in the lavatory right now! Jay called, "H'lo Paddy's Mummy!" as she sprinted through the kitchen. She noted for future reference that sitting on an ice cold log after sleeping all night, then running back into the warmth without relief was begging for an embarrassing problem.

When she returned to the kitchen, Jay found Lucinda already at the table, happily puddling with a bowl of porridge. The McLeans let the baby feed herself without making her sit in a high chair. If she didn't stay still or if she made a mess with her food they simply said she'd do better when she'd had more practice.

Jay thought if she had a little girl one day she'd like to see what would happen if she didn't have a strap at the table. Even though the table customs had unnerved her on the first day, by the second day Jay was feeling that the way things were done at Inch Brae seemed more fun all round. Lucinda didn't seem to be acting spoiled; in fact, she seemed to eat more, more quickly and with less crying.

To test the promises of the night before and to see if the leniency would spread to herself, Jay spoke up. "Lucinda wet her bed."

"Of course she would, dearie, she's just a wee bairn. That's why we put her in nappies at night. Would you like to tell your brother that his brekkie's almost ready?"

"He wets his bed, too."

"Well, now, lots of folks do when they're wee ones and they're all upset. If he did last night just let us know and make sure he's washed up before he gets dressed. Alright, sweetheart?"

"I used to have accidents in my pants. Before. When I was little. A long time ago. Last year."

"Och, you poor wee lamb. Don't worry so. Some children have a problem like that; your not the only one. If it happens don't get all in a dither. Just get washed and changed right away and make sure we know so we can wash the clothes quickly. Is that all the bad news for this morning? It's a good thing that it is, my poor old heart couldn't've taken much more. There's a good lass, fetch your brother in here so we can all have breakfast together. Won't that be bonny?"

Jay ran off to Pete's room in a dazed silence. It was a let-down for her to have risked so much for so little reaction. Puzzled at first and in more of a vacuum than relief, she hustled Joe out of bed. He was wet, so he was whimpering, but she just hurried him off to the lavatory, trying all the way to explain to him that one of their major terrors was now not even a minor problem.

As the children gradually became used to the new way of things, they gave up their old fears to settle into a contented routine.

No matter what the weather, Jay went out to her log first thing every morning to watch Pete take the cows in for milking. The cows came to expect her and Fleabag went up to the fence each day for her to pat his head. The old dog, Skip, barked every time he saw that, getting Fleabag to go back to work. Shy acted as if Jay didn't exist, but Pete said she was just shy. Pete called to Jay as he walked past, his arm always on Sabrina's brown hip. He almost always called something that made Jay laugh. She decided she wanted to be funny like Pete and make people feel cheerful.

Jay formed a habit of waking up when she heard Pete have his breakfast. She'd get up and dressed then, but wait until he left the house before she used the lavatory. The magic was stronger if she didn't see Pete until she was on her log. She started a practice of accepting a glass of orange juice from Mrs McLean on her way back from the lavatory each morning and taking it with her out the window. It became part of her ritual to sit on her log sipping her juice in a private, satisfying routine of waiting for the cows.

After the herd had passed her, Jay ran back to the house, climbed in the window, dressed Lucinda and took her to the kitchen. Most mornings Jay stopped at the kitchen door to watch Lucinda run to Mrs McLean for her morning toss in the air. Jay liked to stand watching, blissfully sniffing the morning smells of coffee perking, bread toasting and bacon frying.

Once breakfast was finished Jay and Joe had jobs to do before they bustled and hustled into their school uniforms. They could hear the school bus rattling and revving up the stony hill long before it reached Inch Brae. To spur them to frantic haste Paddy needed only to tell them she could hear the bus. Goodbye kisses reduced to quick pecks on the run, satchels grabbed ready stuffed with lunch and homework, off they raced, over the gate – no time to open it – down the wheel track, over the cattle stop, to the front gate to stand and wait.

They could hear the bus clattering and lurching up the rough road from Macintyre's farm long before they could see its rusty old head crest the hill. By the time it was in sight the shrill voices of the children on board could be heard over the din of the clanging mud guards and broken running boards.

The engine howled and revved every inch of the way as if it wanted to drown out the children, though it never could for the law seemed to be that a child must scream to be heard even if the ear being screamed into was only an inch away. The petrol tank was held in place with baling twine and the muffler was patched with wads of sacking securely wrapped with string. Some of the windows would never open and those that opened would never close, so they were always full of waving arms and cheeky heads ignoring Reuben's bellow to "keep yer flamin' heads in!"

When old Gertie lurched to a stop under the carved wooden sign that declared 'Inch Brae' in peeled green paint, she bucked and moaned like a live thing. Big brown Reuben had always to kick her door open to let the children on, whereupon Gertie immediately stalled so that the children all cheered that this time they'd be late for sure, for she'd never start again this time. Smarty pants older boys offered to get out and push, when everyone knew all they'd do is dash off to the beach.

Inch Brae's front gate was just where the hill started to get quite steep, so each morning Reuben ordered the 'flamin' kids' back to their seats, got old Gertie rolling and made her engine cough back into protesting life by popping the clutch. Most of the older children scorned either sitting or holding on like sookie babies, so every morning several of them went flying when Gertie jerked back to life, colliding with the back of Reuben's seat so that he threatened to "tell yer ruddy dad what a great nit you are" while he fought to persuade Gertie she'd rather stay on the road than take them all into McGregor's duck pond.

Gertie scoffed at the idea of springs so each and every one of a million rocks on the road communicated itself with vivid tactile imagery through the wooden seats to the boney bottoms of thin children like Jay. The jolting was so constant that the children made a game of saying ahhhhh, laughing at the way the bumping made their voices go up and down no matter how hard they tried to keep them level.

Lucinda spent the long hours she was alone making a fast alliance with Mr McLean. The older two might be disconcerted by the frail, white haired old man for the first few weeks they lived on the farm, but Lucinda's initial delight in him grew day by day into a childhood devotion.

Jay stood in the doorway of Mr McLean's room sometimes, to watch him with Lucinda. Even though Mr McLean couldn't talk in any way Jay could understand it was clear the two understood one another. His wobbling around, mumbling noises and jerky hand movements alarmed Jay, but Lucinda seemed to make some sort of sense out of it. Her efforts to add her gestures and mouthings to his sometimes helped Paddy understand him and about as often added to the confusion.

At that time of year the cows were 'drying off'; getting ready for the two months in the middle of winter when there would be no milking. Since all the cows were heavily pregnant they needed extra food. Each morning Pete loaded his trailer up with hay, silage and whatever extras he'd decided they needed on that particular day.

On the weekends Jay loved to help him. She thought he was wonderfully funny, wise and kind. She couldn't imagine why she had ever been so afraid of him that she hadn't been able to speak in his presence. He said mighty little, being a man of few words and many grunts, but what he did say Jay valued, so when she wanted to know what had happened to Mr McLean she chose a Saturday morning feed out to ask.

Pete told her that his father had been a right brave man during the war. When another soldier was wounded Mr McLean had crawled out under enemy fire to carry his comrade to safety. A shell had landed too close to them, killing the wounded man and leaving Mr McLean hurt inside his head. Pete called it shell shock.

Jay didn't understand Pete's explanation of what had happened inside David McLean's head any more than she had when Mrs McLean had explained it to her, but she noticed that Pete was proud of it where his mother had been sad. She decided that Mr McLean was no threat to them after all.

But she needed to talk it over with Joe to try to sort it out. They played many a game of war in the orchard, each in turn being the bravest soldier the world had ever seen, but they simply couldn't see how shells could be so almighty dangerous. The biggest seashells they had ever seen would hardly leave a bruise if they hit a man right on the head, never mind a soldier who was probably wearing a helmet at the time. As for the part about the shell exploding – how could a shell explode? They pretended to stuff shells with dynamite, but that still didn't make it clear to them how Mr McLean was hurt inside his head. The best they could imagine was that the shell would have cut his skin with flying fragments if it had been filled with explosive.

Then there was the part of the story that said he had shell 'shock'. The only shock the children knew could hurt people was electric shock and they couldn't for the life of them see how that had become mixed up with shells. Even if there were electric shells the way there were electric eels, why would that reduce a man to making funny noises when he wanted to talk?

But as they acted the part of shell shocked veterans they did realise that it would be awful to be unable to say what they wanted or go where they wanted. However shells and shocks had done it, they didn't want it to happen to them. They became extremely cautious about electrical outlets and with whatever seashells they came across, making doubly sure the one came nowhere near the other.

The children became sympathetic and affectionate towards Mr McLean as they pictured how they would feel in his position. Just the same, they couldn't understand why the women were wiping tears from their cheeks and making poignant phone calls the first time Lucinda's antics made him chuckle out loud. When it was explained to them that the only time he had smiled since the war was at Bruce and Sharon's wedding, they stared at one another wondering that anyone would cry over something like that.

Jay caught only a glimmer of the importance of the occasion the day Mr McLean said his first clear word. She and Joe arrived home from school to find the routine at a standstill. Long distance phone calls were being placed. Bruce and Sharon were at Inch Brae and Pete was not out working on the farm. A bit edgy, a bit puzzled, a bit pleased for everyone if it meant so much to them, the children began to regard the old man's progress as a personal crusade.

It seemed as though his first word had been to call Lucinda 'Carrots'. From then on that was her name. They realised months later that he had probably tried to say she was a character, but that didn't matter a jot.

Just as his delight in her had helped him to make recognisable sounds, Carrots efforts to communicate with him and for him started her trying to say words. Her words for things became the household language. Carrots effort to say Grandpa came out like Poppa, so Poppa he was. Grandma Sally was G'ha assie which became Gahsie to everyone.

Amused, even Mrs McLean's friends stopped calling her Sally, and she resigned herself to being Gahsie for the rest of her life.

Only Carrots could fully understand Poppa's mumblings and moanings, which made her feel so important that she'd move heaven and earth to be at his side first when he knocked his little bell on the floor. Her pudgy little legs could get her there even ahead of Paddy. While they were left alone during the day Carrots managed to teach him how to hold and shake the bell, her plump, unsteady little fingers helping shape his thin, bent old claw. He never did learn to put the bell down without dropping it, but he did learn to hold it until someone could put it down for him. Paddy told the family at the tea table that not having to climb around the floor to find the bell was the best present she could have had.

When Jay and Joe got off the bus, they walked along the drive from the front gate to the home paddock gate swinging their satchels and chittering about the games they planned to invent that evening. Gahsie had mugs of soup waiting for them which they sipped while they changed out of their uniforms into their play clothes. As quickly as they could they ran outside to play.

One of their games was making roads and cities of the dirt in the wheel tracks. Until the gong rang they'd live out complicated life stories for their imaginary populations. The gong was the signal to the children to get their evening jobs finished in time for tea.

Jay ran as fast as she could to get the hens fed and the eggs collected. Joe didn't have an outside job yet, much to his chagrin. He was still stacking wood for the fireplaces. After Jay had taken her bucket of eggs to the kitchen the two ran together to the home paddock gate, stretching on tip toe from the second to top plank to see if they could see Pete coming in from the evening milking.

The moment they spotted the top of his hat coming over the crest of the hill they were over the gate yelling greetings. Hearing that noise those in the kitchen set the table for tea.

The children ran down the path to meet Pete, shouting all the way, Jay's plaits bouncing up and down on her back. He was striding along the wheel tracks to Inch Brae carrying a pail of milk in one hand and a pail of cream in the other, Skip, Fleabag and Shy around him. They all continued home for tea, the children chattering like magpies, jumping up and down, skipping and leaping in their efforts to shout each other down and be the first to tell Pete the news of the day.

He smiled at them, egging them on, enjoying their excitement, feeling flattered that it was so important to them to tell him their news and to be with him. He chuckled at their antics and swung the buckets at them in mock threats that set the dogs barking and romping.

Hearing the noise near the house, Carrots ran to meet them, jumping up and down on the kitchen porch, her pony tails bouncing on either side of her head. Pete handed the smaller bucket, the cream, to Jay, then scooped Carrots up with his free hand. "Are you Potatoes?" he teased.

"Nooo," she squealed in her high pitched baby voice.

"Turnips?"

"Nooo."

To the children that was high comedy. They were laughing fit to burst by the time they were inside the house. Gahsie took the milk pail from him so he could throw Carrots high in the air, shouting, "I know! You're Carrots!"

"Yes!" she squealed, pretending to be frightened, but demanding more every time.

Never allowed inside the house, the three dogs flopped down in the nursery room, panting and wagging, to await their meal. The dogs' dinner was served after tea because scraps from tea were part of it, along with plate scrapings from other meals - porridge and bread included with the vegetables and meat, piled into three dishes with gravy poured over the whole thing. It looked absolutely disgusting but it kept them in working trim for good, happy, long, useful lives.

Old Skip was still working, though not as hard any more, at sixteen years old. Fleabag was eight years old, in the prime of his strength and energy. Shy was the young dog, barely a year old when the children arrived at Inch Brae and in her first heat. She was a valuable and talented sheep dog, not too bad with co-operative cattle, but better with smaller, gentler animals.

Tea time was always full of conversations, noise, laughter and good tucker. It never failed to amaze Jay how much food would vanish without it feeling like they were eating. The food all seemed to taste so good when it was served without the strap. They gave thanks before each meal because they were grateful to have it not because they'd be beaten if they didn't.

Not only were the vegetables and potatoes from their own land, but also most of the meat. Pete and Bruce killed sheep, pigs or cattle as they were needed for the table, hunting deer, wild boar, wild goats and rabbit to give variety. They also ate their own chicken, duck, turkey and goose as well as hunting wild duck, mutton birds and swans. They usually bought the fish they ate, but at times would catch trout or bass in the river. They didn't go fishing in the ocean, so Gahsie bought schnapper, harpuku, hake, haddock, herring, marlin or John Dory from the fish shop in town. Most of the time they bought shellfish, too, but once in a while they would go to the beach to collect pipis, cockles, mussles and oysters. They loved toheroa, but it was expensive.

After tea the dogs were fed, each from its own bowl. The cats were fed from cat dishes, but the dogs had a habit of driving the cats from their bowls and finishing their food.

Not a scrap was wasted. Paper rubbish was used to start the fires, every imaginable part of the animals was eaten, including some things that slowed Jay down at first, such as brains on toast for breakfast. In a short time she came to know that Gahsie's cooking would be delicious no matter how repulsive it sounded. The parts that actually were considered inedible were made into a special dog stew and added to the dog and cat food or buried in the compost heap.

The dogs didn't step over the doorstep into the kitchen. Neither did the farm cats, but the children picked out their favourite kitten and persuaded Gahsie to let him inside the house. Pete named him 'Corker'.

Corker slept smugly in front of the kitchen fire or on Jay's bed while the working animals curled in the nursery room with their backs against the kitchen chimney for warmth. Somehow that didn't seem fair to Jay.

The older children were supposed to help Carrots have her bath and get into her pyjamas while Pete fed the dogs and the women cleared the table. When the baby was ready for bed they had their own baths, then got their homework done before bed.

Once, when they had been skimpy with the soap, (as in not applying it to their skin,) Paddy told them that clean children had shiny skin. Every night after that they turned out the light in the bathroom before they dressed, hoping every time to see a glow in the dark from their shiny clean bodies. They couldn't understand why it never seemed to work no matter how much or how hard they scrubbed. Since Paddy seemed satisfied with what she saw, they went to their homework vowing to wash until they shone next time.

Jay dozed off each night with the light from the passage way gleaming through the transom window, giving the bedroom a muted twilight. Corker, the kitten, curled cozily beside her.

Shortly after they moved in Carrots insisted on sleeping on the lower bunk so the ancient cot was relegated to the storage room again. With Carrots in the lower bunk Jay had to move carefully to sneak her Shirley Temple books and her torch under her blankets without waking her sister. She read by torchlight until she fell asleep, drifting off to the cozy buzz from the front room, the seemingly endless conversation of the adults lulling her to a peaceful, dreamy sleep. If ever she did dream of flying then, it was with her special school friends who loved to fly with her, soaring gleefully together above cotton wool clouds in warm sunlight. Her parents no longer invaded her dreams unless she had seen the welfare worker that day.

The welfare worker was supposed to visit the children every week to see how things were going. She found that she was in the way because everyone was always so busy. Once or twice she tried to see the children on a Saturday, but their weekends were just as full. After a few weeks she found it was best to pick Jay and Joe up from school every Wednesday and drive them home, talking to them in the car. She visited with Carrots while the other two changed out of their uniforms.

Jay didn't hate the poor woman quite so much anymore, though she never forgave her for the things she'd overheard on the first day. She refused to speak about her parents in any way, but would chat endlessly about the cows, the dogs or Corker. The harder Mrs Hone tried to get Jay to talk, the more obstinate Jay became.

Mrs Hone spoke to Paddy about it because she thought perhaps Paddy was teaching Jay not to talk about her parents. Jay smiled to herself behind the door as she overheard Paddy laugh out loud at the very idea of anyone being able to tell her what to say.

Paddy challenged Mrs Hone, "Can you make her say anything she doesn't want to? Do you really believe I can?"

Jay decided she liked Paddy more and more every day. She still thought welfare workers were stupid, even if she didn't hate them all the way she had. Besides, their very existence continued to remind her that they had once all lived somewhere else and weren't born to the McLeans.

She particularly resented the times Mrs Hone visited on Saturday because that was the one day of the week that her school friends couldn't come to Inch Brae to play. It was the first time in her life she'd been able to have friends visit her home and she wanted to savour every moment of it without interruption. The embarrassment of trying to explain welfare workers to stolid farming children who had never come across such a thing as a foster child doubled her resentment. Having the weekend routine that she loved disrupted by someone she didn't want to see was the last straw. Paddy and Gahsie tactfully did the best they could to persuade Mrs Hone that the Saturday visits weren't a success, and thanked God she began to pick the children up from school before Jay blew a fuse.

On weekends Jay left the home paddock after she'd fed the hens, her black rubber boots slap-flapping as she trudged along the track to the cowshed. She stayed on the outside of the wooden fence watching as Pete, Bruce and Sharon milked the cows. As the weather got colder more cows dried off, so there were fewer and fewer cows in the milking shed each time Jay went to see and milking was finished earlier each time.

Bruce fed the pigs with the skimmed milk and pig maize. Scary, noisy, bad mannered animals. Jay watched that operation from the top of the cowshed fence; as far from the pig trough as she could be and still see what was going on.

It wasn't until the milking was finished that Jay had the courage to go in the cow yard. She watched Pete load the big, galvanised cream cans on the trailer, marvelling at his strength as he hefted up the heavy cans that she couldn't even wobble. She rode on the trailer with the cream while Pete drove the tractor. They took the cream to the cream stand at the front gate, where it stood in the cool shade until the cream truck came to take it to the creamery where it was made into butter for the city. Since there wasn't much call for the skimmed milk after the cream had all been taken out by the separator, almost all of it was used to feed the pigs, dogs, cats and people on the farm. A casein factory bought some, but Jay was sure she was being teased when Bruce told her that screwdriver handles were made from casein. No magic, no stretch of her fertile imagination could turn white, liquid milk into rock hard, goldy-yellow plastic handles.

Sharon left the shed to make Bruce's breakfast just as they started to clean up after the cows. Bruce walked behind the herd to supervise the walk to the daytime grazing. That left Pete and Jay alone to finish the cleaning when they came back from taking the cream to the cream stand.

Jay loved that part. Pete was not much of a talker, but he grunted in a friendly way and nodded and smiled each time she did something really useful, making her feel that she knew a little more each weekend. They worked in a companionable silence listening to the sounds of the farm around them, along with the crack and pop of static and occasional recognizable music from the beat up radio balanced precariously on the milk pipe above the first stall.

Jay was comfortable enough to dare to tell Pete one of her daydreams while they stood side by side taking pieces of the separator out of the sterilizer and setting them on the wooden rack to wait for the next milking. He didn't call her a liar or stupid or a daydreamer. He just listened as if she were a real story teller. When she was finished he said, "Y'know, you got quite the imagination there, titch. You stay in school, eh? and study that there literature they'll teach you at college and you could be a writer."

She stared at him. "Did you want to be a writer?"

"Nah, takes too much sitting down and writing. Can't make 'em up, anyway. I tell things I heard, but you – you made that up out of your own head. That's a God given talent, that is, and I'd for sure like to see you famous for it one day. C'mon, now, got to get us some brekka afor me old ma eats it all."

Chapter Five:

Rabbits

Soon after she'd arrived, Jay took over the hens from Paddy. She fed them, made sure their water ran fresh and clean and collected the eggs. It made her feel important to be trusted with the job and more like a real part of the family since all the generations of McLean children ahead of her had started their outside work with the hens.

Just before breakfast in the morning and again, just before tea at night, Jay ran to the hen house. During the week she was in a hurry to get to her meals, but on the weekend she was not so rushed and she could take time to watch them eat, talk to them and make friends with any that would let her. She loved to see them come to recognise her as the one who fed them and run towards her clucking instead of running away squawking.

One Sunday when she was sitting quietly watching the hens, she discovered some baby bunnies sneaking through a hole in the wire netting to steal mash and wheat. Their mother couldn't fit through the hole, so she stood guard. When the mother rabbit realised Jay was there, she stamped her feet and in a flash Jay could have been convinced she'd dreamed the whole thing.

Enchanted by her discovery, she confided in Pete while they cleaned the milking shed that night.

He did two things that appalled her. First he fixed the hole in the chicken wire. Second he planned rabbit stew.

For the first time Jay was enraged by the McLeans.

She felt that her trust had been betrayed, yet she couldn't think about them with her burning hate, no matter how hard she tried. It dawned on her that she really loved these people. At the same time she felt double-crossed by Pete. The mixture of feelings threatened to tie her heart and lungs in a bow.

She raged at Joe, "Pete's horrible! How could he even say such a thing! Leaving little babies hungry. Planning to kill their mother and leave them all alone. And to eat her! I'll never eat rabbit again, never! It's cruel. It's mean. It's disgusting. I'll never ever eat any meat again. I'll heave it up if they make me. On the table. That'll teach them! And Paddy and Gahsie are on Pete's side. They're all cruel, mean, horrible and heartless. I hate them all! I'll never eat anything again and then I'll die and then they'll be sorry!"

Frightened, Joe ran to get Gahsie. Gahsie found Jay weeping into her pillow and asked gently, "Jay, sweetie, whatever's the matter?"

"Go away! I hate you! You're all mean!"

"Oh my goodness. What've we done that's so terrible?"

"You're on Pete's side and he's the worst!" Jay broke into loud, tortured sobs, torn between fear of the strapping she'd have earned from her parents for saying things like that, and badly wanting Gahsie to cuddle her and make it all better the way she had that first morning. Too afraid of being turned away to dare ask Gahsie for a hug, Jay was nearly hysterical.

Gahsie stood on tip toe to get her arms around Jay on the top bunk. She stroked Jay's plaits and crooned, "There, there, dearie, don't take on so. Now you tell old Gahsie what our Pete did that's so dreadful."

"He's going to shoot the mother rabbit with Bruce. You know that."

"Aye, I do that, but I don't know why it causes all this upset."

"They'll leave the babies cold and hungry. What if they can't find their burrow without their mother? Then they'd be lost. He won't even let them have any mash, so how can they eat without her? They don't eat hardly anything, so why can't he share a little bit? Anyway, it's the chooks' mash and they don't care so why is he saying they can't have any? They'll need it even worse after he kills their mother. He's evil!"

"Now, now, that's no way to talk. You'll get yerself all in a pother fit to heat the blood. You come with old Gahsie, now, and have a bonny big mug of cocoa, there's a good lass. Down we come, now. I'll help you to understand, but we dinna call our Petey evil. Such big tears! It's hard for a wee one to understand these things, isn't it, sweetie? I cried, too, the first time I saw my daddy kill for the table, and I've cried a lot since then. Pop up on the sofa, there's a dear, and I'll get the cocoa.

You see, Jay, this is the way of it. Rabbits are a noxious animal. We can't let any of them live. They're not meant to be in this country. God dinna put them here."

"God didn't put us here, or cows or deer either."

"Aye, that's the truth, but they don't fit in with the other life in New Zealand."

"They don't do any harm."

"Oh, my, yes they do. I ken how sweet they look, 'specially as kits, but left alone they spread like wild fire and eat too much, like rats and mice. If we feed them we just make it worse. D'ye see, lovey? Too much of anything is bad for us; too much water'll drown a body and too much food makes you sick."

"But there's only a few of them."

"Rabbits dig holes in paddocks that cows and horses and even sheeps step in and break their legs. Worse than that, people can step in them too and get hurt. If a horse steps in one whilst you're on him you can take a bad tumble and die. Why, the MacGregors across the road – their grandad died just that way when he was a young man. Wasn't found until the next day. His horse was still alive, they say, near crazy with pain. Had to shoot it. That's harder than shooting a rabbit, let me tell you. Letting something like that happen by leaving rabbits on your property's crueler than getting rid of the rabbits is.

D'ye see, now? It's a hard choice, isn't it? Which is worse? You tell me, you dear wee soul with a big, kind heart. Can you tell old Gahsie which choice to make? What if we decide for the rabbits this time and it's you who gets hurt? What then?

There now, ye ken how it must be. Our Pete's not a cruel man – he's a kind man with a cruel choice to make.

Besides, ye ken, Jay, Pete has a responsibility to keep meat on the table. With our Poppa sick and our Dave gone it's up to Brucey and Pete to keep us all fed, isn't it now?"

Jay sipped her cocoa, nodded, then sat silently staring into the flames of the kitchen fire. It wasn't supposed to be complicated. Now she didn't know what she felt or thought.

She was still holding the half empty mug in her hands, musing, when she heard the guns. Her head snapped up, shocked, wide eyes staring straight at Gahsie. Sickened, she leapt from the sofa, ran to her room, climbed out the window and shinnied up the most climbable pine until she couldn't get any higher. By the time the crush of little branchlets stopped her climb Jay was high enough to see over the house. She could see Pete and Bruce near the henhouse.

"Murderers!"

She squeezed her eyes tight shut but she couldn't rid herself of the image of what they were doing and carrying. She wept until she was so exhausted she was frightened she couldn't climb back down. No one came to make her get down and her pride wouldn't let her call for help. Tired and cold she slowly made her way back to earth in the dark, shivering as much with the cold as with guilt at seeing Paddy on her way to the henhouse with the egg bucket.

In deference to Jay's feelings, the skinned, cleaned rabbit became tea on a neighbour's table. In return the neighbour sent some pretty yellow place mats that went with the kitchen curtains.

Gahsie was delighted with the place mats and set them out at breakfast each morning. She busily made more from the scraps of material left over from making the kitchen curtains. They looked sunshiny and cheerful but Jay couldn't help remembering they'd been bought with a mother rabbit's death. She was sure Shirley Temple never had to eat breakfast looking at place mats that came from orphaning baby bunnies.

She missed Pete's company painfully. She thought of him more often during the time her anger kept her from his company than she had when she could talk to him any time she wanted. She got into trouble at school for not paying attention because she was thinking of Pete instead of doing sums.

Jay wished she could draw. She could picture Pete exactly, but nothing like him ended up on the paper. She couldn't even sketch the digger hat he always wore as if he were an Australian, complete with bobbing corks on strings to swish the flies away from his face. She had tried his hat on but those little corks swinging in front of her eyes had bothered her more than the flies had.

Then there was the straw that always hung out of the left side of his mouth as if he was aiming for a degree in looking like a hayseed.

She'd like to know how he managed to walk as if he had three knees and no chest. Even if his pants did have about a two yard inseam, she still didn't think legs could move like that. When she tried to walk the way Pete did she tripped over her own feet.

When he did talk instead of grunting, he spoke slowly and softly like he was half asleep. She had once asked him why he always moved and spoke so slowly. He had told her, "I never run when I could've walked. I never walk when I could've rid. I never stand when I can sit and I never sit when I can lay down."

Now that she thought about it, Jay didn't think she'd ever seen him stand upright. He leaned. She had taken smoko to him one day when he'd been mending a fence and saw that in an open paddock with nothing to lean on he had squatted on his heels, his elbows on his knees; leaning on himself when there was nothing else. He'd even found a way to lean when he walked the cows in for milking; his arm was always on Sabrina's boney hip. Jay did try to lean on Sabrina herself one day to see what it was like. She was too short to reach Sabrina's hip, so she leaned against her big, brown, warm side. And fell every few steps. It's not possible for people to lean while they walk.

Yet Pete was by no means a lazy man. The half-closed eyes saw everything and his ambling slow motion carried a higher work load than stocky little Bruce's high speed buzzing around.

Jay needed her foster uncle, needed to hear his ironic, slow paced chuckle, needed to hear his grunts and to see him wink at her. With no idea how to mend the rift with Pete, she turned to Bruce as a substitute.

Tagging along behind Bruce while he walked the cows from one paddock to another wasn't the same as walking beside Pete. Bruce would never wait for her. He tramped along at such a speed she was more trotting than walking most of the time.

"Wait for me!" she called in desperation one Saturday when she nearly ran out of breath.

Bruce looked over his shoulder. "I got to check these here heifers and see how they're coming along, then I got to take Sharon to town. Can't be late, she's got a doctor's appointment."

"Pete always waits for me."

"Go with him, then."

"Can't."

Bruce looked down at her, puzzled, then bustled off to run his hands over a fat heifer who lifted her head to look at him, curious. "Whyever not?" he asked, charging over to another heifer. This one moved indignantly away, earning a round of curses that made Jay's lips twitch with glee. Pete would never have used language like that in front of her. She didn't know what they meant, but they would be good words to trade at school to win the admiration of her friends who, she was sure, didn't know those ones.

"I - er - he - um - I didn't like it when he killed those baby bunnies."

"You still on about that? Don't half hold a grudge, do you? It's life. All of life comes from death. The Bible tells us, 'Lest a seed fall to earth and die, it shall not bring forth fruit'."

"What's that got to do with shooting those poor little rabbits?"

"I shot them too, you know, Jay. You're being silly about this. You won't spend any time with Pete, but you will with me when it was the both of us did the shooting?"

"I didn't tell you about them. I told him and he went and killed them."

"You have to understand about this, Jay-bird. We can't have wild rabbits running about. Everything dies. It has to. There'd be no life if there wasn't any death."

Jay thought about that while he checked the heifers, then protested as they walked along the race towards home, "That makes no sense. If there wasn't any death there'd be nothing but life."

"If there was no death what do you think the live things would eat to stay alive?"

"Plants."

"Plants die too, you know. And they live off dead things in the first place. The compost that makes our garden grow is made of dead things rotted down. The animals kill the plants by eating them. We eat both plants and animals. We have to for health. It's the way we're built. Everything we eat dies to feed us and other plants and animals died to feed them first. Everything in God's green earth lives from other things dying, then dies itself so other things can live. All life is a circle, kid. All you can do about it is make sure when you do take a life you do it with respect and by causing as little fear and pain as possible." They stopped at the cottage. Bruce told her seriously, "You make friends with old Pete again. He misses you just as much as you miss him. Don't let a difference of opinion come between you and someone you love. We have each other too short a time to waste any of it over things that don't matter."

"What do you mean 'we have each other too short a time?' You and Pete have been together your whole lives. That's a long time."

"I was with my brother Dave his whole life, too, and now we've lost him. Don't take anything for granted. You never know when it's going to be gone the next time you turn around."

"Joe won't be gone the next time I turn around. He's not going to war."

"I thought like that when I was your age, too. It changes you to lose your brother, war or no war."

"It changed you?"

"Changed all of us. I wanted to have kids, which I never did before, and Pat got you lot."

"Paddy got us because Dave died?"

"That's about it. And you mean the world to Pete, too. He don't say much, but it was as bad for him to lose Dave as it was for us. He was younger when Dad left, you know, so Dave stepped in, sort of."

"What was he like?"

"Struth. How can you tell a kid what your brother was like? Like us and like himself. Best damned brother you could ever have. Good man. Bloody Reds didn't deserve the likes of him. Broke me old ma's heart. If it wasn't for her wanting us here I'd be over there teaching them Godless Communists not to shoot me brother, and Pete would to, I'm sure."

Jay discovered she loved Pete again, but, instead, hated God and his system. This made Sunday School somewhat uncomfortable, but it made it possible for her to be friends with Pete again. For a long time she ate no meat or fish.

Life returned to its calm routine. Jay didn't find out until much later that the cats and dogs had been set to hunt out the rabbit nest so she didn't add to her confusion at that time by hating the pets. No one punished her for climbing the tree, nor had they demanded she get down, so after the drama was past Jay and Joe added a new adventure to their play.

They began to climb the highest tree they could, look out over the countryside, hang on for dear life in the wind, sing silly songs and dream marvellous dreams.

Since she had discovered she didn't hate Pete, it was alright for Jay to climb on to the trailer behind the tractor when Pete was driving and ride thumpety bumping across the farm. Each time they came to a gate she'd jump down to wrestle with it, riding it triumphantly as it swung open if she succeeded; climbing crestfallen back onto the trailer to let Pete open it if she couldn't.

As they went blatting up and down the rolling countryside they sang 'Jambalaya', shouting the words to each other over the deafening tractor motor. They laughed at each other and wondered about the strange foreign words, finally coming to the conclusion during feed out one Saturday that it had to be an African song. The words sounded more African than anything else they could think of.

Jay and Joe went to Africa on chilly, sunny winter afternoons, turning the strange words from 'Jambalaya' into a native language and catching many a dangerous animal. Except elephants. Elephants were too nice to be shot by big game hunters, so they made friends with the elephants instead and had b-i-g invisible pets on the lawn.

A great peacefulness descended on the children. Sometimes Jay thought her heart would swell with sheer joy, right through her rib cage and burst all over the house like a water balloon. Even the welfare worker's visits didn't dampen their spirits any more.

Chapter Six:

Wee Davie.

One long, rainy Sunday when there had been no milking for two months, the August holidays were almost over and Poppa, Carrots, Joe and Gahsie were all taking afternoon naps, Jay thought she would shrivel from boredom. She could not, absolutely could not read any more Enid Blyton books; nor Heidi, Pollyanna, Nancy Drew nor Shirley Temple.

She stared at herself in the mirror. With no hair on her forehead she had a high domed look that she hoped made her seem intelligent. She was still wearing her Sunday School dress which had a flat velvet bow at the back of her waist. She noted with satisfaction that the ribbons tying her plaits were level with the bow on her belt.

Jay had a tiny frame and a small, pointed face with huge eyes. Her daintiness was ruined by heavy black eyebrows that she hated. She practised thunderous glares at herself in the mirror, using the eyebrows for effect. It didn't help. She sighed. She still hated them.

Sighing again over her shortness and thinness, she looked herself over from top to bottom hoping to see a sign of growth. She was tired of being the smallest child in her standard one class at school. To see how it would feel to be tall she got a chair and stood on it in front of the mirror.

Once on the chair she lost interest in the mirror, staring instead at the transom window. The first morning at Inch Brae she had wondered about getting up to it, but she hadn't thought about it again since then. She got down from the chair, pushed the desk up to the door and climbed on that. By putting the chair and some books on top of the desk, climbing up and down to check the height and add more as she needed to, Jay built a tower so that even a short little girl like herself could see over the door frame.

The thrill of looking through the window into the passageway wore off fairly quickly. She tried hanging by her fingers from the moulding around the room at the eight foot mark. It was awfully dusty. She found out the decorative lintel at the top of the door frame was wide enough to kneel on and strong enough to hold her weight. She drew in the dust then wiped it clean as far as she could reach in both directions. After that she discovered the window could be opened. It pushed up at an angle to the passage. She tried to listen in on the conversation in the front room but couldn't distinguish a single word. It was all she could do to sort out the voices.

'Hey, Bruce and Sharon are here,' she thought. 'I didn't hear them get here.'

Jay poked her head out of the transom window and tried to see through Paddy's transom window. She couldn't see anything but the top of Paddy's wall. Down the other way she could see all the way to Joe's room, but the view from the top of the door wasn't much different from what she could see from the floor.

The steady, heavy rain poured relentlessly down making everything outside dark and dreary, depressing Jay to where she felt like crying over nothing. Yearning for the sunshine, she climbed down and found her paints and crayons. She needed water for her paints, but the idea of moving the desk, the chair and the books to get the door open was too much for her. There was plenty of water outside if she had something to catch it in. She wandered around the bedroom. The little dish that held her hair grips would do. Jay slid the window up a bit and set the empty dish in the rain. By the time she had carried her crayons and paints to the top of her tower then climbed back down, the little dish was full of water. Carefully she carried it to the desk. She had to put the dish down at each stage of her climb so that she wouldn't lose the water, but finally she had her paints and crayons and enough water to do the job arranged along the lintel over the door.

Jay worked with total absorption to create a brightly coloured rising sun with rays extending to the edges of the glass.

Paddy's voice suddenly asking, "Why Jay A.E. whatever are you doing up there?" startled her so she nearly fell. Jay had been concentrating too hard to notice Paddy walk into the passage on her way to check on the sleeping children. Flushing with guilt, Jay stammered, "I made a sun. We haven't had any the whole August holidays so I made one."

To her relief Paddy grinned up at her. "What a great idea! That's very pretty, Jay. You are an original. I thought we did it all when we were kids, but, so help me, this is a new one. What are you standing on?"

"Books."

"Way up there?"

"Nope. I got my chair and desk and books."

"Good heavens! How did you move that heavy desk?"

"Pushed it."

"You're joking! You are very strong for your size. How will you get down?"

"Climb. It's simple. I did it lots of times."

"Are you sure you're safe?"

"Yep."

"How will you get the door open?"

"Dunno." Jay's face fell at the idea of putting everything back. All the strength left her at the mere thought of all that work.

She looked down at the room around her, hunting for a way to avoid hauling that heavy desk all the way back across the room. Then she shrugged and looked back at Paddy, her eyes light with inspiration. "We can use the window."

Paddy burst out laughing. "Jay, my dear girl, you are truly unique; the most inventive child I have ever met. Stay right there. Now don't you move, I want everyone to see this." Paddy stepped back into the kitchen, calling, "Mummy! Petey! Bruce! Sharon! Come and see this! You have to see it to believe it!"

They came, exclaiming and laughing. Jay felt pleased and embarrassed at the same time. Carrots was woken by the noise and started to cry because she couldn't get out of the room.

Pete went out the front door and sloshed over to the window to climb in, cursing the rain. He took photos of Jay on top of her tower and painting her sun, then lifted her down and pushed the desk away from the door to let Carrots rush to Paddy, arms wide, and the others in.

They helped put the things where they should be, laughing all the while. Once everything was back in place and Carrots had been taken to the bathroom, the men sat on the bottom bunk, slapping their knees and laughing loudly, shouting out to Gahsie, "Mum! Do you remember the time . . . "

Much to Jay's bewilderment, her bored fiddling had sparked endless gleeful 'remember when' stories that brought uproarious laughter for the rest of the afternoon, all through tea and even on going after the children were in bed. She had no idea what she'd done, but she came in for more hugs, pats, pet names and tosses in the air than she usually collected in a week.

Some of their stories were about Xantha, which made Jay and Joe wish they could meet her. Then some were about Dave, which made them glance warily at his photo in its black frame with the poppy taped to one corner. Jay saw Gahsie wipe a tear during a story about something Dave had done as a little boy, but a moment later she was laughing as loudly as everyone else.

Jay whispered to Joe, "Who can figure grown-ups? You'd think they'd be mad at me."

"The rain got to them, I reckon," he whispered back.

There were many quips to Sharon and Bruce about the things they were in for. Jay lay awake in her bunk trying to understand those jokes. Sharon had looked silly and pink when she was teased. Bruce had looked sappy and proud.

'Why? Sharon's silly a lot, lately. She doesn't do her work and everyone carries things for her. And she naps almost every day. And sometimes she just sits down holding her big tummy and saying, "Ooo." She's really fat now and she wasn't when we came here.'

Jay turned over and looked up at her sun silhouetted in the transom. Other odd things bothered her about Bruce and Sharon in the last little while. 'They keep saying, "Just as well it's dry season." and, "Maybe he'll be here before calving." Who's coming? I don't see what they're so pleased about. I wish they didn't dry the cows off. Having a house cow is not the same.'

Sabrina now grazed alone in the orchard. Twice a day she was brought to the kitchen steps and milked by hand. Jay had heard Bruce and Pete talk about drying Sabrina off now that the first calves were due.

Jay thought about that. It had something to do with what was puzzling her, she knew. 'The cows they've brought to the birthing paddock are so fat they can hardly walk. Like Sharon. They're getting calves. I wonder if she's getting a baby? What's so funny about that? They laughed about me and told her that's what she has in store for her. They think it's funny the baby might be like me. I don't like that.'

Her feelings hurt, Jay padded out to the front room. Once she got there she didn't know what it was she had planned to do there. She peeked around the door.

They were all cosily around the front room fire in a semi-circle making toasty pies in the fire toaster. Poppa was still there, propped up in an armchair even though it was way after his bedtime. There was a blanket tucked over his legs, his eyes were gleaming with pleasure and he was making weird noises. Every time someone came to the end of a story they all hooted with laughter and Poppa jerked back and forth, arms flinging up and down, making sounds like a car on a cold morning. Jay supposed that sound like a motor that couldn't get started was Poppa's laugh, but she'd never heard him do that before.

The sleepy canary trilled his grumbles each time their sudden bursts of noise woke him. Corker, sleeping in front of the fire, lifted his head and frowned at the disturbance. The ancient fire irons had a kettle hanging from them, making billy tea.

'What did I do to make a party like this?'

The ever vigilant Paddy sensed Jay lurking in the shadows and looked right at her. "Jay! You little imp, what're you doing out of bed?"

"Now, Pats, leave her be. We are rather loud. 'Spect the poor little mite couldn't sleep. Come here, tuppence, up on your Uncle Brucie's knee. There, now. Too much excitement tonight? Couldn't sleep?"

"No – uh – it's not that. I – um – I wonder . . . "

Paddy was instantly all attention, "What is it, precious?"

"I got to go to the lavatory," she improvised.

"Well, come on, then, I'll take you." Paddy took her hand and they went together into the dark. Jay realised there wasn't one light on in the whole house. She shivered, pleased and spooked at the same time.

Paddy snapped on the lavatory light, ruining the delicious creepiness with every day, ordinary electric light. "What is it, dear? Are you cold? You're shivering. You'll catch your death one day with that habit of yours of going around with no slippers or dressing gown."

"I'm not cold. It's spooky."

"I'll put some lights on if you're scared, sweetheart."

"I'm not scared. It's corker. Why're you in the dark?"

"It's better to tell stories around a fire. We do it for fun."

"Why is it so funny tonight? Why is everyone laughing at me? I can clean the window."

"Aha, I see the problem here." Chuckling, Paddy hugged Jay, lifted her off the toilet as if she were tiny again, helped her wash her hands, then snapped the light off so they were left blind in the sudden darkness. "How's that?" she whispered in Jay's ear.

Thrilled, Jay shivered again, clung to Paddy and beamed into the darkness, delighted to creep through the house like a mouse. She looked at her hands. Disappointed, she sighed.

"What is it, dear?"

"Why don't I ever shine? You said clean children shine and Joe and I wash and wash like anything, but we just can't get clean enough to shine. Look at my hands, and that's after you washed them, too. What's wrong with me? Is the dirt right in my skin so we can't wash it off?"

Whooping with laughter, Paddy exclaimed, "So that's why you always turn the light off in the bathroom. I did wonder. Oh, you precious little soul." She knelt down and gathered Jay to her, holding her close and laughing into her neck. More baffled than ever, Jay backed away from her and ran into the front room to stand beside Gahsie. She fidgeted uncertainly as Paddy regaled the family with the story of the children trying to glow in the dark.

As they all guffawed gleefully it became just too much for Jay. Great fat tears rolled down her cheeks.

"Ohhh," breathed Gahsie, gathering Jay on to her lap. She cuddled the little girl, smoothing her plaits, calling over her head, "Take it easy, kids."

Paddy immediately dropped to her knees beside her mother and stroked Jay's back. "Jay, oh my dear, I'm so sorry. Sweetheart, we're not laughing at you. We're laughing because we love you. You make us very happy."

"Why? What did I do?"

"Uh - that's a tough one," Paddy stalled.

Bruce chipped in, "You remind us of when we were kids and the things we did.

"But why is that funny? How does it make Sharon funny?"

"No flies on that one," Sharon commented under her breath.

That stung Jay. "I know that! There's no flies in winter."

A muffled chuckle went around the room, making Jay mad. She turned on Sharon. "Are you getting a baby?" she demanded with her old sharp tone, halting the smiles at once. The adults looked at one another, disconcerted.

Sharon said softly, "Yes, I am."

Jay hung her head, not sure of how to express the bad feelings roiling inside her. She whispered to Gahsie, "They don't like me."

Those who heard her responded with a chorus of denials and assurances, while those who hadn't demanded to know what she'd said.

Unnerved by their reactions, Jay quavered, her chin quivering, "Well, you'll be sorry if the baby is like me."

Thunderstruck, they all spluttered at once.

Gleaning a feeling of power from being the centre of attention, she pouted at them, "I heard you say that. You laughed at Sharon for being 'in for it'. I heard you. Like if someone falls in the mud you laughed like that. You did! You did! Having me is like falling in the mud."

Despite valiant efforts to contain themselves, one by one they collapsed in helpless laughter.

Jay looked from one to another in mingled bewilderment and irritation. She wiggled down off Gahsie's lap affronted by feeling Gahsie shake with suppressed laughter. As she glared at them all like an offended kitten all their efforts at control left them. They laughed until they couldn't speak, until they were hiccoughing and holding their sides, until they couldn't control those silly titterings that happen when people catch the eye of a cohort who's also trying not to laugh. Even Gahsie was in this, one arm around Jay, the other supporting her head while tears streamed down her cheeks. Poppa was sounding like a car that wouldn't start. When he lurched forward Pete was laughing too hard to catch him properly so they ended up propped against each other absurdly. Sharon wailed, "Brucey, please, I'm going to wet myself."

Which started them all again. Bruce stumbled as he helped the ungainly Sharon to her feet, then they staggered out of the room, arms around each other's waists.

Jay frowned. 'What's funny about a big lady wetting herself? This is just silly.' Sulkily she retreated into the dark and climbed up on the big front room sofa. She curled unnoticed under its afghan, hoping to lie there watching them and figure out what in the world had happened on what should have been a perfectly normal evening.

The next thing Jay was aware of was waking up chilled to the bone. The afghan was mostly on the floor, the fire had gone out and there wasn't a soul around. She couldn't think where she was for a moment, but after looking around groggily she realised that it was morning and she was on the front room sofa.

"Holy cow! The front room!"

Shivering, Jay wrapped the afghan around her like a robe and ventured forth. The canary was puffed out against the cold, his head under his wing. She envied him his feathers. In the cold fire place the billy still hung and the toasty pies still sat, abandoned exactly where they had been when she'd gone to the sofa. That sight started Jay wondering. 'What happened? Why didn't Pete carry me to my bed and cover me up?'

The front room doors had been left standing open. Once she'd seen that Jay was seriously concerned. She hadn't once seen those doors left standing like that. Hitching the afghan up so it wouldn't drag on the floor, Jay carefully latched the doors, then turned to look at the kitchen.

The kitchen fire was not yet lit. Teeth chattering, Jay dumped the good afghan on the sofa, wrapped herself in the old kitchen afghan and ran to see where Paddy was. She was lying on top of her bed, snoring. That sight stopped Jay in her tracks. She had never been awake ahead of Paddy, nor had she seen Paddy sleeping with all her clothes on. She decided she was too cold to do anything other than dress at that moment, so she padded to her room.

Carrots was already awake and chilled. Shaking with cold herself, Jay dressed the both of them, then ran to Pete's room. He, too, was lying on top of his bed, fully clothed. Disoriented by it all, Jay was about to run to Gahsie's room when she heard Sabrina lowing. She hadn't been milked yet! Jay ran to Pete.

"Pete! Pete! What's wrong?" Jay demanded, frightened. Pete was unshaven for the first time since she'd met him. Every new detail upset Jay more.

Sabrina lowed again, a note of desperation colouring her moo. Jay shook Pete's shoulder, calling him. He swung his feet to the floor, holding his head with both hands. "Dear Lord, it can't be morning yet. My head's going to fall off." He answered Sabrina's frantic call. "Coming, old girl. Keep your horns on." He pulled himself upright with great care, then patted Jay's head. "'Snothing wrong, poppet. Once we've had some sleep everything'll be hunky-dory. Anyone else up?"

Jay shook her head.

"Gawd struth! Be a good'un and get old Pats up. She's got to see to the old man, sleep or no. 'N you got to see to the hens, m'girl. Time to chaw it over later when she's running ship-shape again. Hop to."

Jay 'hopped to', waking the complaining Paddy while Pete splashed cold water on his face at the kitchen sink, swore under his breath, put his hat and boots on and stomped outside with a "Struth! She's a cold'un with no hot tucker to get a man going."

Jay bundled herself up against the cold and dashed outside to her hens. She ran past Pete squatting at Sabrina's side milking her with smooth even streams of milk pouring into the bucket and the cats hanging around hopefully. As quickly as she could without being careless Jay fed the hens, collected the eggs and brought them back to the kitchen door. She set the egg bucket down to reach up and open the door when a new sound stopped her dead. There was a feeble mewing coming from the nursery room. She turned to open that door instead when she was jolted by a bellow from Pete.

"Hoy! Don't you open that! Freeze the little sod, you will. Get on with givin' Paddy a bit of a hand. Got to get some grub on, girl. Man can't work with no sleep and no grub, both."

Jay shot inside with the eggs. Whatever she'd missed last night, it must have been something phenomenal. 'It's a mystery. I'm going to figure it out like Nancy Drew.'

She set the eggs down inside the door and sat down on the floor to pull her boots off, eyeing Paddy closely. She called out across the kitchen, "The door to the nursery room is shut. Something's in there."

Paddy turned a haggard face in her direction. "Why not? Everything else happened last night. Put the eggs on the table and bring a chair here." Paddy spoke in a flat voice quite unlike her usual warm tones.

Both Paddy and Pete had given Jay orders in an unfriendly way that morning. Jay thought about it as she pushed a chair from the table to the stove. It didn't offend her, it made everything more mysterious. Wincing at the noise the chair made scraping across the floor, Paddy grabbed it and plunked it down in front of the stove.

"Where's Gahsie?" Jay asked.

"She'll be here soon. Up here, now."

"What about Joe?"

"He's going to have to take care of himself this morning, Jay. I need you here to stir the porridge so that we have something for breakfast. Like this, now, watch." Despite the shortness of her tone, Paddy gave Jay thorough, gentle instructions on how to take care of the porridge.

Jay felt as if they had treated her like an adult. Awed by the importance of her job she daydreamed, 'I'm a grown-up lady making a beautiful, nourishing, hot breakfast for my ten children and eight orphans from the starving Belgians.'

Stir and stir and stir.

'You can't stop when your arms ache. I'm a slave in America and if I stop they'll flog me. I'm a black slave. I only look white because they make me stir porridge.'

Stir and stir and stir.

'Won't this ever be finished? I'm never going to make porridge when I'm grown up.'

Stir and stir and stir.

'I think maybe I'll never even eat porridge again. I probably won't ever eat anything again. After this my arms won't be able to lift food to my mouth.'

Stir and stir and stir.

Pete stomped in with the bucket of Sabrina's milk. "Struth! Paddy! What's she doing leaving the kid slaving away like that? Here, poppet, I'll do that." He put the milk down beside the eggs, lifted Jay down from the chair and effortlessly stirred the porridge.

Shaking her aching arms out, tears of weariness beginning to spill, a disappointed Jay protested, "She needs me to. I'm big enough."

Pete picked her up and put her back on the chair. "You reckon? It's finished. I'll cut this here bread and you toast it. Don't burn yourself, mind, nor the toast neither, for that matter. You right now? Okie dokie. I'll see what's going on down there."

He clomped off down the hall to Poppa's room. After a moment Paddy strode back to the kitchen looking more awake and businesslike.

"I'm so sorry, Jay, I just couldn't get back. Daddy was up too late last night. Now he's just impossible. Can you set the table? That's a lass. Hop to, now. We're all at sixes and sevens today."

One way and another, a tolerable substitute for breakfast was pulled together. The first smiles of the day were cracked at Joe's efforts to dress himself. He shuffled into the kitchen, sulky at being neglected, decked out in a slipper on one foot, a sock on the other, play pants, a pyjama shirt buttoned crookedly and hanging out at the back, topped off with his best cardigan inside out on one sleeve and twisted over at the back to be right side out on the other sleeve. Grinning, Pete tried to straighten Joe out, saying, "Regular little ragamuffin, aren't you?"

Joe's bottom lip came full out. He stamped his foot, wailing, "I am not a raggy muffin!"

Pete and Paddy let out a hoot of laughter. Pete swung the little boy up in the air and tossed him at the ceiling, chuckling, "A corker you are, son, a right corker! Got to tell me mates this one, eh, Pats?"

"Everybody sit down and let's eat. Say the blessing, Pete, then we'd best let this crew in on it all," Paddy told him.

Jay could hardly contain herself. The moment they said, "Amen," she burst out, "I know! I know it! I bet Sharon's getting a baby and Gahsie's gone to the cottage to help."

"Not bad, Miss Sherlock Holmes, but you're missing by a bit. You went to bed just as the excitement started last night," Paddy answered.

"I didn't go to bed. You left me on the sofa."

"What?"

"Jay pointed to the front room afghan heaped on the kitchen sofa. "I was cold," she complained.

Pete exclaimed, "Gawd's struth! That right now? Never even noticed. Right as soon as Sharon went to the bathroom, you remember that?"

Jay nodded.

Pete continued, "Maybe that last big laugh did it. Dunno, but next thing y'know they're bellering the kid's coming so we all shoots out in the kitchen here. Sure enough. Time to go."

Paddy interjected, "Bit much for the little ones, Pete."

Pete looked sheepish, mumbling, "Yeah, well . . . "

Paddy shook her head at him, then turned to Jay, "I am sorry we lost you in all the confusion, pet. We all rushed in here, you see. Then, while Gahsie stayed in here with Sharon, Pete and I put Poppa to bed."

"And he warn't half peeved about that, too!"

"And Bruce ran over to the cottage to get his car."

"And the great clot goes and gets it stuck in the mud, doesn't he?"

"Oh, Pete, he was nervous about Sharon, and it was still raining cats and dogs, remember."

"Struth! He's lived on this flaming farm for his whole life and he's been driving on it since he was twelve. Paths haven't changed in living memory. That's 26 years of walking them things and fifteen of driving them and he gets lost in a bit of rain! Strike me pink! So he comes walking back here, soaked to the skin, wanting me to bail him out. My whole life he never figured I knew me right hand from me left, now he wants me to save his hide!"

"The kids, Pete."

"Yeah, and you women sure didn't help none, cackling away like that."

"It was funny. Bruce was soaked to the skin and running around in circles with you barking at his heels."

"Well, he wants me to fart around in that flaming rain storm in my bloody new car, getting it muddy and God knows what all, to get his ruddy great tank out of the paddock what he went and dug it into but good in the first place – spinning his flaming wheels like Gawd amightly circular saws – leaving his poor labouring wife here by herself."

"She wasn't by herself."

"Fat lot of good you two did her, keeping her laughing away in here, fit to be tied! Holy cow! It's a wonder she didn't rupture something!"

Wiping tears of laughter from her eyes, Paddy begged, "Please, the children."

"Yeah, right. First birth on the farm of our generation and they got to run it like a God forsaken circus!" He glared at the children. Even though they only understood two words in three, they couldn't help giggling at the idea of Pete and Bruce shouting at one another in that downpour.

"You think that's funny, do you? Just you wait, it got worse!"

Paddy interrupted, telling the children, "That storm made it difficult for Sharon's Mum to get to the hospital, so Gahsie went with her to make sure she had a mother with her, even if it isn't her own Mum."

"Oh, yeah, right, sure thing, but you know why, don't you? She didn't believe that great nit could get her there in time, so she wanted to go along to be at the birthing to save laughing Madonna there and her kid from Mr 29 thumbs."

"At least Sharon was cheerful, Pete."

"Cheerful! Hysterical, if you ask me. You know what he does? He puts my car in the duck pond. Holy mackerel, me new car! Like it wasn't wet enough already! Then he – you wait, this is a corker! – he wants me to drive the tractor now, in that weather, no less, to pull his car out. Not my new car, oh no, his lollopping great brontosaurus of a thing that he got stuck; I'm to drown meself to free it. There, now, you didn't know that one, did you? Think it's funny, do you? Wasn't you out there getting buckets emptied over your head because his lordship's forgotten how to drive. Can't even get out of his own damned farm, how's he going to get his poor wife to the hospital, I'd like to know?"

Speechless with laughter, Paddy shook her head, trying to get her voice to work. "Mum'll help them," she said at last.

Pouring more coffee, Pete was not to be mollified. "You don't know the half of it! Blow me down! He gets his wife into the car, and then he wants Mum to drive the tractor in case he can't get the car there. Me poor old Mum driving all that way in the pelting rain and he sits nice and dry in the car with his wife."

"No one was dry by then."

"So why didn't he drive the tractor since he was already drenched through? Oh no. He's got to go off half-cocked making an Easter Parade of it; me poor old Mum driving me good tractor in the Gawd's struth awfullest down pour this side of Noah's flood and me dumb cluck brother trying to remember how to drive his hysterical wife to the hospital to have their first kid. Never seen the like in me life! Stone the flaming crows! They got the tractor. They drowned me car. Now the cows start to deliver. Of course they do. Old Sharon sure held off till calving, didn't she now? Good hearted soul, that. Why didn't she just shoot me and put me out of me misery?"

"This part I know about, Pete. I was out there with you all night."

Sudden warmth in his voice, Pete turned to Paddy, "Too right you were, Pats. Good thing, too." His voice went up again as he continued, "That kid of theirs, he's got our Mum who can calm a fidgety cow like nobody's business and he's got our brother so's I got no one to help me with the heavy work. Good, eh? Just perfect. Then that pretty little heifer there, the one with the white freckles - what do you call her?"

"Sylvia."

"It's her first time. She's a bit nervous there, you know. She tries to drop in the water. So that flaming Fleabag, what does he do? He barks at her! Gawd struth! And that's me good cattle dog! So she goes pelting off into the blessed duck pond with me dearly departed car, up to her belly in water, in heavy labour, frightened silly. The water's too cold for her, she starts to bellow, but she won't leave the bloody car! What is it, her baby sitter? I'm going to lose the first calving cow of the year because of me prize winning cattle dog there. Man's best friend, my eye. Me brother's not here to help me, me mother's not here to talk her out of it, and me tractor and me car can't pull her out. They hang murderers, you know. Not legal to torture them to death. But farmers? Now there's good sport, mate, we're fair game."

Jay asked, "Did you get her out?"

"Yeah. Had to wade in and gentle her out, easy like. Took forever. Nearly lost that one. Got a real nice heifer from her. Looks alright now."

Joe asked, "Didn't you help, Paddy?"

"I was busy all night with the sheep."

"I'n'it marvellous? I'n'it just flaming marvellous? The stupid sheep decide to drop their lambs, too. Not enough we've got Sharon and the cows started - now the sheeps got to add to it. Not as if it was raining or anything, oh no, it was a vertical lake! Sheep are the stupidest animals on God's green earth. Only mistake He ever made, they are. Forgot to put the brains in them. Think they'll come down for help like the cows? Not on your life! They got to hide theirselves. Ewes down in that rain, their wool so waterlogged they can't get up if they had the brains to try. Stone the flaming crows! Worst night in the history of mankind, lambs, calves and me great helpful brother all in one night; and it's got to be the night we get we get four inches of rain in twelve hours."

"Could have been worse, Pete."

"How?"

"Could've been windy. A strong wind and we'd've lost those calves and lambs."

Pete sighed. All of his indignation vanished. He looked as if he'd deflated. "Now we're dead beat, you kids. You watch your step today. No one's had enough sleep and the two of us got to do the work of five. Just take her easy today, you got that?

The children looked at one another, nodding. Solemnly they began to help Paddy clear the table. The phone rang before they could finish. Pete and Paddy looked at one another for a moment, then Pete got up to answer the phone.

All the gruffness left him. He didn't look as unshaven, somehow, but he was speaking so quietly they couldn't tell what had happened.

Finally he hung up and told Paddy, "A boy, David Bruce - wee Davie, they're calling him. 7lbs 10oz, just a few minutes ago. Sharon's doing well, she's sleeping. Her Mum did get there in time, so our Mum's heading home now. That was Bruce. He'll hang about a bit. Wants to see her when she wakes up, I 'spect."

Paddy and Pete held one another close, tears in Paddy's eyes. Jay was puzzled. She would have expected leaping for joy at the news of a new baby, not this almost reverent silence.

"Will wee Davie share my room like the girls share?" Joe asked, jigging in anticipation.

"No, lovey, he's Bruce and Sharon's baby. He'll live in the cottage with them." Joe looked so crestfallen that Paddy got down on one knee to give him a hug, adding, "You'll see him every day and he'll grow up right here, so it'll be almost the same. When he's bigger maybe he can visit overnight in your room."

Poppa's bell rang, galvanizing everyone to action.

The house and the farm with all their work were still there to be tended.

Chapter Seven:

Alphie

While she was helping Paddy with the dishes, Jay heard again the strange noise she'd heard when she was carrying the eggs inside. "What is that?" she asked. "Can you hear it? And why wouldn't Pete let me open the nursery door to see?"

"Ah, yes, I meant to tell you earlier, but it sort of got lost in all the confusion. One of the ewes last night had terrible trouble. Her wool had soaked through and it was too heavy for her to get up. When I helped her can you guess what happened?"

"She had a lamb?"

"Not just one lamb."

"Twins?"

"Triplets! Isn't that something? Second delivery of the season is triplets! It's a miracle, God's green earth is. `S a wonderful time, spring, even when it does have nights like last night."

"Pete was very angry with Bruce, wasn't he?"

"No, dearie. He's very short of sleep and very worried about Sharon. We love her, she's family, and it was a bad night to be trying to make a long trip like that."

"But he was angry with the sheep."

"He was worried about them, too. They need more help than the cows do – their wool gets wet and they go down, they won't come for help and they hide. With only two of us out there, he thought we wouldn't be able to do it. That's why he got so loud. When Pete's quiet you worry. That's when he's mad. He blusters when he doesn't know what to do."

"But he's quiet all the time. I've never heard him talk so much."

"That's 'cos you've never seen him so tired and upset at the same time. We're finished here. Come on, I'll show you what's in the nursery." Hand in hand they went to the door, then Paddy said, "Close your eyes."

Jay put one hand over her eyes, the other still holding Paddy's hand. She dropped her hands in fright when Paddy wailed, "Oh, no! How could he!"

Lying in the straw was a tiny new born lamb. The strange noise was the lamb's weak little cries. Tight against the lamb, one paw over it so she looked like she was hugging it, was the gentle, quiet, retiring Shy, her thick border collie coat making a blanket for the little scrap.

"Is she hurting that thing, Paddy?" Jay asked in horror.

"No, dear, no. She saved his life. It's a baby lamb, the littlest of the triplets. He would have died out there, so I put him in here, but in all that caffuful the kitchen fire went out and it wasn't relit until so late this morning that this room must have been like ice. He'd have had no heat but for Shy. Looks like Pete hasn't fed him. I thought he would have done that first thing. He must have thought I did. I put the poor little thing in here to save his life, then we almost killed him with neglect. Oh, Shy, you darling dog. How did you get in here?" Paddy picked the tiny lamb up, which made the timid dog shy away. "There, now, come on, Shy. You're a good dog. Good dog. Come, Shy. You deserve a special treat."

The dog obediently followed them to the kitchen door, but stopped at the threshold. She knew not to go into the house and was too timid to take a chance, even for a special treat. She stood politely at the door, carefully focusing on the floor until Paddy got back to her with a piece of cheese.

"Good dog. Good dog, Shy. There you go, now. Go back to your sheep. You've saved this one." The dog gently lifted the cheese from Paddy's hand, then turned and trotted off, purposefully.

While she watched Paddy make up a bottle of milk for the lamb, Jay asked her, "Why is Shy like that? She never barks or jumps around like Fleabag."

"Everyone has their own personality, Jay. Everyone is unique. All God's creatures are their own selves. Shy is just really shy and quiet. She was born that way. Best sheepdog anyone ever had. She really loves her sheeps. Like she wouldn't leave this little midget by himself. This is ready to feed him, now, see? I'll just sit on the sofa for now. He can go back into the nursery after. Come one, baby, now, you'll like this. Drat!" She broke off as Poppa's bell rang.

"Let me do it. I can do it, Paddy. You can see to Poppa. I'll be careful."

Sighing, Paddy left the lamb with Jay and ran to her father.

When she returned she found Jay sitting in a miserable, tear-stained heap, cuddling the feebly moving lamb.

"He won't do it, Paddy. I didn't help at all."

"Oh, puddin, don't take on so. He's too weak. Poor little thing. He's not going to live."

"We have to keep trying!"

"Aye, I suppose we do at that. We owe him that much, at least, after all we've done to him. Ah, me, what a day. Tell you what, then. You keep him warm whilst I make up a brew for him. Time to get lunch together, anyway."

Jay curled around the lamb, tucking the afghan around both of them to make a warm nest of herself. She listened to the cheerful shouts of Joe and Carrots playing in the passageway and wondered, "Are you sure it's a him?"

"Yes, dear, quite sure."

"Doesn't even look like a sheep."

"All new-born beasts have that look, dear. He was only born this morning. You'll be surprised when you see wee Davie. He'll have that same look, only in a people sort of way instead of a sheepy way. What say we have last night's leavings for lunch? They can heat whilst I make whatzizname's brew."

"He has to have a proper name."

"He might not live, pet. It hurts to get close to a baby just before it dies. Hold off for a few days. Don't get your hopes up."

"Alright, but I'm not going to have no hope."

"That's a good girl."

"He should have a real big name."

"Whatever for?"

"So he can grow into it."

"Oh, Jay, you say the darndest things. What sort of big name can you give a sheep?"

"Didn't you ever have a pet lamb?"

"Oh, of course. We all did. Every year one or two of the orphans that lived were pets. But lots of them die. Lots with better starts than this one had. We found out giving them a name made them more special, somehow, and then it's harder to lose them."

"What did you call your pets?"

"Um - let's see - Frisky and Sammy were mine, and Sukie and Curly – no, that one was Pete's, and Sooty was Xantha's, but I had Snowball and I think Bruce had Clumsy and Noisy or was that one Dave's? Maybe his was Squeaky. I don't remember them all."

"No. He's got to have a more important name."

"How in the world do you decide what name is important for a sheep? Here, this'll do him good. I'll show you how to get something down one who thinks he can't suckle, then you can have a go while I carry on here." Humming quietly to the lamb, Paddy rocked him, gently working the rubber tube into his throat, stroking under his throat as she did so, so that he automatically swallowed. Pretty soon all the `brew' was in his tummy, making it hard and round. The lamb gave a big, shuddering sigh and went to sleep. Jay sat, cuddling him, mentally trying out all sorts of names on him, no matter what Paddy had said.

Paddy was too busy making lunch and feeding Joe and Carrots to take any notice of where Jay had put the lamb, but when Gahsie walked in, in the middle of lunch, she wanted the lamb in the nursery room.

Jay told her the lamb's whole story, running from the table back to the sofa to hold the lamb in her arms.

"Sorry, Jay. If he dies it's too upsetting. If he lives he'll poop on the floor."

Joe and Carrots were no help to Jay. They were delighted with the lamb, but they treated it like a toy, not like a living thing, and they didn't speak up on her side to keep the lamb in the house.

On his way outside after lunch, Pete scooped the lamb up to take it with him.

"No!" Jay shrieked at him. "Don't take him! He'll die out there! He'll be all by himself and he'll just die!"

"Now, Jay, you heard what your grandmother said," Pete warned her.

"She's not my grandmother! You're just mean and cruel! You don't care! You don't care about anything but your stupid car! You shoot baby bunny's mothers and leave them to starve and you'll let a tiny baby lamb not even a day old die all by himself and lonely and cold. You're mean and I hate you!"

Pete gave her a cold glare and said in a menacingly soft tone, "Go to your room, Jacqueline." He turned away from her as if she didn't exist and said in his usual voice, "Mum, now that the tractor's back I want to get my car out of the duck pond. Would you be able to give me a hand, please?" He shut the door ever so softly behind himself and the lamb.

Remembering what Paddy had told her about Pete being quiet when he was genuinely angry, Jay raced to her room, sobbing. This time Paddy came into her room, a stern look on her face. Jay quailed. She wished Gahsie had come in to comfort her the way she had over the rabbits.

She corrected herself. 'No, I don't. She was the one that did this.' She sat up, glaring at Paddy, sullenly.

"Jay, you owe Pete an apology."

"He was taking the lamb outside! It'll die!"

"You must find another way to handle those things. You've hurt his feelings. Today, of all days, when he did warn you this morning. He didn't sleep because he was up all night in the pouring rain trying to save little beasts just like that lamb and you accused him of not caring."

Jay hung her head. She felt like a rat. "But he mustn't take the baby outside. It'll die."

"Then you deal with that some other way. That was the last of those screaming tantrums in this house. We do not use the word 'hate' towards one another in this family. We do not bring up old fights to fuel new ones. You owe all of us an apology for unpleasantness at the table. Plus Pete for all the things you said to him. Carrots is coming in here for her rest. Find somewhere else to pout."

Jay was devastated. To not even be able to retreat to her own bed! Paddy cut her dead as surely as Pete had. 'How can they do this to me?'

She ran out of the bedroom, through the kitchen to the nursery, eyes blurred with tears. She saw the tiny lamb lying on its side, kicking feebly. It had been all tucked in against the chimney, but had kicked its blanket off. Jay settled him down, then lay down beside him so that he was between her body and the chimney with the blanket over him. He'd sleep a little, then whimper and kick, then sleep again. She stroked and soothed him when he was awake and sang to him when he slept.

Gahsie came in with a bottle for the lamb. She stood for a moment looking at Jay lying beside the tiny lamb, then she sighed. Jay was glaring at her, accusingly. Gahsie took the lamb in her arms and crooned to him, helping him swallow the milk the way Paddy had. The lamb went back to sleep when his tummy was hard and round again. Gahsie wrapped him up in his blanket and layed him down by the warm bricks.

"He's comfy now," she smiled at Jay, who had not said one word.

"Yeah. Until we go away and he's all by himself. He kicked his blanket off before I got here."

"Oh, my. I didna think he had it in him."

"Well he does. You just put him out here so he'll die. Gahsie please, please, can't we keep him inside until he's strong enough to be out here?"

"Now, Jay, you just listen for once. Poppa's granddad built this room on the house so that the little orphans could survive without needing to be in the house. We've saved many lives out here. It keeps them warm and dry and we feed them regularly. There isna anything else you can do. After they're warm, dry, safe and fed it's up to God."

"But if he dies out here we won't know if he could have lived if we'd just been with him."

"When they're that weak, dearie, sometimes it's a kindness to let them go."

"Then why don't you just kill him?"

"Oh, Jay. Eveyone deserves a chance."

"But Gahsie! He's not getting his chance out here."

"Oh my, but you are the obstinate one, aren't you? Well, then, we'll give it a try. Seems you're not going to understand until you've gone through it for yourself."

"Oh, thank you! Thanks awfully – and the baby thanks you too, I bet."

"Mind, now, listen here – that lamb is only going to be in the house as long as you clean up after him. Jay? Will you give me your word, now? Anyone else has to clean up after him, even once, through your neglect, and right back he comes. No more scenes. Promise?"

"Oh, thank you, Gahsie! I promise! I promise! But what if I'm at school?"

"He'll be out here while you're at school. It's too much to expect we can watch for him whilst you're not here. Hssht, now, you gave me your word, remember? Anyhow, anything that happens whilst your not here's not your neglect, now is it? And he'll be big enough by then, so don't you worry."

Jay scooped the little lamb up and held him close, beaming.

"Hold him gently, sweetling. Dinna hug him too tight, he canna take it." They went in to the kitchen where Gahsie started to prepare the evening meal, tea. She talked to Jay while she puttered around the stove. "Jay, now, dearie, sit ye down on the sofa and mind what I say. Are you listening? Now, that lamb's too small. He's weak, he's had a bad start, males are nae as strong as females and he's just plain too small. Look at the poor wee mite. See how frail he is? Look at his eyes; see that milkiness? Look at his nose; see how it's cracked and dry? See how he gasps when he breathes? Look, now, when he takes a breath see how his chest heaves? Jay, now, sweetheart, this poor wee mite may not even see morning. But if he dies, now, well, ye canna be carrying on so."

"I know, Gahsie. Paddy already told me. Um – I'm sorry for what I said at lunch time. I apologise. I didn't mean to yell at the table. I have to find another way to – to – uh – when I get upset I have to not say stuff like that."

Gahsie ran over to the sofa to give Jay a hug and a kiss. After that they chatted happily while Gahsie cooked tea. In between discussions about lamb names, Gahsie gave Jay some hints on how to cope when she felt overwhelmed with rage. She told Jay stories about pets she'd had as a child and about her children's pets.

While she was helping to scrub potatoes, Jay finally chose the name `Alphie' for the lamb and asked, "Do you know if that's short for anything?"

"Oh, I dinna ken, poppet. Alfred, maybe."

Jay sighed, tossing the potato she'd just finished into the water with a plop. "Alfred's a dopey name. I wanted an important name, like a king or something."

"Oh, Alfred was a king, dinna ye know? First real important English king."

"Yeah? Maybe I will call him that, then. King Alfred the Sheep."

They laughed happily, Jay thinking to herself that she never wanted to lose that cosy feeling again. Somehow she had to find a way to do as Paddy said; she had to figure out how to behave when she felt desperate so that things never went sour again. She could only pray that if she apologised to everyone they would all be comfortable with her again the way Gahsie was. She flung her arms around Mrs McLean and gave her a big hug of pure love.

It dawned on her that in all the months she had been with the McLeans she hadn't once seen them fight the way her parents did, yet the same number of things went wrong in a day. More, perhaps, since her parents didn't have the care of someone like Poppa. Jay thought she had better watch more carefully to see if she could find out how the McLeans dealt with things without losing their tempers.

By the time tea was on the table, Bruce had arrived home, all foolish grins and pink cheeks. He howled with laughter over the stories of the night, then without sleep and without sitting down to tea, he patted Alphie and headed out to help Pete with the cows and ewes.

Pete didn't even put his head in the door and grab a handful of food the way Bruce had. He had a difficult calving so he couldn't leave the birthing paddock.

Jay had to leave her precious lamb long enough to feed the hens and collect the eggs, so she coerced Joe into lamb-sitting while she did so. She found out Pete's job of feeding the cats and dogs had been added to her list of jobs for the night, then she was asked to do Paddy's job of going down to the poultry shed to feed the turkeys and then to the orchard to feed the ducks, geese, and free range hens.

From the orchard she could see Pete's and Bruce's silhouette's in the twilight. From the way they were crouched she could tell they were cold. The damp and chill of the evening was making her shiver. The house lights reached out to her with fingers of warmth, beckoning her back up the hill. Merely walking towards the light made her feel warmer.

Back in the house Jay stomped her feet and blew on her fingers to stop their fiery tingle. Her noise disturbed Joe who was already in his pyjamas nodding off on the sofa, a cup of cocoa in his hand, Alphie in his lap, Corker purring beside him. "I watched him for you," he reported sleepily.

"Thanks. Where's Gahsie?"

"Getting Carrots into bed."

"Where's Paddy?"

"Getting Poppa into bed."

"Did Alphie have a bottle?"

"Mmm."

Paddy appeared, carrying Poppa's tray to the kitchen sink. Jay waylayed her with "Paddy, how're Bruce and Pete going to have tea?"

"Out of my way, pet, I don't have time tonight. Soon's we're finished here we'll take something to them. Finished with all the feedings and things? That's a good soldier. Pop into the bath, now."

"It's cold out there."

"Yes. Sky cleared 'safternoon. Lose lots of newborns if it freezes. Warm bath'll thaw your toeses. Hop to, love, I have to get out there as soon as I can."

"But how will Pete and Bruce get warm?"

"When we take their tea we'll take blankets and coats and we'll get as many mothers in the hayshed as we can."

"Won't they come in the house to warm up?"

"Likely won't get a chance 'til morning. Another hard night. You could help by putting yourself to bed so's Gahsie can get away quicker."

Jay stood still for a second, listening to Gahsie tuck Carrots in, taking a moment to tickle the little one and settle her down to say her prayers, playing with her even though she was so tired and rushed.

Joe had fallen asleep on the sofa. When she had cleaned Poppa's dishes, Paddy gathered him up gently to carry him to bed. On her way to the bathroom, Jay stopped and asked, "Paddy?"

"What is it, tuppence?"

"I could take things to the men. Then they wouldn't have to wait for you."

Paddy stopped, Joe cradled in her arms, and looked at Jay in a way that made Jay blush and mumble. "And I – uh – want to show you I'm sorry and – um – I didn't talk to Pete yet."

"Aren't you the honourable one! Good girl, but you're a bit little for that, sweetie, and you must be awfully tired not sleeping properly in your bed last night."

"I know where they are, though. I saw them when I fed the ducks, and I know they're cold. You didn't sleep last night, either, did you?"

"No, that I didn't. Didn't get time then. Had a wee bit nap after lunch. It happens at birthing time some years."

"Let me. Nobody's slept right. You're all tireder than me. And I . . . "

"Ah, yes. You have your own hatchet to bury. Alright, then. You get the thermoses down and put water in the kettle. And don't push the chair, it'll wake the kids. I'll be back in a tick."

Not too long afterwards Jay was picking her way downhill. Although she found the moon was bright enough that she could see her breath in the air, she had to step gingerly. The grass snapped and scrunched under her feet. The mud was deceptive in the silver light. Sometimes it was crunchy, sometimes it was slick. She couldn't see well enough to tell which way it would be until she stepped on it. She couldn't carry a light for her feet because the hot food, gloves and coats were almost more than she could manage. Even though she panted and struggled to make her way down the hill on her feet, she was too exhilarated to notice the effort. At last she was doing something grown up and important.

Jay could see Pete's shadow moving, squatting, crouching, then moving again, hunched over. No sign of Bruce any more.

She fell, gasping as the cold ground touched her bare skin when she slid on the frozen grass and her clothes rode up her back.

A shrill whistle from Pete and Fleabag was by her side. She battled her way to her feet, gave Fleabag Pete's coat, adjusted her load without it and trudged on, feeling guilty as she watched the dog drag the coat along the ground all the way to Pete. Without it she traveled more easily, but she was afraid the coat would be useless by the time Pete got it.

Pete had the coat around his shoulders when Jay reached him. He seemed to be warming his hands on a cow that was lying on her side, moaning. He was talking to the cow more tenderly than Jay would have believed possible if she hadn't heard it for herself. She took a closer look. It was Pansy, a silly, skittish heifer. Now the look on her face brought tears to Jay's eyes.

"Pete!"

"Yeh, it's a bad'un. Couldn't get the flaming vet. He's over t' McGregor's place. Having trouble there, too. Bad year. Lost some already. Gawd a'mighty. Caught us with our pants down this year."

"She's – Pete! Pansy's – she's hurt!"

"Oh, my Gawd. What're you doing out here? Little titch like you. What're those women thinking of? Sending a little kid down to a sight like this."

"Pete, I – I wanted to . . . "

Pansy heaved, letting out a gasp of anguish that sounded like a human wail. By reflex Jay slid on her knees under the cow's head, cradling it in her arms, laying her own head between Pansy's eyes. The cow's head was so heavy it instantly cut off the circulation to Jay's legs. On top of that the hard boniness bruised Jay every time Pansy jerked or tossed her head. Nevertheless Jay stayed steadfast in the biting cold, soothing and calming Pansy while Pete did something at her other end that Jay couldn't see.

When Pansy relaxed Pete lifted Jay out from under the cow's head. As he rubbed the little girl's legs he told her, "You're a proper corker, you are. Dynamite comes in small packets, eh?"

"Pete, I'm sorry, I – um – I didn't mean to – uh – well, this morning . . . "

"Struth! You came all the way down here in the cold just to tell me you're sorry for flipping your lid?"

Jay shrugged and reached for the knapsack.

"Righto, then, let's have some grub. We got a couple of minutes before Pansy'll have another pain. How's your mouse?"

"Pardon?"

"Your white rat. Is it still with us?"

"He's not a rat. He's a sheep. His name is Alphie."

"Well now, still going, is he? Alphonse, eh?"

"King Alfred the Great."

"Oh, la de da."

Jay laughed out loud, which made Pansy lift her head and snort.

Pete shook his head. "Poor ruddy sod. It's too blamed cold for her. She's getting muscle cramps 'n all. She went down th' safternoon. Should've had her in the shed hours ago. Should have the vet to her. She's been at this too long. Can't get her up to move her. If she gets through this we're going to have a sick girl on our hands for a long time. Bet the calf's lost already. Here we go again! Take her head, shorty – it seems to help a bit."

Pansy made terrible noises. Jay hadn't known it was possible for a cow to sound like that. As soon as it was over that time the cow's head flopped.

"Yeh, see? She's about had it. Rotten way to go. Should shoot the poor blighter. Got some warm water, Jay? That stuff in the pond's too cold for her, 'n she could do with a blanket."

"The only warm thing to drink is your tea."

"Alright, then. Take the lid off the thermos and pour a little bit in the cup. We'll mix it with the pond water and give it to her. Got sugar in it?"

"Yes. Paddy said you would need the sugar to fight the cold."

"Goodoh, so does Pansy. Let's get it in her, then."

The liquid seemed to revive Pansy slightly. With the next pain she grunted more, moving her upper back leg back and forth instead of howling.

"Ah, you're a good mate, you are. She's getting somewhere now. If she's got the strength left in her another couple of good shoves'll do it. Here now, you don't believe in the stork, do you?"

"Um – Mum said a good angel brings the good babies and a devil's messenger brings the bad ones. She said the stork is a fairy tale like Hansel and Gretel."

"Geez, and we were ordered not to tamper with your innocence! But this is a hell of a way to find out the facts of life. Nah, Pansy's going to have to do it without you. Go back to the house. I'll get Bruce's tucker to him."

"Pete, please, I can't leave Pansy now. It hurts her. The calf's in her, isn't it?"

"Mmm, and how did you figure that one out?"

"From lots of things – and I never believe anything Mum tells me. Oh!"

They leaped to Pansy again. This time she pushed hard, her eyes rolling with the effort. Pete called encouragement to her. "Come on. Atta girl. You're a beaut. Little more, little more. Good girl. Hold on, Pansy, old girl. She'll be jake. We'll do it yet." He patted her flank as he talked to her. She relaxed, blowing. Jay sat beside her head stroking and petting her.

"It's not going to be pretty, Jay. Pansy's in real trouble. The calf's likely dead. Can you bear up?"

"Yes. Was it like this for Sharon?"

"Lord, no! She had no trouble. Nine and a half hour labour. Pansy was showing yesterday. She's been down more'n eight hours already. That's what's wrong, Jay. She's exhausted and too damned cold. You're too young for this." Before he could order her back to the house they were helping Pansy again. Clouds of steam rose in the moonlight from her tail. Two more big pushing efforts after that and Pete had a tiny tail in his hand. He swore under his breath.

"Pete?"

"Ah, stone the flaming crows, the blasted thing's a breech. Figured as much. That means it's coming out tail first, see? `Stead of nose first. Much harder on the mother. Then, too, sometimes the head gets stuck, coming last on the end of the neck like that. Nasty business. I wish you'd go up to the damned house! `Sides, it's past your bed time."

But Jay stubbornly stayed. After a few more hard pushes a calf's body lay on the ground in front of Pete, twitching in the clouds of steam. He took his coat off and wrapped the calf's body in it. Pansy found the energy to anxiously turn around to look.

"I don't believe this little heifer is alive. Must have the make up of a Sherman tank. Got to get her head free before she smothers. You try to hold Pansy. She won't like this."

Jay couldn't tell what Pete was doing because it took every ounce of her strength to hold Pansy's head. The cow gave one last, despairing bellow then laid her head along the ground and coughed once or twice. Her eyes didn't focus any more.

When Jay looked up at Pete again he held a slimy, wobbly, sneezing calf wrapped in his coat. "Give her some more tea, Jay. I'll be right back."

Pete ran up towards the house at a lope, sliding on the frozen grass, but keeping his footing and cradling the calf in his arms. He was haloed in the frigid light by the steam rising from the calf.

It made Jay nervous to be left alone on the icy grass with the downed cow. She spoke to Pansy and stroked her, as much to keep herself warm and calm as to help the cow. After a moment Pansy caught her breath, lifted her head and looked around herself. She made moaning noises, then made an effort to roll more upright. She gave up and put her head back down.

Seeing Pansy flat on her side, her head stretched out for all the world as if she were dead, frightened Jay. She forgot her own nervousness, talked to Pansy, called her, petted her, convinced her to lift her head enough to take some tea and prayed aloud that Pete would be back soon.

Before Pete arrived Bruce chugged up on the tractor and trailer, driving carefully on the icy grass.

"I brought you some tea," offered Jay.

"What're you doing here?"

"I helped Pete. Pansy had a heifer. Pete's taken it up to the house. He'll be back soon."

Bruce leaped down from the tractor, shrugged his way into his coat and wolfed down a cup of tea and a meat pie. "B'Gawd look at the condition Pansy's in," he worried, his mouth full. "She's down. Look, we have to get her to the house. Can you carry a lamb?"

"Course I can."

"Well, then, take this one to the nursery room. I'll stay with Pansy. Run, now."

Jay cradled the lamb against herself and trudged up the hill to Inch Brae. She had to be even more careful with her footing than she had on the way down because the lamb moved which made it harder to carry than nice, quiet bundles of food and clothes.

Skip came anxiously up at one point, then loped stiffly off towards Bruce.

Pete met Jay at the home paddock gate. He was wearing another coat and carrying a cow blanket. "Where'd you get the lamb from? You seen Bruce?"

"Yes, he's with Pansy and he's got the tractor."

Pete set off full tilt, sliding down the hill, pleased that he might be able to save Pansy.

Paddy lifted the lamb from Jay's arms and carried it into the nursery room to set it down beside the wet calf. Fleabag was lying beside the calf, warming it with his body. Jay was surprised to see him because she didn't remember him leaving Pansy.

"Paddy?"

"Yes, pet."

"Can we call the calf Primrose?"

"Let's see if she lives, first. Did you name your lamb?"

Alphie was lying beside the chimney bricks, looking brightly around at all the activity. Jay was surprised to see how mature he looked next to the new one, with his wool all dry, white and fluffy, but she suddenly saw why everyone had told her he was too small. He was far smaller than the new lamb although he was a day older. "He's Alphonse the Fleece King," she told Paddy as she went to Alphie to pet him.

"Where do you some up with these ideas?"

"Dunno. I just thought of it."

"You've had such a big day, dearie, you must be done in. Can you put yourself to bed? Then I can go down and help load Pansy on to the trailer."

Jay agreed, but in actual fact all she did was get a bottle for Alphie and fall asleep fully clothed on the kitchen sofa while Alphie drank his milk. When the lamb woke her during the night she stoked the fire, renewed his bottle and fell back to sleep curled around him on the sofa.

The cold sheets almost woke her as Pete tucked her into bed, but in the morning she wasn't sure whether she had dreamed that part or not.

She had to look in the nursery to be sure she hadn't dreamed the whole thing. There was Pansy, wearing a cow coat and sleeping heavily with her calf and another beside her. More orphan lambs lay beside Alphie. Alphie himself lifted his head and bleated at her, the first lamb-like sound she'd heard him make. Jay hadn't realised how afraid she'd been that he might die until she heard that proof that he was getting stronger. She ran to him, tears on her cheeks and hugged him. He squirmed and tried to suck on her plaits.

"Paddy, Paddy, look at Alphie," she called, carrying him into the kitchen, stepping carefully around the body of a lamb that had not been so lucky.

"Aye. He'll be a fine big ram one day." Gahsie was at the sink. "After ye've fed that scrap there's other orphans as need milk and the poultry could do with some o' ye time today as our Pats is up to her eyeballs in birthing ewes. Our Joey has done the hen house and eggs already whilst ye was asleeping, but he's a mite wee for the rest of it."

Not only did Jay feed the ducks, geese, turkeys and free range hens, but now that the dogs were working at night they were to have a light snack in the morning as well as their meal at night. It fell to Jay to do that as well.

After the first morning Paddy and Gahsie took over the orphans, but Alphie was Jay's responsibility alone and she found him almost more than she could keep up with. He demanded to be with her every second he was awake, following her through the orchard to the poultry shed night and morning and insisting on being with her at her log each dawn as Pete walked the newly calved cows to be milked.

By the time the August holidays were over milking season was well under way, a truck of bobby calves had already left and the paddocks were dotted with fluffy little white beasts bouncing across the fresh green grass.

Pete decided to use Pansy as the foster mother for calves that weren't quite strong enough to join those in the calf pen. She had spent one day lying prone on the floor of the nursery, then Pete and Bruce had rigged up a sling for her, explaining to Jay that the cow would cast if she didn't get to her feet. She wasn't strong enough to support her own weight, so they slung a cow coat from stout ropes tossed over the beams. The coat was fitted under Pansy's belly and held her on her feet. She looked as if she were in a tube, with one coat over her back and one under her belly, but it kept her warm and on her feet.

The first day her head hung listlessly to the floor. They let her down at night so that she could sleep lying down. When she protested and fought against being put back into the sling the next morning, the men rejoiced that it meant she was taking enough interest to live, even while they cursed her for the extra work she cost them by fighting.

On the third day when Pansy got indignantly to her feet and lowered her head at them at the sight of the sling, they left her out of it and the day after that took her outside for a while in the warmest part of the afternoon.

Instead of putting her with the rest of the herd they took her to live in the orchard with her four foster calves so that she wouldn't get pushed around. She was bone thin and slow moving so Pete and Bruce didn't think she could stand up for herself in the herd.

Pansy took to poking her head over the orchard fence to greet the others as they walked past on their way to milking, but she didn't seem to mind living apart from them. She needed her coat and the tonic the vet prescribed for her for some weeks after the birth. She was never again skittish, but became gentle and calm.

Sylvia caught bronchitis from standing in the duck pond the first night, so she kept Pansy company in the orchard with foster calves of her own.

When Sharon arrived home with wee Davie, Jay didn't know if she was pleased to see her and the baby or just glad that she would be taking some of the work load. Sharon's Mum stayed with her for the first week she was home, but Jay hardly saw the woman since she rarely left the cottage.

Alphie lived happily in the nursery at night and tied to a stake in the back garden any time Jay couldn't have him with her. As soon as he was old enough to spend the night out of doors Jay convinced Pete to move the lamb's stake to the front lawn so that she could see him from her bedroom window. He quickly learned to call to her in order to get her to climb from her bedroom window to feed him. He set up such a commotion if he saw her try to go anywhere without him that she was soon never seen without her little white shadow. He was with her as she watched the milk herd go past each morning, while she fed the ducks and hunted in the reeds for their eggs and while she filled the feeders for the rude, rough geese and turkeys.

He bleated anxiously for his breakfast when he saw her feed the others, for all the world as if he thought she would miss him. When he knew it was his turn he'd race her back to his stake in the front garden, bouncing up and down as if he had springs under his tiny hooves. She always carried his bottle with her. She was afraid she would never get him back to the stake if she didn't distract him with his breakfast.

It was almost with relief that Jay took her leave of Alphie when school started up again at the end of the August holidays. Jay and Joe were filled with stories for their friends on the bus about the new calves and lambs and their new jobs. Joe fed the hens and collected the eggs twice a day as Jay had done before she had so much else to do.

They were amazed to discover that their astonishing time didn't even rate a comment as far as the others were concerned. Everyone had suffered from the freeze. It had been the worst cold snap in living memory. All of the neighbouring farms had lost lambs, kids, calves, and foals and some had even lost the birthing mothers. Those who were listened to were not Jay and Joe, but the ones who had horses. Everyone, it seemed, had at least one pet lamb or calf.

The jeers of her schoolmates ringing in her ears, Jay settled back onto her seat letting the rough thudding of old Gertie over the stones pound her rear end to numbness while she listened to the stories around her. The children were planning on entering their pets in the show. They were arguing with one another about how best to train a lamb or a calf to walk on a lead.

Jay didn't know what the show was, but she made up her mind there and then that not only would Alphie be entered in it, but he would show all these scornful brats up by winning at everything. That'd teach them not to call her a townie!

While Alphie attacked his bottle; sucking just didn't seem like the right word for that wild frenzy; Jay watched him, imagining how he was going to look wearing a blue ribbon. It would suit him perfectly, she thought. Surely none of the ordinary pets the other kids had could get so worked up over their bottles that they ended up on their knees, tails whirling like aeroplane propellers, almost jamming themselves into their bottles. Alphie was the only lamb around with such talent.

Despite the melodrama Alphie could put on when he was tied up and left at the stake, he was quite happy trimming the lawn in circles around his stake all day while the children were at school. Jay felt rather foolish that she had wept quietly in the girls' bathroom over having to leave him the first day back at school. She was glad no one knew she'd done that, they would only have laughed at her for being a sookie-townie. The first thing she did each night after changing out of her school uniform was free Alphie and give him a bottle. Seeing the way he pounded away at the bottle, Jay began to feel sorry for mother sheep.

Fortunately, lamb docking day was a school day, so it was all over when Jay returned home to find her darling tailless. In spite of the fact he didn't seem to notice, Jay had nightmares about baby lambs screaming with human voices while blood squirted out of their tail stumps like water from a split in a hose. She missed seeing his little tail spinning like an aeroplane propeller.

Joe became upset that Jay didn't have time to play with him anymore. "He misses your company, poppet," Gahsie explained.

"But I have so much to do. What about Carrots?"

"Carrots is nae you. He loves Carrots just as much as he loves you, but you have to remember he does love you, too. Ye dinna have so much to do that ye canna give your only brother the time o' day."

"He's being a pest, Gahsie."

"Well, now, have we ever said to you that you're a pest when you need us and we've other things to do? Would you treat the wee man any different than we treat you? He hasna any other to play with, ye ken. If he runs just as hard as his wee legs can carry him after school he gets to McGregor's just in time for tea, so there's no time to play 'fore he has to be getting back for for bed. Can ye no let him play with Alphie with you? 'Tis more fun to share such things most times, ye ken."

After that the two children spent many hilarious hours trying to teach Alphie to walk on a leash for the spring fair. All of the adults gave them advice, all their school friends and some of the teachers chimed in. All to no avail. Alphie was not of show lamb stuff.

Chapter Eight:

A Hint of Darkness.

The household settled into the familiar routine of milking season. The new jobs that Jay and Joe had to do made them feel grown up and important. Each day the weather was that touch warmer than the day before that made spring such a joy. Looking forward to summer added a new facet to the everyday, comfortable rhythm of Inch Brae.

As they got off the bus from school each afternoon Jay and Joe found some new preparation for spring. The market gardens were tilled, then planted in nice, straight rows of pig maize, sweet corn, and potatoes. The kitchen garden was planted with onions, peas, beans, silver beet, radishes, tomatoes, beetroot, lettuce, cabbage, cauliflower, Brussels sprouts, and carrots. The rhubarb, asparagus, and kumara patches were tended.

Along the fence on the east side of the house paddock, flower patches daily gained more freshly turned soil that Jay supposed would reveal all sorts of flowers later in the year. Spring flowers popped their heads up in the flower beds along the fence and made brightly coloured patches of snowdrops, daffodils, pansies, tulips, and crocuses. Under the windows facing the front lawn were more spring flowers, filling Jay with joy at the sight of them. The east fence ran along beside the wheel track which meant the children could enjoy the spring flowers as they walked from the front gate to the house paddock gate.

There was another, small gate that led directly from the front gate to the front lawn, but no one ever used it. Every day the children went right past it to the back of the house and in the kitchen door. With Alphie at his stake crying pathetically at the sight of Jay the two ran, swinging their satchels, to be with him as soon as they could, but not once did they break their habit and go through the front garden gate straight to him.

On weekends Jay ran down to the cowshed after she'd collected the duck eggs, taking a thermos of tea for the men. They cheered to see their cuppa. Alphie cropped the grass alongside the cow yard fence, staying close to Jay while she perched on the top rail to watch the milking.

She jumped down to help Sharon feed the calves in the calf pen. Aside from the calves being fostered in the orchard by Pansy and Sylvia all of the good quality heifer calves were in the calf pen. All of the faulted ones and all the bull calves were sent away on the bobby calf truck. The calves that were kept lived in the calf pen, a small paddock of their own. They were fed skimmed milk when the cows were milked, with tonic added to the milk to make up for the missing cream. They were also fed molasses and bran to make them strong and healthy when they were big enough to begin to graze on the fine grass grown only in the calf pen.

Jay thought they looked sweet, small and helpless until she tried to help feed them. Then she discovered that even the young ones were strong and rough. She was too small and light to control them, so after trodden on and bruised feet and one scary time when she was knocked right over and would have been badly trampled if Sharon hadn't leaped in and lifted her up, she helped as much as she could from outside the fence.

In the separator room Jay loved to watch the fresh, warm milk foam into the big stainless steel vat, pouring in a rich, creamy-white, warm, sweet smelling stream from the milking shed pipes to be separated into skimmed milk and cream. Since the herd was mostly Jersey and Guernsey cows, the milk was so high in butter fat that it had a richer, creamier colour than the milk Jay'd had in the city. The whole milk was fed through a pipe in the bottom of the vat into a separator that hummed and whined as it sent the cream in a thick, gurgling stream into the cream cans and the skimmed milk in a whiter, foamy, thinner stream into the larger milk cans. Since the cream was the main source of income for Inch Brae it was treated almost with reverence.

Milk for the house was ladled from the vat as whole milk, or a milk pail was placed under the separator instead of a milk can if skimmed milk was wanted for something. The wonderful house cream came from putting a small bucket under the cream side of the separator to take pure cream, then letting the cream pail sit until the cream settled so that the very top, super-thick layer could be skimmed with a spoon for cocoa and for porridge. After the cream pail had been skimmed the rest of the cream was whipped for desserts or beaten into butter for house use.

The cows took themselves from the milking shed along the runs to the paddock chosen for daytime grazing. They went in the first open gate they found along the run. All Bruce had to do was make sure the right gate was open. The cows wandered off as they were let out of the stalls, some waited for their friends, but most wandered dreamily, slowly, chewing their cuds.

Those who could hear their calves milled unhappily, lowing. Every now and then one would push at the fence, roll her eyes and let out a moo that ended in a high pitched shriek, startling for Jay and enough like a factory whistle to wake wee Davie, even over the racket of the milking machine, the separator, the radio, the pigs and calves.

Wee Davie was put in a miniature hammock swung across the corner of the separator room nearest the outside door where he would be warm and safe while Sharon fed the pigs and calves.

When a cow bellowed he'd jump, then wail angrily, his red face wrinkling up and getting redder. If Jay couldn't soothe him and Sharon didn't come at once, his nose would go purple.

Looking at Davie like that, Jay thought it remarkable how ugly a human could be. New born lambs were pretty in comparison. Besides, by the time other animals were six weeks old they were full of fun and frolic. She wondered why it took babies so long to be people. Yet when he was asleep, rocking in the baby hammock in the corner, she thought he looked sweet, like a baby chick.

After milking the shed machinery was all pulled apart and cleaned. In the morning the cream cans were set on the trailer with the cooled ones from the night before ready to go to the front gate cream stand. The milk cans were set in the cooler where they sat until needed for the house, calves, pigs or what few sales there were.

Sharon left with wee Davie just as one of the men was finishing milking the last cows and the other one began to shovel out the holding pen. She walked straight to her cottage to make breakfast for Bruce, never taking part in any of the clean-up.

Jay thought Sharon missed the best part. She thought the clean-up was more fun than anything else. The music was turned up loud enough to give the cows fidgets the moment the last cow went out through the stall door. In time to the music, having to shout at the tops of their voices to be heard over it, the men cleaned the cow shed.

When the holding pen had been hosed down and swept with great yard brooms too stiff for Jay to push, the shed yard and stalls got the same treatment. The brother taking the machinery apart was wading in the flood made by the one hosing down the concrete. Jay helped carry the smaller parts of the milking machine into the separator room to be sterilized. She cheerfully ran back and forth. She loved this part. The music was loud, the men singing and the brooms swish-scraping in time. She waded through the swirling water having lots of fun.

Once the milking area was spotless, all the equipment sterilized and air-drying on scrubbed wooden racks, one brother tackled the separator room floor while the other went out to supervise the cows to their daytime grazing.

When it was Pete's turn to shut the cows in Jay raced to keep up with his long strides, her clumsy black rubber boots slap-flapping on her legs as she ran. She was so fascinated by the way Fleabag reacted to Pete's whistles that she ran until she could hardly breathe, afraid that she might miss something.

Fleabag wandered behind Pete for all the world as if he'd no interest in cows at all. Just the sight of Pete, Jay and Fleabag started most of the stragglers ambling off along the run after the rest of the herd. Sabrina waited until Pete was leaning on her hip before she admitted there was to be any walking done at all.

The few who were too upset about their calves to move of their own accord were turned by hand and gently urged down the run. Pete called each by name, speaking gently and rarely needing to slap one on the flank to get her moving.

Every once in a while one was too distraught or too stubborn to be eased down the run. Pete only needed to whistle once and Fleabag suddenly showed full interest in the cattle, herding the cow down the run even if he needed to bark to do it. Most of the older cows knew what the whistles meant and obeyed them without needing the dog to enforce them.

"Wouldn't it be quicker if Fleabag drove them all?"

"It might at that, but if cows're driven hard they give less milk. Happy cows are high yielders."

When the Taranaki gate was hooked behind the herd Jay and Pete walked back to the shed, whistling and singing. He showed her all the calls and whistles for the dogs and just about collapsed with laughter over her efforts to copy his whistles. If her boots weren't too muddy she sometimes rode back on his shoulders, hooking her toes around his chest under his arms so that she didn't need to hold on with her hands. She put his digger hat on her own head and together they laughed at how frantic Alphie got that she'd vanished.

Bruce finished the separator room while they were gone, then drove the cream out to the stand. All that remained for Jay and

Pete to do was to pick up the cream and milk pails for the house, tuck the empty thermos under Jay's arm and walk back to Inch Brae for breakfast. Bruce and Pete swapped the jobs around each day so that every second day it was Pete who drove the cans out to the cream stand. When he did that he dropped Jay and Alphie off at the house paddock gate on his way back to the shed and she rushed out to meet him with Joe and Carrots when he walked home with the milk and cream, for all the world as if she hadn't been with him only minutes before.

Every now and then the welfare worker, Mrs Hone, visited the children. At first she'd been there every week or more, but once the judge had decided the children should be left undisturbed for six months the visits seemed to fade away.

The six months were up just before Jay turned eight. Paddy had to go to court, which was a great nuisance because it meant leaving Poppa all day. The only thing that made it only a nuisance and not a major upheaval was that Xantha had decided to visit right then to help out.

In the six months the children had lived at Inch Brae Xantha hadn't been home once. She hadn't met the Eastons, nor seen wee Davie. In the letter that said she would visit that week so that she could help out, she announced she was expecting another baby.

Paddy set out with Jay and Joe in Pete's car before Xantha arrived. The children hadn't been driven to school since their first morning. They enjoyed the novelty and had a fine visit with Paddy on the way. They didn't once mention the court, not because they were too young to understand, as Sharon claimed, but because they were too afraid to think about it. They didn't fully understand what it was all about, but they lived with a dread of being taken from Inch Brae and being sent back.

By the time Jay and Joe got off the bus that afternoon Xantha and Gahsie had the household humming along exactly as usual. Carrots seemed to like Xantha, though she wasn't calm and comforting like Paddy. Jay was shy and timid around the stranger for the first little while, but soon realised that Xantha was fun. A slimmer, taller, high octane version of Paddy with a lilting voice and bubbling laughter.

When Paddy arrived home the entire family had gathered for tea. Bruce and Sharon were there with wee Davie, now three months old, propped up in his baby chair staring around. Poppa was at the table in his wheel chair, smiling, wobbling around and making gurgling noises. Xantha was so pleased with his progress she could hardly talk about anything else. She kept patting Carrots, saying over and over how wonderful it was to see the difference she had made in Poppa.

Jay looked around the table and counted the number of people there. Seven McLeans, if she counted Davie, three Eastons and Xantha. In a way she wished Xantha's husband and three girls had come with her to make an even bigger crowd at the table. She thought she had never felt as happy as she did at that moment with the family all together, the canary singing in the front room, the smells of the food, the happy chatter and the friendly teasing.

After tea Xantha helped Jay feed the dogs and cats, admired Alphie, then returned to the house to give Carrots her bath. She had been a teacher before she had her children, so she was quite a help with Jay's and Joe's homework.

In their bath the two told one another that they each felt they were Xantha's favourites. "I don't feel scared to meet new people anymore," Joe confided.

"I don't, either," Jay nodded. "Everybody new here is nicer and nicer."

While Xantha tucked Joe into bed, Jay read her Shirley Temple books. She practically knew them all by heart, but still dreamed over the photos. A beaming smile of surprise and delight lit up her face when Xantha crept in to wish her good night. "Those were mine when I was your age," Xantha whispered, pointing to the books.

Keeping quiet to avoid waking Carrots, Jay promised, "I'll take really good care of them."

"That's a good girl. When you don't want them any more my oldest girl, Sally, would love to have them."

"Sally's Gahsie's name, isn't it?"

"Yes. I named her after Mum because she couldn't do any better than to be like my Mum."

"She wanted us to call her Grandma Sally when we came, but we wouldn't. Now I wish I did."

"Don't worry about it, 'Gahsie' is kind of a special name. At least, it's a name no one else on the face of the earth has."

Jay covered her mouth with her hands so she wouldn't wake Carrots by laughing out loud. She slid down in the bed, letting Xantha put the books back on the shelf and telling her how she came to choose Alphie's name.

Xantha thought Alphonse the Fleece King was a wonderful name for a pet lamb and told Jay all sorts of stories about the lambs and calves she and her brothers and sister had had as children.

Plucking up her courage, Jay asked Xantha about her name.

"Mum was very young when I was born and given to reading romantic novels. There was a city once called Xanthus and the people from it were called Xanthians. Mum read about it while she was waiting for me to be born and she thought it was a pretty name. She wanted her new baby to be a classic beauty and so she gave me what she thought was a classic name. Too bad I looked like this instead, eh? To top it all off, do you know what xanth really means? Yellow colour."

"But you've got a name no one else has."

"That I do, though half that see it written can't say it, and half that hear it, spell it Zantha."

"At least everyone knows how to spell J.," Jay giggled. Feeling comfortable with Xantha she dared to ask, "Do you know what's going to happen now?"

"You're going to sleep and I'm going to swap photos of our kids with my little sister."

"No, I mean, is that court place going to take us away?"

"Wouldn't you like to see your real parents again?"

"No! They scare me. They won't let me just see them and be here. They're not like that. I never want to leave here, never. I want to grow to be a lady here. I want to be like you and Paddy when I grow up. I want to be like Gahsie and be old with lots of family around me and have big teas like tonight all the time and lots of pets and everyone laughing a lot. I want to live here forever and have Paddy's room when I grow up and Gahsie's room when I'm old."

"Maybe by the time you've grown up on the farm you'll feel like Dave and I did and want to live in the city. I'd had enough of the backwoods by the time I'd finished school. I like raising my kids with all the conveniences of the town."

"Then I'd come back all the time and visit everyone here. I'd always want to have times like tonight."

"You make me feel guilty, sweetypie. You're a very nice little girl. Paddy did the right thing when she took you all in. I hope my kids turn out as loyal as you are."

"But I'm scared if Pa finds out where we are he'll take us away."

"Don't you ever think about the nice things? Do you ever long to see your Mummy again?"

"I hate her. I know we don't say that here, but it's the really truth. Promise me you won't tell Paddy I said that? Please? I don't want her to think I'm wicked, but I'm scared to see them again. If I think about them at night then I dream about them and they hit me and lock me in the wardrobe. Then I can't sleep and my head hurts."

"Jay, have you ever told this to the welfare workers?"

"No. They're so dumb. I never tell them anything. I tried but they didn't do anything, and they told Ma and she hit me."

"You should tell that to Mrs Hone, too, while you're here and nothing can happen to you. You don't need to be afraid any more. Mrs Hone and some other people are going to be asking you lots of questions in the next little while. It's important for you to tell them the truth."

"Why?"

"The judge ordered them to study you and make sure the courts know what the right thing is for all of you. You can help yourself to get what you want by telling them the truth."

"I'm scared of them."

"I'm sure you are, sweetheart. I would be, too, if I were in your shoes. Maybe it would help if I wrote a letter to that judge. Don't worry, Jay, we'll all fight for you."

She tucked Jay in and settled her down to sleep. Jay lay awake for a long time thinking about what would happen if she changed the way she behaved towards the welfare workers enough to be truthful with them. She finally dozed off without knowing what she wanted to do, but feeling safer than she ever had in her life just knowing that for the first time there were people fighting on her side.

Not only did Mrs Hone visit more often, being more nosy than ever, but she picked Jay and Joe up from school one day and drove them to the city. The children didn't know what astonished them more, that they were excused from school for the afternoon or that Carrots was in the car with Mrs Hone.

Although they'd gone shopping in the little township where they went to school, they hadn't been back to a city since their first day on the farm. Jay wanted to visit Xantha while they were there and sulked when she was told there wouldn't be time. Joe was satisfied with being told they might phone her, but Jay wanted to see her house and meet her family.

She didn't cheer up until they arrived at a building Mrs Hone told them was the university. Then she was too awed to remember she'd been disappointed and annoyed. Her disappointment came flooding back when she was told she wouldn't be allowed to explore the university.

All they saw was a white room with tables in it and a big mirror on the wall. Some strangers asked them questions, played games with them and gave them puzzles and things to do. The strangers gave one another those secret grown up looks when Jay told them she needed to know her way around the university because she was going to go there one day. She was so angry with them for the look that she nearly didn't tell them anything they wanted to know, but then she remembered that it was Xantha who had wanted her to tell.

Joe was horrified when Jay spoke up against their parents. He tried to shush her, but she was too angry with the strange people to care what they thought of her. Partly to shock them and partly to punish Joe for not understanding how she felt, she said crushingly to him, "No one's got a Ma and Pa like them. My friends don't. Your friends don't. Even we don't any more. I'm going to tell anyone I want to. You can't stop me." She told him that right in front of the strangers in the white room. He was shocked speechless.

When the strangers went out of the room to get some milk and biscuits for the children Joe turned on Jay furiously. "You stupid idiot! Just like you to say something like that. You would!"

"Shut up. You don't know everything."

"They'll tell like they did before and you'll really get it."

Carrots got down from the table and ran to the door shaking her head and whimpering, "No, no, no."

"Now look what you did," Jay hissed at Joe. "I hope you're satisfied."

"You sound just like Mum."

"Do not! You take that back!"

"Will not. It's the truth. She's the only one who says `I hope you're satisfied'."

"I don't sound like her! I sound like Paddy."

"Do not. Paddy never says 'shut up'."

"She never says 'you stupid idiot', either."

"But when they tell Mummy what you said we'll all get it."

"They won't tell Ma."

"And don't call her that where they can hear you!"

"I won't call her Mummy. I won't. I don't care who hears me, she's not a really Mummy. She never hugs and does things like Mummies do. And Pa's not like a Daddy, either, so there."

"But if they know we'll get it." Joe was shaking with rage and fear.

"You're not being truthful," Jay told him selfrighteously. "You call them that, too."

"Not where they can hear us!" Joe flew at her.

"They can't hear us in here," Jay scoffed, hitting back.

Carrots gave a wail of fear just as the strangers opened the door to bring in the milk and biscuits.

"Now, now, what happened in here?" they asked brightly as the children sat glowering at one another, pretending they hadn't been anywhere near one another.

Joe was still angry with Jay on the way home. They snapped and snarled in the car, but kept their distance from one another until they were home and away from welfare workers of any type.

Then their spat boiled over into a full scale fight, leaving them rolling on Joe's bed bruised, exhausted and tearful but so evenly matched that neither could win. Gahsie found them, separated them and sent Joe off to explain himself to Pete while Jay had to tell her story to Paddy.

Then one night at the tea table Paddy told the family that the courts had decided the children should stay as they were for another six months. Released from the pall that had hung over them, Jay and Joe raced around the house paddock after they should have been in bed, laughing and calling to one another the way they had before the trip to the city. It wasn't until then that the children were friends again.

Chapter Nine:

A Golden Time.

By the time November rolled around the weather was so warm that the children talked to one another about the fun they'd had at the beach when they'd lived with their parents. Jay's birthday was approaching. When Gahsie asked her if there was anything special she would like for her birthday she took her chance and voted solidly for a day at the beach.

"I thought you would be wanting a dolly to hold."

"Well – dolls are alright. I play with them sometimes, but what I really, truly want is to go to the beach."

"If that's what you've got your heart set on, precious, then that's what we'll do."

Delighted, Jay raced all over the farm telling everyone the good news.

At the tea table it was decided that Jay could chose anyone she wanted to go with them all for her day at the beach.

"Can I have anyone at all?"

"Anyone."

"Then I want Poppa."

"Poppa?"

"Can't I have Poppa? You said I could have anyone."

"We thought you would choose one of your little friends."

"Oh, can't he come? I would make him so happy and you said."

"Just a second, now, J.A.E. Don't be so hasty. Pete, how could we take him to the beach?"

"Bruce and me could carry him to the car and lift him into the wheel chair when we get there."

"How would we get the wheel chair across the sand?"

"Isn't there any beach around here that doesn't have those flaming dunes?"

"Not for miles."

"Yeh. Rats."

"Can't we take him? We'll all help push." Jay's chin quivered.

"It won't make much of a day for you, pet. Now don't take on. You'll have a better time with one of your school chums."

"But Paddeeee, he'd love it so and if he can't come you can't come. It'll ruin everything. Besides, you said."

"Struth! How that child can wail. Fair puts a lost calf to shame."

"But Pete . . . "

"Uh uh. Don't start on me. Bruce 'n me'll see what we can do 'bout getting the chair across the sand. Strike me pink. She could talk holy water past the Devil."

"Oh, thank you, Petey, thank you. Now Paddy can come."

"Uh."

"I still think she should have a friend of her own age."

"What's to stop us taking another bairn with us too? What d'ye think, Pete?"

"Uh."

"We'll have to take both cars anyway, won't we?"

"Uh."

Paddy beamed at Jay, "There, that's settled then. You invite your best friend to come to the beach with us."

At school the next day Jay was mortified to find that her best friend didn't want to be seen on the beach with Poppa. The kids in her class laughed at her and said her grandfather was crazy.

Paddy had to go to the school the day after to explain to the headmaster why Jay had been fighting in the schoolyard like a boy.

After Jay calmed down from the outrage of hearing her dear, brave, lovable Poppa made fun of she invited a girl who had not joined in the name calling, Ngaire Macintyre, from the farm right beside Inch Brae.

Seeing how much it meant to Jay, Pete and Bruce set about finding a way to take Poppa with them and to take care of him outside the house. When he had been taken for an outing in Pete's car while Paddy went shopping in the little township he had never been taken out of the car. They needed to be able to take care of his needs on the beach and to be able to get him across the sand. They solved the latter by making wooden runners as if they were making a sled so that they could put the wheel chair on the runners and pull it across the sand instead of pushing it.

The day itself turned into such a treat for the whole family that even standing in line for fish and chips was fun. Jay stood with her eyes half closed against the glare of the sun on the white sand, listening to Ngaire chatter while the seagulls whirling overhead squalled insults at one another and the breakers crashed rhythmically on the beach. The scents of the sea, salt, fish and hot frying fat filled her nose with the smells of summertime, carrying her away to a paradise out of reach of the woman trying to take her order.

"Jay," Ngaire nudged her.

"Huh?"

"C'mon, luv, give us yer order. There's others waiting."

"Oh, sorry. Fish cakes . . . "

"Ugh."

"Sharon wants fish cakes. Two schnapper and chips, whitebait fritters . . . "

"Don't they have hake?"

"Out of hake, luv."

"I always get hake, Jay."

"Get John Dory."

"I always get hake."

"I'll have John Dory, too."

"How many's that, then?"

"Two John Dory and chips . . . "

"I don't want John Dory."

"You girls aren't ready to give your order you can wait in line."

"We're ready."

"What's that, then – whitebait fritters, fishcakes, two schnapper and chips, one John Dory and chips."

"A haddock and chips, too, and two just chips. And we'd like tomato sauce, vinegar and salt, please."

"But I didn't get anything, Jay."

"What do you want, then?"

"I'll have a savaloy, please."

"Oh, yes, we should get one for Carrots, too, on account of the fish bones."

"What's that, then?"

"Two hot dogs, please."

"With batter or without."

"With, please."

"Yes, both with batter."

"Ha'penny more for batter."

"'Salright, it's my birthday today. I can have what I want."

"Kids these days get too much, I always say. Got no appreciation for things the way we did in my day. That's seven shillings and fourpence ha'penny."

"Cor, Jay, will they let you spend that much?"

"It's for eveyone's lunch. There's lots of us here."

"Here, how are you kids going to carry all that, then?"

"We'll get help, it's alright. I'll just run and get the money, alright?"

"Alright, then. Wait for your order over there. Next."

They ate the fish and chips straight from the newspaper, burning their fingers, laughing and teasing one another. They sat in the warm sand, the sun in their eyes, the wind blowing sand onto the food.

Paddy thought the stick in Carrot's hot dog might be too sharp to be safe, so she took it out. Carrots cried. She could see Ngaire eating her savaloy on its stick and she wanted to do the same. Ngaire took her stick out and ate her sausage in her fingers, dipping it in the tomato sauce and dripping red on her legs. Carrots promptly stopped crying and did the same, including flicking tomato sauce on her fat little legs until they were twice as spotted as Ngaire's.

Trouping across the sand with Ngaire and Joe to put the newspapers in the dustbin, Jay said, "Paddy liked it when you took your stick out for Carrots."

"It's a shame for a baby to cry at a birthday lunch."

"I'm glad you could come."

"Thanks for asking me."

Joe spoke up. "I'm glad all of us came."

"Me too. It's my best birthday ever."

"I want to come to the beach on my birthday, too. I miss the beach."

"Did you used to live on the beach?"

"Pretty close. It's the only thing I miss, being able to go to the beach all the time."

"Me, too."

"Some kids say the McLeans're not your real parents. I'd die if I had to go and live with strangers. Don't you miss your Mum?"

Jay and Joe looked at one another and didn't answer.

It was still too early in the season for swimming, but since there was warm sun, sitting back from the water tucked in between the sand dunes out of the wind was heavenly warm. Paddy wanted everyone to sit still for a few minutes after they had eaten. They obediently settled in the warmth, but almost at once the children were giggling and shoving one another.

Bruce had loaded the dogs in the back of his big car with the children and then had tied the dogs to the back bumper where they could lie in the shade of the car. As Paddy was trying in vain to make the children keep still until their lunch settled and Sharon was having just as much trouble keeping Davie still so she could change his nappies, Bruce sneaked off and let the dogs loose.

"Men!" the women snorted to one another in exasperation when the dogs set off on a wild run up and down the beach, the children up and after them.

Old Skip nosed about, barked once or twice, then limped over to Poppa and flopped down beside him. He slept for the rest of the day. Fleabag chased every stick, jumped in every moat, trampled every sandcastle and generally totally forgot he was a working dog. Even Shy forgot herself enough to chase seagulls for the first little while. After that she sniffed around the sand dunes following fascinating smells and pretending she didn't know that lout, Fleabag.

The shore that the children had known before was dotted with islands out to the horizon. Mayor Island had been a haze on the left and White Island's smoke plumes had appeared just where the sea dived over the edge into the sky on the right, with none of the sulphurous land visible at all. Jay was disoriented to find the smoke on the horizon, right in front of her, floating up from a craggy hump of rock and sulphur.

"Ngaire, isn't that White Island?" she asked her friend, not able to believe the volcano could be in the wrong place.

"'Course. What else would it be?"

Jay ran to check with Pete. It was true. He told her how clever she was to know what the smoke was, but she hardly heard him. She went back to the edge of the surf and stared out at the smoke, feeling for the first time the distance between herself and her old home. It was as if she had found an invisible wall protecting her.

As she stared and stared she felt a lightness well up in her until it felt like she finally really could fly.

Along with herself, Pete, Gahsie, Poppa, Carrots and changes of clothes for everyone 'just in case', Paddy had managed to squeeze the cake into Pete's little car.

Jay was called from her daydream for her birthday cake. They made hilarious and mostly futile efforts to light the candles in the seabreeze, then gave up and sang happy birthday. Paddy handed the knife to Jay to make the first cut. She hesitated, used to cake cuttings that led to slaps because she hated fruit cake, which was the only cake her mother ever made for birthdays.

Seeing Jay hesitate, Paddy offered, "Here, pet, I'll help you. You don't need to be afraid of the knife."

With Paddy's strong, square hands over her own guiding the knife into the cake, Jay wondered how she could ever have doubted Gahsie. Because it was her birthday, the cake was her favourite – a thick, heavy, gooey, fudgy chocolate cake iced with loads of the rich whipped cream from their own cows. No layers of jam, not even a hint of almond paste. Just chocolate and cream. Jay licked her fingers in utter bliss, eyes closed.

Strapped on top of Pete's car with Poppa's wheelchair and sled, Pete had brought the makings for kites. After the cake had been devoured to the last smear on the plate, Pete and Bruce set about putting kites together and racing across the sands trying to get them to fly at least out of Fleabag's reach.

No longer in the mood for charging about with the others, Jay lay down on the old, grey, woollen army blanket beside the sleeping baby Davie. In the shelter of the sand dune she watched the other children scream and chase around trying to fly the kites with Bruce and Pete and rescue the ones Fleabag triumphantly yanked out of the sky. She chuckled quietly to herself watching as one by one the dog caught all of the kites by the tail and brought them crashing down then ran as hard as he could to avoid the wrath of thwarted kiters.

The women were digging for pipis as the tide receded, chattering with one another and straightening up every now and then to laugh at the men. Fleabag heard their laughter and took it as approval of his efforts to keep the skies free from dangerous cloth-tailed kite-birds. Gahsie looked like a young woman with her pants rolled up, feet bare, squealing like a child when a cold ripple rolled around her ankles over the sun warmed edge water.

Passers-by turned to point and laugh at Fleabag's fight against the kites, but there were no other people playing on the beach. For all the crowds at the fish and chip shop, it was too early for most people to go near the water. To have the beach to themselves made the day perfect.

Pete and Bruce had dug a chair in the sand for Poppa and he slept there, worn out with excitement, fresh air, fish and chips and too much cake. The breeze which was flying the kites sneaked around the dunes to tickle his face. He moaned and reached for his bell. Jay leaped to his side. "Poppa, Poppa, the bell's not here. We're at the beach."

He looked frightened for a moment, then waved his hands and bobbed his head like a pigeon until he managed to say, "Shaygh," with a smile so full of love that Jay just had to hug him before she ran down the beach, shrieking, "Paddy! Paddy! Poppa said my name!"

Everyone came running. Poppa needed to use the toilet, which meant both men were needed to lift him into the wheel chair and pull it across the sand to the changing rooms. Suddenly the children needed to go, too, so they straggled after the men, battling the sliding sand with every step. Carrots started to cry with weariness before they got there, so Paddy trudged over to carry her.

By the time they had all collected together again everyone agreed it was time to go home. They hauled their belongings back to the cars, tired, happy and dirty, packed and loaded the cars and had time to admire the bucket full of fat pipis the women had collected for tomorrow night's tea while the men tried to catch Fleabag who didn't want the day to ever end.

The wheel chair and its sled were lashed to the top of Pete's car wrapped in the army blanket to protect the car's paint. It was decided that the kites weren't worth taking back home, so they were left sticking up forlornly from the dustbin in the parking space. Pete and Poppa sat in the front, Paddy in the back with Carrots on her lap, Gahsie beside her cradling the bucket of pipis. Shy lay on the floor on Paddy's feet and old Skip sat up on the seat with the women as if he thought he was a person.

Bruce and Sharon sat in the front of his big car, Davie in Sharon's lap. Jay, Joe and Ngaire wrestled with Fleabag for room in the back.

Part way home Pete's hand came out of his window, waving up and down. "What's he doing?" Sharon asked.

"Wants us to stop."

"Hope nothing's wrong with your dad, love."

"Soon see."

Bruce stopped the car, yelled at Fleabag, "Get in behind!" when he tried to jump out, then went to see what Pete wanted.

"What could be wrong with Poppa?" Jay asked, worried. But Sharon was too busy calming Davie, frightened by his father's shout, to answer.

A cheer of mingled relief and delight broke out when Bruce reported, "Mum doesn't want to cook tea tonight. Thinks we should pick up meat pies to eat on the way. You want to?"

Sharon wanted to, though she worried, "Fleabag'll get into the kid's tea the way he is tonight."

Bruce turned to Fleabag, who was trying to pull the ribbons out of Jay's plaits, and said with his fist raised, "He better not, I'll brain him."

Fleabag suddenly remembered he was a sober, responsible, well trained, hardworking, large cattle dog and not a spoiled poodle puppy. He quietly lay down on the floor of the car and pretended he hadn't acted like an idiot for one second of his entire life.

Jay couldn't believe how tired she was when she was plodding through her evening jobs. She tried to enjoy a reheated meat pie with tomato sauce before she went to bed, but she was too tired to taste it. It seemed a waste of a rare treat to not taste it, but she couldn't help it. Before her usual bed time she was in her bunk, wiped right out.

Waking with a start in the middle of the night, Jay lay still for a moment trying to figure out what was bothering her. She hadn't said thank you. Afraid if she didn't show gratitude for all the niceness it would all stop, she clutched the cloth doll that Gahsie had made for her birthday, guilt stricken. She slid silently down from the bunk and tip toed from the room, then glided into Paddy's room. The sleeping sounds stopped with a sudden snort.

"Jay? What's wrong, pet? Tummy ache?"

"No. I'm sorry I woke you. I tried to be quiet."

"You were very quiet. That's what woke me. I'm sensitive to tip toes. Are you alright?"

"I'm sorry I didn't thank you for my birthday."

"Oh, you sweet little thing. You didn't have to get up in the middle of the night just for that."

"It was the best birthday I ever had in my life."

Paddy hugged her and Jay spent the rest of the night sleeping in Paddy's sweet smelling bed.

Jay was woken very early in the morning by Paddy gently slipping out of the bed. Poppa's bell had rung. Jay lay where she was, listening to a part of the morning she usually slept through.

Before cock crow, before first light, Paddy tended Poppa, put the coffee on to perk, washed, dressed, then woke Pete and Gahsie with their first cup of coffee. Hearing their hushed voices and soft footfalls, Jay could see why the beginning of the morning normally didn't wake her.

While Pete shaved, washed, dressed, then helped Paddy bathe Poppa and change his bed, Gahsie made breakfast so that Pete could eat before he went out to bring the cows in for milking. 'So that's why everything's ready by the time I get up,' Jay thought.

She heard the dogs bark, Pete's whistle, the rooster crow, Alphie calling her. 'This is when I usually wake up.'

It gave her a strange feeling to lie there when she was normally up, as if she was listening in on herself. She could hear Paddy and Gahsie visiting over their coffee, starting the first load of wash, tidying their rooms. She pretended to be asleep when Paddy puttered in her room.

'So that's when they do those things, when I'm watching the cows.'

Carrot's crying, puzzled that Jay wasn't there to help her get up, prompted Jay to join the day.

The front room was kept shut all day to protect the children from it as much as to protect it from the children. Gahsie thought it a cruelty to make it too easy for them to bump and break precious things. They would peek through the glass, but only on Sunday had they spent any time in the room. The first time the children were invited to sit around the front room fire for toasty pies after Sunday School, Jay stood as still as she could with her back against the wall just inside the doors looking around herself with her hands behind her back so they wouldn't accidently disgrace her.

The room faced north, as hers did. On the south wall, beside her, was the fire place with a wide, polished wood mantle shelf over it. There were ornaments all along the mantle shelf, over which hung a very old painting. The children were told it was a portrait of Poppa's grandmother before she married his grandfather. They couldn't imagine that much time.

On the east wall were bookshelves lined with ancient, leather bound, gold tooled sets of books. Jay admired them with pleased awe. She wondered how old she had to be before she would be allowed to touch books like that. There were more ornaments artfully placed on the shelves between sets of books and beautiful handmade wall hangings in between the columns of bookshelves.

The north wall was almost all windows with white lace curtains. There were double doors there, too, leading out onto the veranda, but only the top half of these were square window panes like the inside doors. The lower half was white painted wood squares. The doors to the veranda were flanked on either side by the same tall windows as there were in the bedrooms, except that here instead of the heavy, dark, light-blocking curtains there were the white, antique lace curtains that Jay thought were exquisite. The veranda shielded the room from the winter winds and the midsummer heat.

On Jay's left was the piano against the west wall, lovely vases arranged along its case, each sitting on a round, white crocheted doily. Some of the vases held flowers from the garden; blooms, blossoms or dried flowers depending on the season so that there was always fragrance and beauty in that room.

All along the wall above and around the piano were photos and paintings of five generations of McLeans families. On either side of the piano were china cabinets displaying cut glass and crystal.

Around the fireplace there were armchairs and along the east wall under the bookshelves were sofas. Under the windows were wooden window seats padded with hand embroidered cushions. All the stuffed furniture had hand embroidered cushions, plus handmade afghans and hand crocheted arm rest covers. The little tea tables in the room had hand crocheted doilies to match the ones on the piano. Jay was breathless with admiration for such a weight of heritage, never mind the enormous amount of work that had gone into making all that stuff.

The ceiling had moulded borders and patterns of flowers all painted with pastel colours so many years ago that it was hard to tell what all of the colours used to be. In this, the best room, the ceiling was yet higher than in the rest of the house so Jay could fully understand why the ceiling had never been touched up. What she couldn't grasp was how it had been painted so prettily in the first place.

During the winter Poppa was wheeled to the front room after tea and lifted into an arm chair by the front room fire. After the evening work was finished and the children were in bed the adults joined him for their evening chats in front of the fire before they all went to bed.

The doors were left standing open when Poppa was put in there and Jay loved to look in while she was sitting at the kitchen table doing her homework. Each night she was soothed to sleep by watching the red glow from the fire flickering on the ceiling of the kitchen, and the muted buzz of voices rising and falling in a peaceful rhythm of contentment.

In winter the front room fire was the focal point of evening life, but in the summer after tea the family drifted out to the veranda that opened off the other end of the front room. As soon as it was warm enough the children did their homework out there, joined one by one by the adults as each finished his or her evening jobs.

They all lingered in the longer, warmer summer evenings to watch the sun go down. Rocking chairs appeared from the storage room as if they had been summoned by warm weather genies, and a hammock swung invitingly from one pole of the veranda to the twisted trunk of the old totara tree in front of Gahsie's room.

The children played on the front lawn if they got their homework finished in time, while Poppa smiled at them from his rocker. Gahsie sat beside him, serenely rocking, her lap full of hand sewing of one sort or another. Jay never saw her foster grandmother seated with empty hands. No matter what she was doing, if she were seated for only a moment, she was mending or making something.

Poppa dozed in his rocker in the waning light, stirring now and then to chuckle at the antics of Shy's pups, Alphie or whatever batch of kittens joined the fray. At times looking up from the lawn to Poppa and Gahsie rocking side by side Jay could pretend nothing had ever gone wrong with Poppa.

When Paddy joined her parents on the veranda the children played harder knowing that bed time wasn't too far off once Paddy was outside. For a few moments Paddy and Gahsie chatted, rocked, stitched and sipped tea, then Carrots was called and the evening was at an end.

Carrots didn't always take kindly to the idea of ending her play when Paddy said so and the chase was on. It never lasted long, for Pete scooped her up and handed her over when he sauntered around the corner of the house, then Paddy hauled her off, ignoring her shrieks of rage. Usually by the time she was called Carrots was too tired to care and went willingly with hugs and kisses.

Sometimes Pete perched on the veranda steps, his cuppa beside him, the children around him and the dogs at his feet. The children watched, fascinated, as he made toys for them, mended pieces of machinery and broken toys or made a new leg for a broken chair. He hummed, whistled and sang while he worked, his mellow tenor leading the twitterings of the sleepy birds settling in the pines and the frog chorus tuning up for their night concert.

When Poppa had been tucked into bed Pete stretched out in his hammock with his guitar to sing the day away until he was ready to sleep himself. In the heat of the summer he was known to actually sleep right where he was until the dawn woke him.

Although the curtains in her room were intended to block out the light and make it easier for her to sleep, Jay liked to wait until Carrots was asleep and open the curtains enough to let the twilight in. Many's the time she drifted off to the sound of Pete's guitar, the cows lowing restfully in the distance, a morepork trying for lead in the frog choir, the crickets strumming up just as the horizon smoothly swallowed the last of the light.

Chapter Ten:

Christmas.

Each week of December had its own special task, marking the time to the big day until the tension was almost unbearable. Although the children took turns to cross off a day on the calendar every morning, the time seemed to drag so that the day never drew any closer.

At last, at last, school was out for the summer holidays. Then the children were free to make total pests of themselves hanging around the kitchen tasting Christmas baking and prying remorselessly for clues about their presents or where they might be hidden.

Fortunately for the adults' sanity and the children's survival, the onslaught only lasted two days. The day after school was over Xantha and Malcolm arrived with their three girls. Not only did the adults have help, but also the children had a marvellous distraction; more children.

They weren't too badly matched in age; the Eastons were just turned eight, almost seven and almost three, and of the

Murphys Sally was almost six, Pam had just turned four and Tui was twenty months old.

Sally set out at once to be shown over the farm by Jay and Joe while Tui was content to muck in the dust beside the kitchen door with Carrots. Pammy couldn't keep up with the older children and resented being left with the younger. She started an irritating whine to be allowed to go with Sally, but at once fell and cried when the trio were made to take her. Forced to stay in the home paddock, she fought with Carrots who was her equal in size and pushed over Tui who was not.

To try to give Pammy something close enough to what she wanted to give everyone a rest from her tears and tantrums, Xantha suggested the four children stay in the orchard. There was enough to explore there to keep Sally and Pammy happy, it was close enough to the house to allow Pam to stay with the others, yet they weren't made to stay in the home paddock with the babies.

After trees had been climbed a game of hide and seek was started. The moment it was Pammy's turn to hide her eyes the other three ran off over the hills, way out of her sight by the time she tried to look for them.

To their immense relief Pam had to lie down for a rest after lunch. They badgered Gahsie for glass jars and set out for the duck pond where they spent a blissfully smelly afternoon scooping up jars full of tadpoles and dirty water. They were made to strip and be hosed down outside the kitchen door before Gahsie would let them into her house to be scrubbed for tea. And what a tea it was, with bannock slathered with Gashie's home made jams, eaten out on the dust that passed for a back lawn. The back steps worked as a table, holding the plates and tea pot, while adults and children alike sat on the ground and ate with their fingers. Cheerfully dusty, Jay wondered why in the world they'd needed to scrub up for tea.

Jay and Joe were too busy showing off for Sally and Pam to do their jobs properly. One or the other was calling to Sally, "Come over here!" every few minutes.

"Those chooks'll never be fed at his rate," Gahsie muttered.

"Their hearts aren't in it, Mum. It is Christmas holidays, after all. Why don't we give them a breather?"

"Are you going to do their jobs, Xan?"

"Why not? I haven't done the like for years. Be a change of pace for me and give mine a lift to see their old Mum puddling about."

"Take her easy, Xan."

"I'll be jake. You did more when you were preggers, didn't you, Mum?"

"I was used to it, though. You've been away from it for a bit."

"I can still remember, besides, it'll give our Patsy a rest from trying to watch that lot and get the babies ready for bed at the same time."

Freed from all work except taking care of their own pets, Jay and Joe spent all day long tramping over the paddocks with Sally. They had to use more and more elaborate schemes to escape from Pammy, but that only added to the fun. They haunted Pete and Bruce, raided the orchards, dared to cross the fence into McKenzie's place, replaced the tadpoles as they died in the jars and scratched themselves to ribbons picking blackberries.

Malcolm Murphy had never lived on a farm. He found no joy in eating tea in the dust, in hosing down stinking children clutching jars of slimy tadpoles, in butchering a calf for dinner with Bruce and Pete, and no matter how wide Sally's grin, he didn't take to seeing his golden haired princess reduced to a grubby waif with grazed knees and scratched hands. He tried valiantly to join in with the McLeans, but they were too close a group. He had thought to find a kindred spirit in Sharon, who was also an in-law, but she had gone to school with them, had grown up on a similar farm and was some sort of cousin to boot.

In an effort to get to know Pete and Bruce, Malcolm took smoko out to them when they were mending fences within sight of the home paddock. He was heartened to hear them cheer at the sight of their sandwiches and beer, but so upset to see Pete holding Sally on the back of a horned cow that he all but broke the beer bottles dropping them to rescue Sally.

"Hey, watchit!" Pete snapped in exasperation when Malcolm lunged at his daughter, startling Sabrina. As Sabrina jumped away Pete swung Sally up in the air out of harm's way.

"You fool! What do you think you're doing?" Malcolm yelled at Pete. The loudness offended Sabrina, who took two steps backwards and shook her horns, and looked at Pete for comfort. The dogs woke up and ambled over to see what the noise was, Fleabag with his hackles up just in case. "Watch out for the bull!" Malcolm shouted, torn between grabbing Sally from Pete and diving for the fence.

"Bull?" they all said, looking around themselves over towards the bull paddock, then back to Malcolm to see where he saw a bull.

Seeing that he was looking at Sabrina, they all burst out laughing, including Sally who at once tried to swallow her laughter and hung her head to think she had laughed at her father.

Pete put Sally down and stepped over to Sabrina to give her friendly clout on the shoulder. "That's Sabrina. She wouldn't hurt a fly," Bruce explained.

"It's got horns," Malcolm said, unhappily. He tried to clutch Sally to him, but she danced off, not noticing, to pet Sabrina.

"'S got an udder," Pete told him, pointing.

Malcolm looked doubtful, so Jay tried to clear it up for him by saying, "Like ladies have breasts and men have . . . " she stopped, embarrassed by the way the men were looking at her.

"Sabrina wouldn't hurt me, Daddy. She doesn't mind if Pete sits me on her, and he was holding me so I wouldn't fall." Sally petted Sabrina's brown nose and reached up to grab one horn, giggling as she tumbled to the ground when Sabrina shook her off.

The dogs flopped down again, panting in the broiling sun.

"It didn't look so safe," Malcolm muttered.

"Uh," Pete grunted, going over the beer to make sure it wasn't broken

"You're a good bloke, Mac, but can't you figure we wouldn't do anything to hurt your kid?" Bruce said the words amiably, but his eyes were on the beer as if he were more anxious that it was not hurt than his brother-in-law's feelings.

Mumbling apologies, Malcolm headed back to Inch Brae. Sally hesitated, watching him go, then ran after him and caught his hand.

The others looked at one another, uncomfortably. "Ruddy beer's so shook it'll foam to hell," Pete grumbled under his breath.

"Gawd," Bruce complained, looking at the sandwiches. "Squashed flat. Nothin's worse'n squashed tomato sandwiches."

"Uh," Pete disagreed, holding up a beer. "Foamy beer."

"Well, you great clot, why'd you have to scare the poor blighter like that?"

"Wasn't me. Was the bloody bull." Pete jerked his head in Sabrina's direction.

"Sounds like a load of bull to me," Bruce growled, throwing a soggy sandwich at Pete.

Pete flicked the cap off a bottle of beer with his belt buckle, expertly jamming his thumb over the neck of the bottle while he gave it a couple of good, hard shakes. Seeing what he was doing, Bruce jumped backwards, but a spray of beer foam caught him from his hat to his belt while Pete grunted, "Yer foamin at the mouth again."

Bruce dived for the beer bottles while Pete tried to kick them out of his way. The dogs jumped back up, barking, Sabrina trotted indignantly away, her tail held high in the air, and Jay and Joe scrambled to dodge the men's flying boots.

Pete got his hands on another bottle ahead of Bruce but before he could let loose another spray, Bruce scooped Jay up and held her in front of his face, calling, "You wouldn't squirt the squirt, would you?"

Hesitating only long enough to see the look of delight in Jay's eyes, Pete let loose a stream of foam at about Jay's knees. Covering her eyes with her hands, Jay pulled her knees up out of the way, which let the beer catch Bruce in the crotch. The sight of the wet stain spreading on Bruce's pants was too much for Joe, who threw himself on the grass and howled with laughter.

"Teach you," Bruce threatened, dumping Jay on the ground and lunging at Joe.

But Joe was laughing too hard to run away. He just lay there, shrieking with laughter while Bruce grabbed a handful of tomato sandwich and mashed it into his hair.

"My boy," Pete grunted, bravely going to Joe's defence by taking his sacred hat off and hitting Bruce on the back with it.

With a roar Bruce reached for a bottle of beer and straightened up with it in his hand and aimed at Pete.

But Pete had one, too, so they circled one another, fiercely shaking their bottles, feinting and lunging, each waiting until the other made a mistake.

Joe found the bottle Pete had first sprayed Bruce with and quietly tasted the remains. He pulled a face, but finished it anyway, then picked up Pete's hat and made a task of collecting the spent weapons, draining them whenever he was sure no one would notice what he was doing.

The foam began to squirt out around Bruce's thumb, so he let it loose at Pete, who ducked and squirted back. Bruce dived for the last two bottles, trying to grab them both, but Pete was right behind him, trying to kick them out of his way. Under the flying boots one broke.

"Clot!" Bruce growled, trying to get the cap off the other, hampered by Pete pulling at it trying to get it from him.

"Twit," Pete gasped back, losing the tussle over the last bottle and getting a face full of foam. He took a mouthful and sprayed it back at Bruce.

Bruce tossed the bottle aside and dived for the sandwiches, landing in a heap with Pete who'd had the same idea at the same time. They rolled around on the ground smearing soggy bread, mashed tomato, salad dressing and butter into one another's hair and chests until there was nothing left but handsful of grass to add green stains to the mess.

Stopping at last, they sat side by side on the beer and tomato soaked grass, slapping their hairy knees and laughing at one another. "Sharon'll have a burk at the sight of you," Pete warned Bruce.

"Think Mum'll let you in her house?" Bruce returned, unconcerned.

"Uh." Pete looked at the fence they'd been working on.

"Gotta clean up and have some smoko before we finish that."

"Uh," Pete agreed, getting to his feet.

Bruce found his hat and hit Pete with it, so Fleabag tore it from Bruce's hand and ran off with it. Bruce and Pete slapped one another on the shoulder, laughing, and trudged off towards Inch Brae with a glance over their shoulders to make sure the children were following.

Jay was clutching her sides, sore from laughing so much. Joe was carrying the empty bottles in Pete's hat. Pete called Fleabag back, took Bruce's hat from him and carefully gathered up all the pieces of the broken bottle and placed them in Bruce's hat to carry them back to the houses where they couldn't hurt anyone.

No one noticed Joe wore a silly grin or that his eyes weren't quite focused.

Sharon was getting her washing in off the line when she saw them making their way up the hill. At the sight of them she scooped Davie up and dashed into the house, shrieking, "No you don't!"

They detoured off the path to Inch Brae to go to Bruce's door. It was locked. "Told you," Pete grinned.

"Front door," Bruce whispered, darting suddenly off around the house.

Sharon was too quick for him. She locked that one, too, calling to him when he tried it, "You're not coming in my house in that condition, Bruce Allan McLean!"

Bruce pressed his nose to the living room window, whining, "Very nice. Is that any way to treat a poor, hardworking man? And right on Christmas, too."

Even though she was laughing hard enough to have difficulty talking, Sharon threatened him, "You'll have to clean that window." Then she pulled the curtains so that he couldn't see her phone Inch Brae to warn Gahsie.

The ambush was sprung on them after they were through the gate, trapping them in between Malcolm with the hose at the gate and Xantha with buckets of soapy water at the kitchen door. The only escape was past the hen house and there was Paddy. Jay and Joe ran to Paddy, but Bruce and Pete let Malcolm get his revenge by hosing them down thoroughly.

When the dust had been well turned to mud they dashed at Malcolm as one, taking him by surprise and rolling him in the mud to howls of laughter from the women. One of the howls gave away that Sharon had sneaked over from the cottage to watch the fun. Seeing she wasn't holding Davie, Bruce took off after her with one of the buckets of soapy water. No one saw what happened, but they all heard the shrieks. When Bruce and Sharon reappeared both were soaked to the skin.

Bruce and Sharon had tea at Inch Brae that evening. The evening felt hotter than the day had been, to everyone's groans of discomfort. Davie had heat rash and wailed dismally from the shade of the pines while tea was eaten on the veranda. Joe grizzled and held his head in his hands, refusing to be comforted.

Puzzled, Paddy asked, "Are you fellahs sure you didn't knock him on the head?"

"Nah," Pete shook his head.

"I just rubbed his hair. I wasn't rough with him, was I Joey?" Bruce said.

Joe sniffled, not lifting his head.

"Touch of sun. Needs a hat," Pete decided.

"Could be," Gahsie nodded. "Could be a summer bug, too. We'll see how he is in the morning."

Joe sobbed out loud when Gashie went to take him to his bed before he'd had tea, so Pete carried him off. "Poor wee man," Gashie murmured and went to the kitchen to make something to make him feel better, but he promptly brought it up, convincing her he had a bug and convincing Pete he had heatstroke.

From then on Malcolm was called 'sport' and 'mate' by Bruce and Pete, even if he didn't know the difference between a bull and a cow. A valuable place was found for him; he took all four older children to the beach in Bruce's battered car, along with Shy's last remaining ownerless pup. The children stayed out of trouble, Pammy stopped being such a pest and Malcolm didn't feel so useless.

Running on the sand, digging moats and castles and swimming by the hour, the children were so tired by the end of each day that they fell asleep as soon as their heads hit their pillows. Since none of the others came down with Joe's 'bug', it was decided that Pete had been right after all, and Joe was given a hat to wear. He was delighted to have a cowboy hat, but as soon as the novelty of playing cowboys and Indians wore off, he spent hours making it look like a battered digger hat, even to demanding corks to hang around the rim from little strings.

No matter how she told herself she was going to stay awake and see how Santa made his sled work in the hot dust, Jay was too tired to last to sundown. She was fast asleep while it was still warmly sunny outside.

When she woke in the morning she felt cheated and angry that she'd slept through Christmas night, but the moment she spotted the bulging pillowcase at her feet she had only one thought, 'New toys!'

She hung upside down off the bunk to look down at Carrots who was sleeping flat on her back. Sure enough, there was another pillowcase at Carrot's feet, just as lumpy as Jay's.

The cot had been put back where Carrots used to sleep as a bed for Tui. She was curled in a little bundle and – yes – there was a pillowcase with things in it at her feet, too!

"Carrots! Tui! Wake up! Santa came! Santa!"

Carrots leaped straight up in the air from a sound sleep, landing on her knees in front of her pillowcase.

Jay flipped over, landing on her feet facing Carrots, calling, "Wait! Wait. Let's don't open them yet. Let's get the others."

"Yeah!"

They hauled the sleepy, complaining Tui out of the cot, dragged their pillow cases behind them and burst into Pete's room where Joe was sleeping while the Murphys were staying. Pete had already left to milk the cows. "Joe! Santa came! Let's get Sally and Pam."

Joe grabbed his pillowcase and joined the parade to his room where Sally and Pam shared his bed.

Gahsie found them all in Joe's room later in the morning, all gleefully playing with their new toys and feasting on the oranges, apples, nuts, chocolates and lollies that had been tucked into the pillowcases to keep them happy. "Merry Christmas, kidlets, aren't you ever going to eat?"

They ran to her, all yelling at once.

For once they ate in their pyjamas, which would have been special enough without their being able to see through the front room doors that a Christmas tree had magically appeared in there. They peered through the curtains in open mouthed wonder. The tree was covered with lights and glass balls. Under it were presents. But the sight that rooted the children to the spot was the balloons. All over the tree, the packages and out on to the floor were dozens of balloons of all sizes, shapes and colours. Entranced they watched the warm summer breeze waft the balloons around.

All morning the children played with the toys from their pillow cases and wandered through the house looking at the ribbons, wreathes, candles, bells, flowers and crepe paper decorations that had appeared in every room during the night.

At long, long last it was lunch time. Bruce, Sharon and wee Davie arrived from the cottage. Poppa was dressed in his best and sat up in his wheel chair, all excited. Poppa's younger brother, Ian, and his wife Fiona had arrived. The children were as much exhilarated by the crowd as they were shy.

Aunty Fi looked in the front room and exclaimed, "Why, Sal, where on earth did you get all those balloons? There must be dozens of them!"

"A hundred, to be exact, and my cheeks will never be the same again! You see, we thought the bairns would like them and besides, if they got to the tree before we were up we'd be bound to hear them this way. You never can tell, Christmas morning, ye ken."

"Aye, you're a canny one, Sal. I'll remember that one for next year. Our Andy'll be at our place with his wee ones next Christmas. Be worth a try, that will."

While the children had spent days at the beach, Bruce and Pete had dug out the hungi pit in the corner of the front lawn under the pines. Gahsie, Paddy and Sharon had cleaned it, fired it and got the stones good and hot while Bruce and Pete had slaughtered and hung the inevitable pig, as well as a lamb and a goose.

With lots of stuffing and every imaginable vegetable, the meats baked in the pit for twenty four hours to be uncovered in succulent, steamy wonder for Christmas dinner. They ate from paper plates out on the front lawn, trying to find some relief from the gruelling sun in the shade of the pines, the totara tree and the veranda. The bamboo blinds had been unrolled all the way down all sides of the veranda to make it as cool as possible for Poppa who sat in his rocker enjoying every moment.

The dogs and cats found a Christmas of their own, following people around to catch the dropped scraps.

There was a trestle table set up under the pines to hold pitchers of lemonade, big bowls of salad, and beer for the men.

Sitting on the grass in the shade of the totara tree where she could watch everyone, Jay thought she had never eaten anything so delicious in her life. She had never seen a hungi before and rated it the best meal she had ever had. They were allowed to eat with their fingers and to stuff themselves to the point of sleepiness. The pleasure of it outranked opening the presents from under the tree, especially when the ones under the tree included a doll for each of the girls from their parents and a truck for Joe.

Jay promptly let the puppy run off with her doll by accident. Joe started to cry for his mother and Carrots fell asleep on Poppa's lap.

Chapter Eleven:

The Bubble Bursts.

The morning started with the laughing sounds of cock crow.
Jay listened for a moment to see if she could hear Pete, then she
slid from her bunk, dressed, slipped into the kitchen for her glass
of orange juice, back through her room and out the window into
the crisp dawn air. She sat on the cool dampness of her log to
watch Pete and Fleabag bring the depleted herd around the home
paddock. Dry off was well under way and even the cows that
were still in milk were wide with pregnancy. These, too, would be
dried off before the month of May was out. Then for two months
there would be no milking, except for Sabrina who was bred two
months later than the others so that she could be the house cow
again until the hectic month of calving.

Jay waved as she did every morning, then watched until Pete
vanished from her sight around the corner. He was leaning on
Sabrina as he did every morning, whistling a tune around the
straw he held between his teeth, walking as if he had three knees.
Jay smiled to herself when she remembered trying to walk like

Pete and falling over her own feet. Perhaps that was why he always leaned on something, even if that was a walking cow.

Fleabag and Shy followed obediently at Pete's heels, more out of habit than need as the well trained, experienced cattle peacefully ambled along the path, chewing their cuds, their breath making puffs of steam. Skip didn't go with them every morning any more. He was getting too old and stiff to keep up. In his place Pete took Shy's pup, Leafless, teaching it to walk to heel first before it started to listen to whistles. When Jay asked Pete why he had named the pup Leafless, all he said was, "Ever see leaves on a dog?"

Alphie had long since joined the rest of the sheep. Pete explained to her that he had out-grown his stake the day he pulled it out of the ground and wandered off down the road after the school bus. She missed his company at her log, but the first frost was in the air so she knew it wouldn't be too long before there were more orphan babies. She liked the idea of raising and training a calf to win prizes in the show and grow up to be a life time companion like old Sabrina.

Corker, now a mature cat, trilled at her for a moment, then loped off to the cowshed to take his chances on some new milk. He angled across the home paddock, threading his way between the bushes as only a cat can. While she watched him Jay spotted the remains of the truck her mother had sent Joe for Christmas, now a forgotten scrap in the tangle under the hedge. The memories of the gifts they'd received were already buried in the layers of time, but that hungi stood out clearly in her mind.

The hungi was clearer to her than the meals of baked ham and hot cross buns they'd had at Easter and the special anniversary meal Gahsie had made to celebrate the day they had been at Inch Brae for a year.

Jay could hardly remember the way they'd been when they arrived. She laughed at herself when she thought of how scared she'd been of foster homes and wondered why they'd plotted against Paddy. She felt a twinge of regret that they had refused to call Gahsie 'Grandma Sally'.

She stood on her log to look out across the paddocks for a moment before she went in, feeling the cool dampness of the dew on her toes, glad that the mornings were chilly enough for the kitchen fire to be lit. She'd missed the cosiness of it when the weather had been hot. Having it back reminded her of her first morning, of how comforting Gahsie had been, of how afraid of Pete she had been. She was looking forward to dry season when Pete would have more time at home with her. She hoped the cows wouldn't calve until the end of the August holidays so that they could be home together.

Paddy had to go to court again, since their second six months was up, but they had been through that twice before without any trouble. Looking over at the discarded truck Jay felt a tweak of fear, but nothing as strong as the fear she used to feel. Life hummed along in its usual routine so smoothly that Jay hadn't noticed the time passing. Even the major days, like Christmas and everyone's birthdays had blended in because they had the same feeling of joyful tranquility.

Jay jumped down from her log and dashed to the window where Carrots stood waiting for her, complaining that she'd had to wait.

Joe had the 'flu, so Jay did his work of feeding the hens and collecting the eggs. As she always had before, Jay filled the bucket with warm water for the mash. As she did every morning, Gahsie scolded Jay for running barefoot in the cold; as she did every morning, Jay ran out barefoot anyway.

She mixed the warm water with the chick mash, loving the toasty smell. She whirled the air above the hot mash so she could watch the steam rise in swirls and eddies. She fed the impatient hens, scattered wheat and poured the warm food into the feeder, made sure the water trough was clean, then closed the door and peeked through the cracks between the boards to see whether or not there were any baby bunnies stealing food.

Quietly so that she wouldn't scare off a laying hen, Jay opened each nest box in turn, carefully lifted out each egg she found and set it gingerly into the bucket still warm from the water. Some of the eggs were still warm and she fondled those, letting their warmth soothe her chilled fingers. She liked the soft feeling of the eggs with the bloom still on them and always tried to set her fingerprints into the shell, something that can only be done in the first few seconds after laying, but looks magic in the cooled, hardened shell of an ordinary looking egg.

By the time Jay set the empty kettle gently on top of the eggs and hurried cautiously towards the warmth of the house, her toes were beginning to hurt from the cold.

As she did every morning, Gahsie chirruped about how well Jay'd done, how fine the eggs were, how many there were, how beautiful they were, for all the world as if Jay had laid them herself.

Joe was tucked under a bundle of blankets on the kitchen sofa, looking miserable. Sick as he was, he had taken it on himself to get up and tend the fire. In his turn he heard how well he had done, how the whole family would stay warm because of his effort. Jay listened to Joe's chest being swelled with half an ear. Although they had been at Inch Brae for a year, she still found praise to be a novelty and took pleasure in the sound of it whether it was aimed at her or not.

Carrots appeared in the kitchen proudly bearing Poppa's breakfast tray, babbling at them as she walked about the way she had fed him. They couldn't always understand everything she said when she had a long story to tell, or when she was excited. If both happened at the same time there was no point in trying to make out what she actually said and asking her made her upset, so they all nodded in what they hoped were the right places and told her what a great help she was. At three she had the widest eyes in the country and two wispy blonde ponytails that bobbed as she nodded her head with the earnestness of her story. Even Jay and Joe acknowledged she was sweet and they thought she was a pest most of the time.

Jay ate her breakfast dreamily, listening to the sounds of the morning kitchen. The fire was crackling, the canary was singing, Rosemary Clooney was inviting them over to her house, the coffee was blurping, Gahsie and Paddy's voices buzzed contentedly around her. She was glad the winter sounds were all together again.

The children huddled over the table, watching Jay pour the milk just so around their porridge. It took great concentration to make the porridge float all in one piece so that each bowl became a desert island floating in a milk ocean. Mountains and palm trees were sculpted from brown sugar and top cream. Eating the islands was a complex system of forming harbours, lagoons and volcanic eruptions. Jay didn't remember that they had once loathed porridge, it tasted so different when it came with shark attacks instead of parental attacks.

So absorbed were they in supervising the erosion of one another's islands that they didn't notice the phone ring. Gahsie called Paddy to the phone. When Paddy hung up the phone she sat, watching them without a word.

Joe sat back in his chair to catch his breath and stayed there, wheezing slightly, watching Paddy with a nervous frown. It took the girls a moment to notice that Joe wasn't playing any more, then their chatter faded and they stared at Paddy, too.

"What is it, lovey?" Gahsie asked.

"You have a new baby brother," Paddy told the children in a soft voice that frightened Jay.

Joe beamed at Paddy. "Did you have a baby, Paddy? Can I see him?"

"No, sonny, your Mummy had a baby. Yes, you can see him. She wants to bring him here to show you."

Then Jay knew why she had felt that stab of fear. "No," she pleaded. "Don't let her come here. Don't let her find us."

"There isn't anything we can do to stop it, sweetheart. The court has given her permission to get in touch with all of you again."

"No, you have to stop it. She'll take us away."

"Don't worry, Gashie and I will be here. It'll be the same as ever. They have only been given permission to visit. You won't be going anywhere. They haven't seen any of you for more than a year, and they just want to see you all. It's only natural."

"No, no, no. She'll hit us. She'll wreck everything."

"Jay, Jay, stop it. You're frightening your sister. Now, calm down, dearie, no one will hit you. I'll be right here with you."

"I'll run away."

"Now, that's just silly talk. Come on, let's finish breakfast and get cleared up."

But Jay ran from the table in tears. She climbed up on her bunk, her head throbbing. She stared at the photos in the Shirley Temple books, tears blurring her sight so that she could hardly focus. No matter, she knew all of the pictures by heart and looked at them whether she could see them properly or not. There were some of Shirley swinging on a white picket gate. In her mind Jay could see the gate move back and forth, could hear the laughter of a Jay with blonde curls who lived in far off America where little girls could swing on gates without ever hearing about courts.

No matter what she was told, Jay couldn't believe that nothing would change. It was all changed for her already.

She had no idea how the time passed until the day she found herself standing in the front room after lunch. It didn't feel like Inch Brae any more. It was all wrong. Here they all were, all dressed up and it wasn't Sunday. She should have been at school at that moment with her friends in standard two getting ready for the physical education class after lunch, not standing in the front room at the wrong time of the week watching Poppa mumble and wobble in his chair. He was excited. He knew something was going on. Jay watched him, realizing sadly that she loved the old man and didn't want him upset by one of her mother's scenes.

A car drove in the front farm gate. The world went into slow motion. The car pulled up beside the front garden gate that no one ever used. Their original welfare worker, Mrs Phillips, got out of the driver's side of the car. Their mother got out of the passenger side, carrying a baby. They seemed to float towards the house. The world was roaring in Jay's ears. Paddy, dressed in her city suit, greeted them on the veranda. They came in through the front doors. The edges of the world were tinged with black fog. Gahsie in her Sunday dress said hello and gooed over the baby. It was wrapped in a white shawl that hung down. The baby was put down diagonally on the big brown arm chair under the window where he'd be safe and every one could see him. The shawl was folded over him so it wouldn't hang on to the floor. Jay could only see right in front of herself.

Ursula Easton was shrilling at them. Calling them darling. Jay backed against the wall by the kitchen door. Joe ran forward and hugged his Mummy and talked a mile a minute about Alphie and Corker and school and being big enough to carry wood for the fire, only he'd been sick and hadn't done it this week, though he still was a brave little man and tended the fire when he was sick and would the baby be in his room?

Their mother hugged him and cried and said sappy things and called him darling. Jay remembered that word with dread. They'd been called 'darling' before; when other people were around. When there was no one around to hear they were called names they hadn't heard since they'd been at Inch Brae. Until that moment Jay had forgotten those derisive names. No one else she'd met ever used them.

Carrots stood by Poppa's chair, her fingers in her mouth. Jay thought Carrots didn't remember their mother until she realised Carrots hadn't sucked her fingers since they'd first arrived. After that she wasn't sure.

"Come to Mummy, darling," trilled their mother. Jay hated every inch of her. Carrots edged forward. Jay pressed her back to the wall. She couldn't stop this from happening. It wasn't stopping. It wasn't a bad dream. She couldn't wake up from it. Paddy wasn't stopping it. They weren't safe. The nightmare had come to life.

Carrots was coaxed forward to look at the baby and hug their mother. She stood in front of the woman shifting from one foot to the other, sucking her fingers, saying nothing, her head slightly lowered as if she'd become suddenly shy. Remembering how Carrots had run giggling around all the strangers at the

Christmas hungi, Jay tried to send tangible waves of loathing at her mother. She wanted to knock her over with a solid lump of hate.

Abruptly Carrots spun and ran to Paddy, arms wide like a bird to fly up to the safety of Paddy's neck.

Their mother scowled, which made Joe leave her side and rush to the shelter of Paddy's skirts.

Ursula snapped, "Jonathan! Come back here!"

Carrots at once wriggled down from Paddy's arms and ran to Poppa. She climbed on his lap and hid her face in his chest.

Mrs Phillips made soothing noises, quickly putting a hand on their mother's arm as she lunged towards Joe.

That started Mrs Easton saying a lot of things about keeping little children separated from their mother until they forgot her. Mrs Phillips made soothing noises.

Gahsie went to get refreshments. Poppa mumbled softly to Carrots. He seemed upset. Jay patted his arm to comfort him. Paddy caught the movement out of the corner of her eye and turned towards them, starting, "Jay, precious . . . "

"Jacqueline! Her name is Jacqueline!" Mrs Easton snapped so sharply they all jumped, even Paddy.

Jay shrank back against the wall.

Mrs Phillips made soothing noises.

The canary stopped singing.

Ursula Easton ordered, "Jacqueline, you come here and don't be stupid!"

The old, forgotten feelings of terror swamped Jay. She couldn't move. She couldn't talk. She could barely see. She shook her head.

"Don't you shake your head at me, young lady! You do what you are told when you are told. You come right here right now!"

Jay thought if she tried to move she'd wet herself. She looked away.

Her mother lunged forward. Paddy and Mrs Phillips caught Mrs Easton's arms. Mrs Phillips made soothing noises.

Ursula yelled at Paddy about poisoning the children's minds against their own mother.

Joe shouted at his mother not to yell at Paddy.

Gahsie ran back into the front room.

Mrs Phillips tried to shush Mrs Easton.

The baby started crying.

Jay ran from the room choking with indignation. 'Paddy never, ever gave us anything poisonous. Now she's telling lies about Paddy. I hate her! I wish she was dead!'

The children's welfare worker must have arrived after Jay ran from the front room, because that's who turned up in the bedroom, tapping lightly on the door but not waiting to be told to enter. Mrs Hone found Jay hunched up on the top bunk, rocking back and forth, staring into space, the Shirley Temple books open around her.

Mrs Hone had to call more than once before she got the response, "Get out of my room!"

"Now, Jacqueline . . . "

"Don't call me that!"

"It is your name, Missy. It won't do you any harm to use it to please your mother while she's here."

"I don't care! I hate her! She's ruined everything!"

"Now, now, we don't mean that, do we? That's a terrible thing to say. Come back to the living room with me and we'll have a nice visit with your Mummy before she has to leave. She can only stay a little while, you know, and she has missed you all so much. You have a new little brother, isn't that nice? I just love the really new ones don't you? They're so sweet and helpless, just like that lamb of yours the first time you showed him to me."

"Alphie."

"Alphie. Now, let's dry your eyes. We don't want anyone to think you've been crying, do we? Your Mummy has missed you, you know. She's been fighting for today for over a year. She loves you so much she's been going to counselling every week to learn how to be a good Mum. You didn't know that, did you? She's very unhappy that you won't even talk to her. You don't want to make your Mummy cry, do you? Now be a nice little girl and don't make a scene. You haven't behaved this badly in all the time I've known you. Your foster mother says you are a brave and loyal little girl. How can I believe her if this is what I see?"

Jay swallowed. In her need to escape her mother she'd accidentally made Paddy look bad. Paddy, who she admired more than anyone in the world. In miserable confusion a solemn, silent, white faced Jay climbed slowly down from the bunk, the only time she ever used the ladder. She meandered, a hollow shell, until she was in the front room.

Gahsie was serving tea with little cakes from the good china off the shelf in the front room. Paddy was helping Carrots feed a piece of cake to Poppa. Joe was leaning way over the arm of the chair watching his mother change the baby and comparing it to wee Davie.

The welfare workers nodded and smiled at one another. Mrs Phillips signalled with her eyes, "How did you . . ?"

"Tough nut," Mrs Hone said out loud.

Jay hated them both. Did they think she couldn't hear them? Did they think because she was only eight she wouldn't know what they meant? They meant she was a tough nut and they'd been clever enough to crack her. They weren't on her side at all. Xantha had been wrong. They were on her mother's side and Jay knew she would lose, Paddy or no Paddy, if those two smug women wouldn't fight against her mother.

She sighed, looking across the room at Joe enjoying the new baby. Jay had nothing against that baby. In fact, she would have liked to know him. But she didn't want to lose everything she had come to know and love at Inch Brae. She was deeply fearful of showing approval of the baby in case that led to her being expected to live with him. At her parents'. No matter what the cost she had to fight against that. Just had to.

Then it started. "Just where do you think you've been?"

Mrs Phillips made soothing noises.

Ursula Easton gave orders.

Jay stood with her back to the wall, saying nothing.

In a short time she couldn't have spoken even if she'd tried; her heart had stopped pumping and sealed her throat off. Not long after that she felt as if she were going to wet her pants. She looked towards the sleeping baby, but couldn't properly focus her eyes. After a little more yelling she couldn't properly focus her ears, either, which proved to be a blessing in the long run because she didn't hear everything that was said. She heard the part about how wicked she was, how she'd hurt her mother very much, but she missed parts of how it was her fault the family had been broken up, and she didn't understand the parts she did hear of how it was because of her Ursula had had to marry that man. Jay knew she had ruined her mother's life, she just didn't understand how she had done it.

Jay was never sure how the shouting went past the point of the welfare workers making soothing noises to Gashie insisting, "That type of language is not to be spoken in my house and if Mrs Easton cannot control herself she will have to leave."

That snapped Jay to attention. In all the time they'd been together, Jay hadn't once heard Gahsie use that deadly tone. It was startling. Its hushed venom was somehow more powerful than all her mother's shouted threats. On the spot Jay decided she would use that quietly lethal tone whenever she was outraged. Unfortunately it opened Jay's ears so that she clearly heard her mother complain to Mrs Phillips that she would never have had to get married in the first place if those damned pills had of worked so that she'd lost the baby. Jay didn't know what that meant, but it made her feel as if her life was in danger. She saw the reactions around her and had bad dreams about her mother's visit for twenty years.

Mrs Phillips escorted the furious Ursula Easton to her car, making soothing noises all the way. Mrs Hone followed with the howling baby, saying she'd be back in a moment. Gahsie told her to leave them alone and shut the door behind the lot of them.

Paddy and Gahsie had their hands full trying to calm Poppa who was making wild-eyed noises, waving his arms frantically, nearly overturning himself out of his chair. He had tears on his lashes. Jay thought perhaps he'd wet himself. She turned dumbly to Joe and Carrots. The three of them stood in a bedraggled knot of misery.

Jay was numb. She felt as if she'd stood under a bell as it was struck. She couldn't hear properly and work crews were using wrecking balls inside her head. Joe was snivelling. Carrots was growling furiously, "Bugger bum, bugger bum."

Having wrestled Poppa to his room and left him with Paddy, Gahsie turned her attention to the children. She stopped, shocked. "Carrots! Wherever did you hear such terrible words! Don't you ever say such a thing again!"

Jay started to giggle and couldn't stop. She tried to control herself, but it was like waves washing over her that she could do nothing about. Gahsie looked at her for a moment, then wordlessly patted her head and rushed off to call Pete.

The car horn sounded in Pete's code. Short, long, long, short, for P. Very soon they could hear the tractor roaring full throttle towards the house.

Pete lifted Poppa onto his bed for Paddy, then strode into the front room, muttering something about getting those darned kids to earn their keep from now on. Jay thought he didn't know what had happened until she realised he was trundling around tidying the front room, talking non-stop. The only other time he'd been blustery was the morning wee Davie was born. Knowing that helped start Jay's stalled motor. She detached herself from Joe's clinging hands and picked up a plate to carry it to the kitchen.

She got only as far as the sight of the kitchen sofa and its afghan. Seeing it was like coming up from underneath crushing tons of dark water. The weight left her, the darkness left her, the drowning feeling left her. She bolted to the sofa like a rabbit with a dog on its tail and had no further contact with reality that day.

Chapter Twelve:
Tarnished Gold.

The children remained quieter and withdrawn for weeks after their mother's visit. Joe wet his bed again. Carrots didn't talk any more. Jay day-dreamed. She and Joe got into trouble at school.

When the quietness wore off it was replaced by a rowdiness they'd never had before. By the time the ponds were edged with ice, as thin and clear as glass, they were rackety enough to stampede outside and smash it by jumping on it. They screeched, yelled, shouted and laughed, exploding back into the kitchen in clouds of breath, red cheeked, their toes, noses and fingers stinging in the sudden warmth.

When they had Carrots with them they were careless of her so that Gahsie had to blow the car horn, long short long short, for C, which she had never needed to do before. At that Carrots was sometimes so chilled she was in tears when she got to the warmth of the kitchen, yet the children didn't want to leave her behind. They might not have wanted to take care of her, but they also didn't want her out of sight.

Came the day Sharon and Bruce were at Inch Brae all day because Paddy and Gahsie left right after breakfast for the court. The children were driven to school instead of catching beat up old Gertie, but this time there was no nice visit on the way. This time the children were terrified of the court and the adults no longer had enough faith in the wisdom of the law to convince the children there was nothing to worry about.

When Jay and Joe climbed off Gertie's wooden steps at the end of their day they stood for a moment looking at Inch Brae, hand in hand, before they trudged slowly along the wheel track to the home paddock gate. They were in no hurry as they climbed one by one over the gate and walked towards the kitchen door. They stalled a moment more at the threshold of the kitchen door to stroke Corker where he slept on the hay inside the nursery room door.

Inside the kitchen they found Sharon tired and upset from trying to take care of Poppa. She and Carrots were cross with one another. From listening to the gripes from both of them Jay and Joe figured out that Sharon thought it wasn't right to leave someone as young as Carrots to give Poppa his lunch, even though Carrots knew how to help him and wash his face afterwards. Poppa had fussed, Sharon and Carrots fought and no one had a proper lunch.

Wee Davie didn't like having his nap in a strange bed and had cried all day. He was almost a year old and very loud when he wanted to be. Carrots got mad at Davie for disturbing Poppa. Poppa was tired and cross from not having a proper lunch or a proper rest. Sharon was tired out by Davie's howling, Carrots temper and Poppa's uncooperativeness. Her troubles had started after the men had eaten their lunch and left for the afternoon and her pride had prevented her from blowing the horn and calling them back to help her.

By the time the children were home from school she was cross enough to say that Poppa was dirty and not good for the children. In fact she thought he'd be better off in a home. Sharon didn't realise that just because Poppa couldn't always make himself understood it didn't mean he didn't understand what other people said. At times she talked in front of him as if he weren't there. That day was one of those times.

Poppa was even more upset after she said that and Carrots started storming all over again.

Bruce arrived to fetch smoko for himself and Pete, walking right into the middle of the uproar. He lifted Poppa into bed, then he and Sharon had a fight. Jay and Joe changed out of their school uniforms and left to do their jobs with the fight still whirling in the air, Davie, Carrots, and Sharon all in tears.

The day at school was roughly even with the day at Inch Brae in sheer rottenness, which Jay reckoned was about the right level of things considering what she expected to hear from the courts.

After the dogs, cats, and poultry were fed Jay ran down to Poppa's room to see what she could do to fix things for him. He was fast asleep, propped up on his pillows, snoring slightly. Carrots was asleep on top of the covers, Poppa's arm around her shoulder, her head on his stomach, her arm across his waist. Jay tip toed out, shushed Sharon and led her down the hall to peek. She thawed a little then, and began to smile.

With Jay and Joe helping her get tea on the table and trying to cheer her up, Sharon was able to laugh at her day, albeit a bit sheepishly, when Pete and Bruce teased her about it while they ate their tea. She admitted it was remarkable how motherly Carrots was for her age. She even joined in the conversation Bruce and Pete had about how good it had been for Poppa to have the children around him. It was possible he wouldn't have been talking at all if they hadn't been there.

When the conversation turned to how the children had benefitted from Poppa, all of them stopped talking and looked pensively around the table. Just the idea of the way Carrots had learned to talk brought to the surface how worried everyone was about the court's decision.

They were all friends again, but too depressed to talk to one another when Paddy and Gahsie drove up in Pete's new car. No one ran to meet them. No one moved. Not a word was said as they waited for the women to enter the kitchen.

Paddy and Gashie settled themselves at the table with only the briefest of greetings. Then almost the entire family was sitting around the tea table not talking. Some were too nervous to eat, as well. Like Jay, who soon couldn't bear the suspense and burst out angrily, "What did you do in that court place?"

Seeing the adults glance uneasily at one another terrified Joe, who began to cry. "Do we got to go? They going to take us away?"

Gashie shook her head, glumly. "No, no, dearie. There, there, my brave wee man. Hssht, now, dinna ye cry. Paddy, dear, we'll have to tell them."

"They said we were to let the welfare workers tell them, Mum."

"Oh, my, well, they canna see how scared the bairns are, can they, now? Tsk, tsk, tsk, the poor wee lambs, look at them, they'll have to know something, ye ken." Gahsie gathered Joe onto her lap and crooned into his hair, "Dinna ye worry, now, we'll take care of you all. 'T'll all work out, you'll see. 'All things work together for good for those who love the Lord'."

Despite the fact that they weren't supposed to hear about it and in actual fact didn't understand much of it, the children were told that they had been made permanent wards of the courts with Paddy as their legal guardian, largely because of the scene the day their mother visited.

Everyone was excited that the children didn't need to be afraid ever again about being taken away. Jay wondered why Gahsie and Paddy hadn't been more cheerful when they'd arrived home. The day had been so all 'round bad that she couldn't believe it had suddenly turned good. "What's wrong, then?" she muttered under her breath.

The glad shouts faded as the others around the table looked at her, realised for themselves that all was not as it appeared to be and turned to look at Gahsie.

Paddy put in quickly, "Mrs Hone will be seeing you more often."

"I don't care about her," Jay sulked, knowing full well that Mrs Hone wasn't what was making Gahsie and Paddy so glum.

Gahsie leaned forward over Joe's head and said, "Jay, both those welfare women told the courts a lot about what things were like for you before and what the difference is now. Try not to be so scornful of them, pet, they really put their necks out for you kids."

She spoke seriously, which left Jay stolidly staring at her unconvinced that there was nothing to worry about. The look on Jay's face made Gahsie sigh.

"It was the welfare workers more than Paddy and me that got the judge to leave you here for good."

Jay didn't even blink.

Paddy carefully explained that when Mrs Easton realised she had lost her children for good she set out a very well prepared argument about her right to see them. No one was ready to argue against it. They hadn't expected it. The woman had gone to court all set to fight any possible outcome. The judge had been persuaded that both parents should be allowed to see the children every second Saturday afternoon.

Everyone but Jay relaxed, glad that the bad news had finally come out in the open. As the picture of both her parents coming to Inch Brae regularly became clear to Jay, all the hope, all of the stuffing, all the life drained out of her. She slumped in her chair, her head hanging, her plaits swinging slowly back and forth as she shook her head.

Gahsie gave Joe to Pete to hold and knelt beside Jay, telling her ever so softly, "Jay, puddin, please dinna be afeared. They likely will nae come all this way that often. When they do they have to be supervised. The courts want someone with them all the time to make sure what happened last time never happens again, because if it does they will nae be allowed to see you again at all. All right, sweetie?"

Jay shrugged without lifting her head. "They had that before," she mumbled.

"Oh, sweetheart, you must have hope. It is nae exactly the same, ye ken. When she came here before she dinna ken she could have you taken from her for that. She thought she was right and we were doing a terrible thing. Now she does know things will get better, you'll see. Some folks dinna ken what's right, you know. It's hard for a wee lass to understand, I know, but some grown up people just didna learn the right things when they were young. You see, lovey? But she's not stupid, Jay, and she wants to learn the right thing. It will nae be the same as that time."

Jay's chin quivered. "It won't be the same here, either, and they'll still hate me if there's someone watching them or not."

"Oh, my goodness, what a terrible thing to think. I wish you could've seen her after she knew she'd lost you, puddin, she was heartbroken. I think she does love you, really, but she doesna ken how to show it. She'll learn, Jay. Now that she knows what can happen."

"She always knew or why would she tell us about how we'd be taken away and locked up if the police knew?" Jay lifted her head, jutting her chin defiantly.

There was a rumble of agreement from the men, a shuffle of anger at the threats that had been made to the children.

Gahsie glanced around the table, telling everyone, "But she has something to work for now. We go back to court in six months, again, to see how they've been behaving. If they're doing all the things the judge said they have to, they'll be allowed to take the kids out, so you know full well they'll be working as hard as they can to do the right thing."

Too late Paddy realised what her mother was about to say and motioned frantically for her to stop.

Gahsie saw her mistake with a gasp. She scooped Jay up from the chair and sat on the sofa, rocking back and forth. "Oh, my. Oh, my. Oh, I'm so sorry, sweetheart. There, there, it's nae for a long time. The judge will be very, very careful before he lets either of them alone with you. Try not to worry, pet, it's a long way away. You'll be nine by then, ye ken. Did you know that? 'T'will give them a chance to learn to be a good Mummy and Daddy. Everyone deserves a chance, remember?"

Jay had the underwater feeling again. She thought to herself, Learn to be a good Mummy? That's a laugh. She'll figure out how to trick the court people. We've had it.

She stared into the flames of the kitchen fire, unmoving, oblivious to everything else.

Once the younger ones were in bed, after Bruce and Sharon had taken wee Davie home, when Pete and Paddy were bathing Poppa for the night, then Gahsie went back to Jay. She took with her a mug of hot cocoa with top cream floating on it. She gathered the forlorn little figure onto her lap and rocked her back and forth, crooning soft old Gaelic lullabies.

Jay curled against her, nestled like a baby chick. In the tiniest voice Gahsie had heard from Jay since they'd first met there came, "They'll take us away."

"Oh, my. They have no way to get you away. They're not allowed."

"One day they will. That court place can't stop them forever."

"Oh, my wee lamb. My brave wee Boudicea. Can ye no find any more fight in your heart?"

"I won't grow to be a lady here."

"No one can see the future. Ye canna tell what may happen."

"I won't be with you when I'm big. Not even when I'm a teenager girl." The tears finally came, sliding slowly down her cheeks and dripping into the untouched cocoa.

Sally McLean had never seen Jay look so defeated. It was all the harder to watch for being so rare. Sally was speechless with grief and outrage. She was doing her level best to accept the court decision, to maintain her respect for the law and its wisdom, but she was losing the battle. With tears dripping off her own lashes, Gahsie sat silently rocking Jay, undoing her plaits to brush her hair out for the night.

Jay took a sip of the cooling cocoa and demanded in her old, sharp tone, "Why'd you get us, anyway? If you'd left us alone we'd never've known this."

"But you would have been put somewhere, anyway. Maybe even in three different places."

"Why?"

"Because the welfare couldn't have left you there to be beaten up like that."

"Why would they put us in different places? Ma told me Joe 'n me'd never see each other again if we were so bad the police got us. After we were here we thought that was a lie."

"Oh, my, well, ye ken, that's nae quite the way things're done. The welfare doesna take bairns because the bairns're bad. You three didna do anything wrong. D'ye not ken that yet? You see, they try not to break families up if they can help it. It's just that it's hard to find homes that will take three kids all at once."

"Why did you?"

"Because we couldna get any fosterlings any other way and because we didna like the idea of kiddies losing each other as well as their home and Mummy and Daddy."

"Why did you want to get foster kids? I heard you tell Paddy you didn't like it when she was getting us."

"Oh, my. It's not that I didna like it, ye ken, it's that I was that worried about our Paddy. She has so much on her plate already with Poppa, you know? I was afraid she'd wear herself out taking in so many wee ones as well."

"Then why did she?"

"Well, you see, pet, she feels she canna have a family of her own any other way whilst she takes care of our Poppa."

"Why?"

"Oh, my. D'ye ken how hard it is for her to get away? How can she get out to meet anyone? And besides, ye ken, even if she did, she doesna really have time for a husband. She's never really free, is she? So we have all of you. Our new twigs on the old branch, so to speak. Ye see, pet, we couldna let anyone take you from old

Inch Brae, you're our wee ones now. So don't you lose heart, you hear? We are your family now. All of us love you and need you."

"How did you get us?"

"Ye ken we nearly didn't. They usually willna let an unmarried lady have fosterlings. Especially in our case with Poppa in the house, they told us we were nae in a position to take care of a child. But when we thought we had room for a family and then they needed a place for all of you suddenly in the middle of the night and they needed it a good long way from your parent's house, well, it was our lucky day."

Jay lifted her head to look into Gahsie's eyes to see if she meant that.

Gahsie smiled at her. "It was our lucky day, ye ken. They wanted to move you to a more suitable home as soon as they found one, but you settled here so well they could be talked out of it. Even though Xantha and Sharon have their bairns now, the three of you are still our dream come true."

She hugged Jay. "You're our big, brave lass and such a help, too. Joe is our wee man. He reminds me of my Dave when he was seven. Regular wee bloke. He's such a strong heart. Though Davey had lived with what had happened to his Daddy for six years, he didna hesitate to give his own life when his turn came in Korea. We're able to live the way we want to because of brave men like my David and our Dave, ye ken. And our Joe's made of the same stuff. He'll not be hiding from his duty if, God forbid, there's another war in the 1970's when he'll be the right age."

"There won't be another war, will there, Gahsie?"

"'Course not, not unless the Russians do something stupid. What else would there be to fight about? We taught the Chinese their lesson in Korea."

"What about Carrots?"

"Well, now, Carrots is surely the answer to our prayers for Poppa. Jay, you canna ken the change in him since you've all been here. Eight long years we've been taking care of him and him hardly knowing. And now, just one year of new life in old Inch Brae and there he is, laughing and listening again. And trying to talk, too. We do love all of you. You're our future. New blood in the family. A grafted on branch, just like Pete put granny smiths on that mackintosh tree. D'ye ken? We canna let anyone just up and take you off. You're our bairns for good and all, now, the judge said."

When Jay finally did fall asleep she slept too heavily to be disturbed when Pete carried her to her bunk. She felt safer knowing what it meant that the judge had made them all permanent wards, but fear of visits from her parents weighed on her mind and darkened her dreams.

The first few visits were terror filled disasters, but gradually the time their parents spent at Inch Brae became less threatening for the children. The main reason was that the man the court had assigned to supervise the Eastons was not the type to make soothing noises. He demanded obedience.

Seeing that even their father had to obey the man or leave, the children were greatly comforted. The turning point for them came the day that their father had insisted that it was too far for him to travel to Inch Brae and that the children should be brought to him. The welfare worker, Mr Potae, saw how afraid the children were and refused to hand the request on. Knowing that there was someone in the world more powerful than their father let the children relax as nothing else had.

Once the children believed no one could take them from Inch Brae for any reason, life on the farm ran again more or less as it had before the visits. The feeling that their home had been violated didn't completely leave them, but the regular routine was like a balm over the sore spot.

From then on the days seemed to have a brighter shine to them, as if the finger of danger had spread a glittery hardness over the soft golden air of Inch Brae. There was an urgency about life. Jay tried to memorize each moment so that she would always know what it had been like. She couldn't shake off the feeling that it could all vanish in a blink, no matter what welfare workers, teachers and family told her. It took longer for the sameness of routine to work its healing for her.

There were no midnight dashes to the hospital in the middle of the night that August. Xantha's fourth daughter, Jane, was born in the city, causing no more than a phone call to ripple the calmness at Inch Brae.

The birthing days went more smoothly in the paddocks. New calves and lambs were not born in the worst freeze of the fifties and all hands were there to do the work. More of the new borns were hale and hearty, healthy, happy and loud. There were fewer orphans in the nursery and not one of the mothers.

Each morning brought another delight for the children to exclaim over before school. They knew better than to act as if it was all new magic on the bus in the morning, but they found a fascinated audience in Mr Potae. Joe infuriated his mother when he descibed to Mr Potae how Shy had given birth to her latest pups.

Claiming that the McLeans had destroyed the children's innocence, Ursula Easton filed a complaint about corrupt home atmosphere with the courts.

Jay didn't know what that meant, but she resented it. Knowing that the story her mother wanted her to believe, that babies were brought by good or bad angels was a lie, but what was supposed be hidden was the truth, Jay boiled with anger. Her rage overcame her fear so that instead of trembling and stuttering in front of her mother, she began to bait her.

To Jay's amazement her mother rose to the bait with monotonous regularity. Any other grown up she tried her tricks on only fell once, if at all, but here was the woman she feared tumbling over and over again to the simplest things. It gave Jay a feeling of power over her mother to know she could lead her on any time she wanted to. Her nervousness evaporated, leaving behind a film of pitying contempt.

Joe the soft hearted remained open and chatty with their mother even after Pete had been dragged off the farm for his day in court for corrupting the children, but after each visit Joe wet his bed for a couple of nights. If their father visited Joe wet his bed for a week.

Fortunately, Mr Easton rarely visited, even in the beginning. After he had words with Mr Potae they didn't see him again. Gahsie told Jay that her father hadn't shown up in court, either, so the fear that he would take them all away faded.

The rowdiness that the children had taken up in the winter got worse after the visits started. After school Jay and Joe raced through the house until their noise got them sent outside where they racketed around the home paddock. They roared about so much that they wound Shy's pups up into a frenzy of shrill yapping. Shy got so upset she carried her pups one by one into the back corner of the nursery room.

Whether they were feeding the hens, collecting the eggs or getting firewood, Jay and Joe were just as rough and noisy. For the first time eggs were broken and the children had to be warned not to frighten the penned hens off the lay. Carrots went running in to Paddy crying that the bigger children had hurt her so many times that they were sharply told to keep their roughness away from the house altogether.

The loose poultry were in for it every night as whooping wild Indians bounded down from the home paddock to the pond at the bottom of the birthing paddock, back up the hill and to and fro through the orchard. Duck eggs were broken by frantic ducks, new lambs and calves were frightened, new mothers and mothers-to-be were panicked.

At the tea table one night it all came to a head when Jay and Joe couldn't stop giggling, shoving and kicking long enough for the adults to have a conversation. Pete smacked the flat of his hand on the table, causing a shocked, open mouthed silence. He launched into a list of the children's crimes. They glared back in chin-jutting defiance.

Gahsie sighed and placed herself at the head of the table. Jay and Joe glanced at one another, not sure what would happen next. "Now, now, everyone settle down. No more of this carry on. First I want each one of ye to tell one other person why ye love them. Peter?"

Pete blinked to hear his full name, looked directly into Jay's eyes and said, "I love Jay because she's braver than I am."

All of the tension in the room folded in on itself.

Jay was stunned. She couldn't imagine such a thing being true.

Paddy took her turn. "I love Joe because he's our hard working little man."

Jay looked around the table feeling very inferior. She couldn't think how she would take her turn. She swallowed a lump in her throat and whispered, "I love Paddy 'cos she got me."

Joe spoke up as clear as a bell, "I love Gahsie 'cos she never calls me stupid."

They all looked at Carrots, wondering whether or not she understood enough to join in. In her lisp she added, "I love Poppa 'n he loves me."

"Now," Gahsie started firmly. "You bairns need to let off more steam since these visits started. The way you're doing it is not helpful to Inch Brae. How can we let the wild animals roar without broken eggs?"

"It's just that I always want to yell," Jay tried to explain. "I want to yell and yell and yell. I feel like I'll burst if I don't."

"Then call the cows in," Pete snapped, sarcastically.

"Not a bad idea," Paddy put in. "She could get up earlier in the morning to call them before she gets her glass of orange juice and she could call them first thing when she gets home from school before she feeds the poultry."

The adults nodded to one another, although Jay sat still, wondering whether or not there would be any time left for her to play.

"I want to hit," Joe announced before Jay had a chance to sort out what she wanted to say.

"Is he too little to split kindling as well as carry the wood in?" Pete asked his mother and sister.

"No, I'm not. I'll be careful. Can I? Can I, Gahsie?"

"Me too!" Jay yelled, jumping to her feet. "I want to chop wood too!"

Both children were shown how to handle the little hatchet with the utmost care. From then on they split kindling every day after school as well as their other jobs. It seemed to do the trick. The worst of their explosiveness was gone.

Chapter Thirteen:

Poppa

The evenings were warm enough for Gahsie to sit on the veranda to do her hand sewing after tea. It was a warm spring that year so that, although they still had fires in the mornings, the children were able to watch the sun sets while they did their homework.

One of Jay's favourite things was to take her homework out to the veranda and settle beside Gahsie while Paddy got Carrots ready for bed. Poppa rocked away in his rocking chair wrapped in blankets like a parcel because he felt the evening chill. Joe did his homework, then went in for his bath.

The new lamb that had taken Alphie's place was Joe's pride and joy. He had named her Misty. Misty cried after Joe went in until she curled up under the pines for the night. Old Corker, now a grown, sensible, sleepy cat, purred in Gahsie's lap as she rocked and stitched.

The dogs flopped down. Old Skip could hardly walk any more, but he always spared a lick for Poppa before he went to sleep. Strong Fleabag settled his shiny, smooth brown head on his big, black forepaws, giving out grunts and great gusting sighs as he fell asleep. Gentle Shy stayed only a moment beside Fleabag before she went back to tend her pups. Fleabag wagged at her and licked her face. Their son, Leafless, wanted to play some more. Gahsie called him brainless more often than she called him Leafless. When he did finally settle down the long coat he had inherited from his mother warmed Gahsie's toes. Fleabag snored in his sleep.

Jay worked away, trying to make her homework last until Paddy called her in for her bath so that she didn't go in one second before she had to. It hadn't been warm enough to sit on the veranda until much later in the year the previous spring. She listened to the sounds of the night, comparing them in her mind with the sounds of summer evenings. It was too early for frogs, for one thing.

At the precise moment Gahsie stood up and Jay climbed on the veranda sill so that they could watch the sun slather butter across the one view of the sea they had from Inch Brae. Between the hills and trees a streak of horizon showed itself when conditions were exactly right. A lovely, clear, spring sunset was one of those conditions. The sky coloured up as the sea gilded; pinks, reds and oranges rushing to flood the world before they were chased off by the pale blues, dusky violets, darker plums and finally the black of night.

When White Island was active once they saw a liquid pale lemony green as rare as it was beautiful. Gahsie explained that it was caused by the yellow of the sulphur fumes White Island threw in the air combining with the normal blue to make green.

Jay tried to make up a chant about green skies at evening to go with the one about red skies at night, but she couldn't get the rhythm of the words to fit.

She thought there was no place in the whole world as happy as the veranda at twilight. That's when Gahsie told her about things. All she needed to do was ask in the right way and her foster grandmother rattled on all by herself.

One night Poppa was being difficult so both Pete and Paddy were needed to handle him, neither of them able to relax after tea. Jay protested to Gahsie, "Why does Paddy always have to be the one? She never even gets to sit down."

"She's the only one left, sweetie. Xantha's all settled in the city, married to her young man, having bairns of her own. We lost our Dave in the Korean War, you know, just the year before you came. Bruce and Sharon have their wee Davie – besides, they moved out into Uncle Ian and Aunty Fi's cottage when they retired. He put his back out, ye ken, and couldna farm anymore, so they've gone all the way to Auckland where their Andy lives. All their boys grown and gone from Inch Brae, though I did hope their Gary'd stay here. He's share milking in the Wairarapa.

The only ones left here in old Inch Brae with David and me are Pete and Paddy. Ye ken my Pete is courting that nice little Margaret McGregor from over the road, don't ye? She's from good farming stock – Scottish, too – so chances are they'll live here if she'll have him or maybe swap with Bruce for the cottage. Even if they do live here doesna mean Margaret could take care of our Poppa the way his Paddy does. As you've seen, Sharon canna and she's been in the family nigh on three years now, and I certainly canna lift him.

You see? If our Paddy would leave us our Poppa would likely have to go into a nursing home. I do believe that would kill him, you know? So our Paddy doesna feel she can leave us, even for a holiday. But she doesna have any life just taking care of her poor old Dad. She did so much want a family of her own. Especially a wee lass. She talked about having a little girl of her own since she was about yer age, pet, and here's Xantha with four of them and she never did get as excited about it. Silly, isn't it?"

"But Gahsie, why did Xantha just go off and leave Paddy alone to care for Poppa?"

"When their Daddy was brought home from the War in 1944, Paddy was just 15 and still in school, but Xantha was already 22 and away from home taking her teacher training so it fell to Paddy to bear the brunt of it. She hasna been free since that time.

Part of her is off having fun every time she sees you lot running and playing. When you're a young lady a wee bit of her will always be with you having the good times she gave up for her Daddy."

"It makes me sad that Paddy gave her life to Poppa. Maybe I can take care of him when I'm big enough so she can have some good times of her own."

"Oh, you precious wee lamb. There's no need for that. She isna sad, dearie, she's as brave as her Dad was. All her life she'll know she did the right thing when she was called on. How many people can say that? Sometimes the right thing is very hard to do, you know. Then doing it and staying with it is more courageous than being a hero. But everything that's truly worthwhile costs a lot. Paddy knows that. She knows the price and she's willing to pay it. That doesna make her sad and you shouldna be sad for her. Other's lives are sadder."

Jay snuggled down in her bunk thinking about the new meaning of the word 'brave'. She wondered how anyone's life could be sadder than Paddy's. Yet Paddy seemed happy, always humming as she worked, chatting with her family and friends. She seemed to have a lot of friends who phoned to chat or dropped over for a spot of tea. Jay wondered if her parent's lonely house was what Gahsie had been thinking of, but she knew for sure her own life would be sadder if ever she found herself back there.

Their mother's visits carried on, relentlessly, no matter how the children tried to avoid them. Tummy aches and tears made no difference, Mr Potae herded them in to the front room regardless.

Carrots was shy and suspicious unless Poppa was with her, which was difficult because the sight of Mrs Easton upset Poppa so much Paddy didn't want him in the front room with her. Carrots had never spoken in her mother's presence, so their mother called Jay a liar right in front of Mr Potae when Jay repeated something Carrots had said.

After that Jay didn't try to tell stories to make her mother laugh. She kept to one word answers or tried to find stories to tell that would upset the woman. Lurid stories about animals being born were fun for a while after the complaint had been investigated and dismissed, especially if Jay talked about things like that in front of Carrots. The best time was when Mrs Easton got so angry that Mr Potae suggested Jay leave the room. Immediately Jay and Joe began to plot ways to be sent from the room.

Sometimes that ploy worked and sometimes it didn't, but the best one of all happened by accident. Joe was talking to Mr Potae about the games he liked to play when he mentioned quackers without thinking. Mr Potae wanted to know how it was played. It was an easy game. The children interrupted ducks while they were mating to see how mad they got. They scored one point of the ducks just quacked, two points if the drake chased them and three points if both ducks chased them. Mr Potae laughed, which made their mother so angry that the entire visit was called off by her shouting.

Jay heard her mother being warned very firmly that unless she ceased those violent outbursts she wouldn't be allowed to see the children.

Pleased to have a new weapon, Jay and Joe tried to think of things to say that would have the visits cut short. Jay tried more often than Joe, because he felt sorry when he thought his mother was in trouble. Jay was hoping that if her mother stayed in enough of a fury the court wouldn't allow her to have unsupervised visits at the end of the six months.

The visits went more smoothly when their baby brother, Alexander, was brought to Inch Brae. Joe was very interested in his little brother and asked endless questions about him. When the weather was warm enough for them to have the visit on the front lawn, their mother asked Joe if he wanted to live with his little brother. Mr Potae was swinging Carrots in the hammock and didn't hear the question. Joe was busy showing off how Misty walked well enough on a lead to win a prize at the spring fair, so he wasn't watching his mother's face, or being as careful about what he said in front of her as the children normally were.

Off-handedly Joe said there was plenty of space in his room for Alexander's cot. Not noticing how angry that made her, he rambled on about how good it would be for Alexander to grow up on the farm and how good it would be for wee Davie to have someone his own age to play with. Mrs Eastons fury was great enough to have the visit cut short and to have the next one skipped to teach her that she was not to hit the children like that.

Joe never again mentioned having Alexander at Inch Brae. He didn't appear to notice, but Jay knew he'd taken a low blow. He had a fantasy of Alexander living on the farm from the time he was too small to have the kind of memories the rest of them had. In secret they had called the baby Sandy and had dreamed of teaching him each new job as he grew. Joe dropped that game, but where Jay raged he didn't seem to bear a grudge. He simply didn't mention it again. He didn't swear, he didn't cry. Jay envied him his untouchability.

Resenting her mother for hurting Joe like that, Jay got back at her by ignoring Alexander. She remembered how it had upset her mother when she'd been too afraid to go near the baby, so now she did it out of spite. Successfully.

Carrots showed no interest in the baby if she didn't see him and jealousy if she did. Either annoyed their mother and that kept Carrots wordless and suspicious. Jay's resentment became tinged with contempt.

Jay's sneering remarks earned her almost as many sharp reprimands from Mr Potae as her mother's temper earned her. Jay didn't care about that. All she wanted was to be sure their mother never earned the right to take them out without Mr Potae there. She was terrified of what could happen if there was no one there to keep her mother under control. Instead of being good, hoping against hope that her parents wouldn't punish her for some unknown crime, she took a risk that she thought might cost her her life if it backfired, desperate to convince the faceless people who controlled her life that she shouldn't be left at her parent's mercy.

During the respite granted to them by the visit Mrs Easton was made to miss after her tantrum on the front lawn, the McLeans planned a special birthday for Paddy. They were having so much fun that they didn't let it bother them that Mrs Easton had filed another complaint against them. This time it was that the children were mistreated.

While the plans were underway for Xantha and Malcolm to visit for Paddy's birthday, Jay found out that something was spoiling the fun for her. She sat off by herself to try to figure out what was wrong. There was something about Poppa that was upsetting her and she didn't know what it was.

Jay started watching Poppa, trying to find out what it was that bothered her about him. The bad feeling made no sense. The old man's hands were steadier, he was able to hold things and could feed himself finger foods on good days. He could point and wave, stoke and pat. His speech kept getting better until some people outside the family began to understand him.

To give him a change of scenery he was sometimes taken to town when they went shopping, but one day he caused one of his sensations by remembering an old friend's name.

One evening when Jay was sitting on the veranda darning socks with Gahsie, she suddenly saw what it was.

Gahsie finished her pair and tossed them to Jay to put in the basket of finished mending, teasing Jay for being slow with hers. A flock of starlings flew across the lawn on their way to the orchard to argue over the sunset with the other thousands of starlings collecting there, when a hawk dive bombed the flock causing a tremendous ruckus. They all looked up and laughed, but as Jay looked over at Poppa she caught the sudden impression that he was becoming transparent.

She thought she could see right through his skin to the shrivelled old muscles underneath. She wondered idly if she would be able to see the bones one day.

Then she thought she'd imagined the whole thing because Poppa was much clearer in his thoughts. He was remembering more and rambled on in gibberish if something said at the table caught his attention. If they could pick any words out of the babble it was obvious he was really saying things and not just making noise.

Jay remembered how pleased they'd all been when he first showed enough awareness to wonder where Alphie was when the sheep out grew his pet-hood and joined the flock. By the time Misty had replaced Alphie on the front lawn no one was surprised to see Poppa point at her and chuckle. He was improving enough for them to take it for granted.

It tired Poppa out and made him cross when wee Davie constantly got into things and cried all the time, but when the Murphys arrived with baby Jane he laughed and made noises almost like cheering, waving his arms around. Carrots said there were tears in his eyes when he was tucked in that night.

Paddy's birthday was a great success. Not only was it a treat to see her have fun, but Sally, Pam and Tui Murphy made the weekend without Mrs Easton's visit into a Christmas for the Eastons. Sally and Jay were allowed to troop over the paddocks to Mcintyres and visit with Ngaire, then, when Ngaire's mother drove the girls home, the women had a good gossip over a cup of tea. Ngaire's Mum had gone to school with Xantha and was delighted to see her again.

Paddy said that the best present of all was when Xantha took care of Poppa for her so she could go to an Ingleside on Saturday night with Bruce and Sharon, Pete and Margaret.

Xantha tucked all the children in because Paddy wasn't there. Jay was glad that Paddy was having a good time at last, but she sympathised with Carrots for crying for Paddy. It felt all wrong with Paddy not there. Xantha got to Jay's bed after the other little girls had giggled themselves to sleep and Joe had begged to have wee Davie with him because he was lonely, then fussed because Davie's crying for his Mum and his own bed kept Joe awake.

Jay decided to ask Xantha about Poppa. She wanted to know all about him. She was trying to find a way to put her bad feelings into words. She thought Xantha might notice any big difference in him because she didn't see him very often.

Xantha told Jay about a Daddy with dark brown hair who looked a lot like Pete and helped her train her calf to walk in the ring at the spring fair so well that it won a ribbon. Xantha had been seventeen when war broke out. Her Dad had said from the beginning that he had to do his duty. Xantha could remember hearing him argue with Uncle Ian and Mr MacIntyre and Mr McGregor about whether his duty to his country was to stay with his wife and five children or to go to Europe and fight the Nazis. By the time Xantha had turned eighteen, Dave was sixteen and Bruce was fourteen. They could run the farm with the help of Uncle Ian, Aunty Fi and their teenage sons who were living in the cottage at the time.

Poppa decided he wasn't needed at Inch Brae as much as he was needed overseas. He joined the New Zealand Army. In 1944 when he was shipped home Xantha was living at the university learning to be a teacher. Dave and Bruce had both enlisted, but neither was taken. Their cousin Gary had been old enough to go in 1943, but he came home unhurt after the war.

Xantha went to the airport with her family to welcome her father home. They all knew that he'd been wounded, but she had been expecting to see her Dad; a hurt man, but still her Dad. Nothing had prepared her for the sight of him; a white haired, sallow skinned, moving skeleton. He didn't know anyone. He didn't walk or talk. He couldn't feed himself or use the lavatory. He'd been decorated for bravery, but for nothing. The man he'd given his life to save had been killed by the shell that had taken Poppa's mind. Xantha hadn't been home much after that. Dave, Bruce and Pete were all at home to help Paddy and Gahsie with Poppa. She hadn't felt needed.

Jay found herself unable to put her worry about Poppa into words. Xantha seemed too pleased with his progress for Jay to have the heart to put a pall over it. It was then that the full meaning of things like Poppa's first words became clear to Jay.

Sally's birthday was only a few days after Paddy's, so they had a little bonus party on Sunday after church before the Murphys went home. Ngaire was invited which Jay thought made it feel as if it had been her birthday and not Paddy's or Sally's.

That year her own birthday fell on a week too rainy to think about days at the beach. Ngaire came for the day and gave Jay the same book, the newest Nancy Drew, that she'd given Sally. When Pete drove Ngaire home that evening Jay went along for the ride and made Ngaire laugh with the story of Davie's birth night.

"Flaming car never has been the same since then. Listen to how she knocks now."

The girls dutifully listened and agreed out loud, though privately they couldn't hear a thing. Jay thought it more likely that the stony road was shaking the poor machine to pieces than that a bit of a bath had hurt it.

Jay dropped in to Poppa's room for a moment before she went to bed. Bruce had lifted him in and out of the bath for Paddy while Pete was driving Ngaire home, leaving him all sweet smelling and clean with his hair all fluffy and soft like a white cloud.

He smiled and chuckled when Jay told him about her day. He fell asleep while she was talking, so she gently tucked him in and tip toed out of his room feeling grown up and responsible.

Jay thanked everyone for her lovely birthday, rain or no rain, and settled happily in her bunk to start her new book. She had to have imagined the whole thing about Poppa. After all, if any of them were upset they went to him to tell him their woes. He focused on them gravely, listening with a solemn face and patting them with his shaky old hands. That didn't sound like a man who had anything new wrong with him.

Poppa liked to have his tea with the family every night now that he was steadier. He couldn't sit still enough to balance on a kitchen chair, but Pete and Bruce made a ramp for his wheel chair. When the chair was pushed up the ramp and its wheels locked he was the right height for the table and safely strapped in. During the meal they needed to help him, wipe him up and make sure he didn't knock things over, but with Carrots on one side and Paddy on the other he did well. It was worth it to see how his eyes shone.

Moreover, they were sure he was genuinely listening to their conversations. He seemed to follow jokes and laughed in the right places, he made pleased or angry or disapproving sounds quite fitting with the things that were said and he made obvious efforts not to interrupt. Every now and then he became involved enough to launch into a long, expressive ramble that made absolutely no sense, but the whole family paid him full attention and tried to pick out words so that they might know his point.

It felt fair to Jay for Poppa to have as much attention paid to his rambling as the most brilliant speaker. She began to have dreams about him being totally well again. In her dreams he was a bent old man with a walking stick, but he did the things Xantha had described to Jay. One night she dreamed he helped with the milking, another he went fishing or helped train a pet lamb for the spring fair.

Then, in a nice dream where Poppa was playing darts with Bruce and Pete, Jay dreamed that the soldier in the photo with the black frame was watching the dart game. Then Poppa melted. She sat bolt upright in her bed and found her pillow was wet with tears. 'But why? It was a nice dream until the very end.'

Spooked, Jay slid down from her bunk and ran to the kitchen. She had to run across the kitchen to get to the light switch by the back door, but once the light was on she felt less afraid.

She walked warily to the table and leaned on it looking at the pictures on the wall as she had the first morning. Now she knew who all the people in the photos were. In the one of Gahsie with all her children, Jay knew that the soldier was Dave and the photo had been taken the day before he left for Korea, about a year before the children arrived at Inch Brae. The photo in the black frame with the poppy pinned to it was also Dave, taken that same day. Beside it was the photo of Poppa when he left for the Second World War, in his uniform.

Suddenly terrified, Jay ran down to Poppa's room. He was snoring gently, sleeping peacefully. Jay spent the rest of the night on the kitchen sofa where she could keep an eye on Dave's photo and make sure he wasn't watching.

Sitting there in the wee hours, waiting for Pete to get up, trying to think of a way to explain why she was there, Jay knew for certain that while Poppa was getting better in so many ways, he was melting away before their eyes. She had dreamed what she couldn't quite see during the day. She knew it as surely as she knew her name, but she couldn't for the life of her find the words to say it to anyone.

It seemed to be the year for riotous birthdays. A few weeks after Jay had turned nine, Pete had his mates over for his birthday with loud singing and noisy laughter until much later than they were usually up.

"We didn't have noisy birthdays like this last year," Jay whispered to Paddy.

"It was too soon after we'd lost our Dave last year, pet. We none of us had the heart. We're making up for lost time, now. Besides, something exciting's going to happen soon that's got our Pete all in a dither."

"What's that?"

"Can you keep a secret just for us at Inch Brae and not tell anyone, not even Ngaire?"

Jay crossed her heart.

"Pete's going to propose to . . . "

"I know! I know," Jay interrupted, too excited to wait for Paddy to say it. "Margaret McGregor."

"How do you know that, you little baggage? You're absolutely right. Secret?"

"Secret." They kissed and Jay lay sweating on top of her sheets trying to read her book and doze off in the heat and the noise.

They all slept in the next morning. After Pete had been hauled out of bed and teased about how old he was that he couldn't even take a late night once in a while and a couple of beer, Carrots was sent down to Poppa to wake him for breakfast. It wasn't often that they didn't hear his little bell first thing in the morning.

As they rushed around trying to catch up, they were all giggling, pulling faces at one another and teasing.

Carrots walked very slowly part way in to the kitchen and just stood. She stood very still. They quietened, staring at her. She said in a peculiar, hushed, grown up sounding voice, "Paddy, Poppa won't wake up."

Everything was quiet and still.

Paddy dropped the toast and ran down the hall.

They followed her, walking slowly.

He was still and white. A Poppa-doll with candlewax skin.

They were all silent.

'There should be screaming. There should be screaming and crying. Why doesn't anyone say anything?' But Jay couldn't say it out loud.

There was only a dream-like, aimless walking around.

Gahsie said, "Oh, Davey."

Paddy said, "I'm sorry, Mum."

Very soft voices.

Very little crying.

It was shocking to hear the loudness of the horn when Joe blew it, short short short long long long short short short. "I didn't know what else to do," he whispered to Jay. "I had to do something. I'm the little man and I don't know what to do."

The horn not only brought Pete, Bruce and Sharon in, but the McGregors and the Macintyres and the McKenzies.

There was no talk, just a sort of suffocating heaviness that made it hard to walk or talk or breathe.

The neighbours finished the milking and fed the poultry.

Inch Brae felt empty, as if there was a crater in every room.

Nothing looked familiar.

The hungi pit was dug out and cleaned, a calf, a pig and a turkey slaughtered. Uncle Ian and Aunty Fi came and stayed at Inch Brae, crammed in with their sons and their wives, Xantha, Malcolm and their daughters. The cottage was full to bursting with Sharon's relatives, the house had no beds or sofas left so there were bodies in sleeping bags on the floors at night.

Jay crept past snoring mounds on her way to the lavatory wondering how Inch Brae could possibly still feel empty when it was so crowded the floors groaned. "I hate you for this!" She hissed at Dave's photo. "You might have left him with us a bit longer. I know this is your fault." Then she sobbed into her pillow with guilt because likely poor Dave had been lonely in Heaven and had needed his Dad.

During the hungi they sang hymns. Pete did so well with 'The Old Rugged Cross' that even the men had tears in their eyes. It was a broiling, searing hot day. The old soldiers never seemed to stop arriving, crowding on to the lawn telling stories about David McLean, soldier, farmer and friend.

Everyone who came brought something to eat, something to tell and something to drink. Jay thought she'd never seen so much beer in her life. Even the minister had his share of swigs and had to be prompted with some of the words.

The thing that Jay couldn't understand was the laughter. Some of the stories the men told made people laugh. She crouched under the pines, trying not to mess her funeral dress, angry with everyone for laughing.

Aunty Fiona found her and asked, "Are you alright, Jay?"

"Why are they laughing?"

"Your Poppa wouldn't want us to be sad on his account. He's watching us and laughing too, glad that we can remember when he was happy and strong."

Jay was confused. When Aunty Fi took her to Paddy, saying, "Here's a wee mite that's taking it hard," she clung to Paddy for all she was worth.

They picked up the coffin from the front room and put the lid over Poppa's face. It tore Jay's heart out to know that no one on earth would ever see that dear face again, but at least she didn't have to hear any more, "Oh, doesn't he look peaceful at last? I am glad he's finally at peace. It's a blessing in disguise."

'That's one hell of a disguise,' Jay thought, ducking away from someone she didn't know who mistook the sour look on her face for grief and was about to kiss her.

Pete, Bruce, Malcolm, cousin Andy, cousin Gary and Uncle Ian shouldered the coffin and off they all walked through the front garden gate, through the front farm gate and off up the hill, shuffling in the hot, fine dust on the road. When it got to be too much for Uncle Ian's back Mr McGregor took a turn.

There wasn't a cloud in the sky, not even a smoke plume from White Island. The dust was like brown talcum powder, yet as they lowered the coffin into the grave, way up on top of the hill overlooking the sea, it began to rain.

"Why did it have to rain? It was bad enough already," Jay whined.

"Always rains at funerals. God's crying with us," Pete muttered, squeezing her shoulder. He smelt of beer and sweat.

Chapter Fourteen:

Afterwards

It offended Jay to be expected to take the bus to school again. She couldn't believe the world was still doing the same things. She didn't know how it should be different, but it should all be different. If nothing had changed it seemed to her that God didn't care that Poppa had come and gone.

She stared at the bus rattling over the hill as if she'd never seen it before. "They must've driven right past the cemetery," she told Joe.

"Mmm." Joe never spoke about Poppa or about what had happened. He wet his bed, but he didn't talk.

Gertie shuddered and wheezed to a stop, then conked out as Reuben kicked her door open so that the children could get on. Reuben cursed Gertie in Maori, too busy trying to crank the bus to notice the children. Jay thought they should at least have been noticed.

The boys cheered Reuben, laughing, offering to get out and push. "Sit down yuh load of ratbags, yuh'll only run off t' th' beach," he yelled at them to their cheers and applause.

They were all sitting in the same seats, fighting over the same pointless things, laughing at the same silly jokes. Reuben gave up on Gertie, kicked her tyre, hauled her door shut with brute force, threw the fish out the window that someone had put on his seat and yelled, "Get yuh ruddy heads in the winders yuh dozey lot of culls." He took the brakes off, letting Gertie start rolling. Though he yelled, "Hold on!" still some boys went flying when she jerked to roaring, sputtering life.

"Get off me back, Te Kanawa, that's the third ruddy time this week. Tell yuh Mummy to show yuh how to hang on."

Hoots and jeers greeted that and Te Kanawa was applauded as he picked himself up and made his way back up the slope of the bus as she shuddered down the hill determined to dive into McGregor's duck pond.

"You missed it, Reuben, go back and try again," a voice called as the corner was safely negotiated. They'd come close enough that time to tear off chunks of grass from the side of the road.

"Yuh mother's prayin for the day you leave home, Marshall."

Ngaire made room for Jay. Her silent squeeze of Jay's hand was more comforting than anything else could have been. Jay couldn't get over how inane the big boys were. She forgot that she used to think they were funny. It made her angry that someone had put a fish on Reuben's seat, though she would have laughed until she was giddy only a week before.

All the kids wanted to know what a body looked like, who had found the body, what Poppa's last words had been. Even kids that had never spoken to her before came up to her in the playground to ask. She ended up in the sickbay to wait until the bus left for home because the day was too hard for her. The school nurse sat down on the bed beside Jay. "How are you feeling?" she asked in such a kind voice that Jay's chin quivered.

"How can they act like that? Nobody cares at all. How can everything be just the same as it was?"

"Life goes on, Jay," the nurse started, but Jay didn't hear anything else she said, just the kindness of her voice. Those three words blocked everything else out of her mind. It just wasn't right.

That evening she sat beside Gahsie on the veranda, her back turned to Poppa's empty rocking chair. The sunset was beautiful, but Jay was glad that Gahsie didn't call her attention to it the way she normally did. Somehow it was obscene that the world was unchanged by Poppa's leaving it. She stared at Gahsie's face.

The staring bothered Gahsie so much that she put down the shirt she was mending and asked, "What is it, pet?"

"Aren't you very sad?"

"Oh, my, yes. Your Poppa was my husband, poppet. I loved him dearly. Oh, I know he didna seem like a husband the last few years, but now, ye ken, all my hopes that he would get well are gone. I always hoped for a miracle, you know? A wee bit more time - maybe he would have got better, you think? He was happier at the end, wasn' he? That's my one comfort. He did what he believed was right and he saw it through and we never let him down no matter how hard it was. Aye, lovey, I'm very sad."

Jay got up and climbed onto the arm of Gahsie's rocker. They hugged one another. "Are you proud, Gahsie?"

"Proud? My goodness. Aye, I suppose I am at that, but all I can think of is how we hoped and dreamed and planned. Now he's gone. He was strong and honest and brave. A good man, dearie. When your time comes, dinna be in too much of a hurry. Wait. Be sure you find yourself a good man."

"Did you wait, Gahsie?"

"Not really, I don't suppose. We were married when I was sixteen. I was only eighteen when I had Xantha, you know. But hardly anyone's as lucky as I was. Prancing peacocks, sweet talkers, hard drinkers – they're a penny a peck. But a true friend? They're as rare as hen's teeth. Worth the wait, though. First class or nothing, you know?"

"Poppa was your friend?"

"My dearest friend. The single most valuable thing in a home. Friendship."

"I didn't know – I didn't think – it's weird to be friends with someone and be married."

"Oh? Have ye no watched Bruce and Sharon?"

"Well, yeah, I s'pose, but that's us. I mean other people."

"What 'other people'?"

"Ma and Pa."

"Look at me, now, Jay, this is important. Your Mummy and Daddy are not the same as everyone else in the world. You do not have to do things the same way they do. You can love your mother, try to understand her, be respectful, but copy only her good points. Leave her faults out. You can be like anyone in the world you want, anything you dream of, you know? Everyone on God's green earth is a mixture of good and not so good, d'ye ken? Love the good, leave the rest."

"Sometimes I don't think they've got any good and they don't like me, either."

"Oh, my, what a sad state of affairs. D'ye not ken if that's so it's not evil, it's pitiable? Hunt for the good in them, pet, seek it out. Love them because God loves you. Poppa would be proud if you would try to do that. So would Paddy."

"Paddy's not sad for Poppa."

"That she is, dearie, she is. But she's free now. For the first time she can be a young lass, you know? Don't begrudge her, Jay. She did her duty, smiling, uncomplaining. Don't you think she's earned the right to play?"

"Yeah, I suppose so, but is she going to try to get back all that time?"

"She never can. Ye ken, that's the only thing there is that can really be wasted. Time. If you waste it, you can never get it back, never replace it."

"What do you do, then?"

"Spend your time wisely, pet. If you can look back with pride like Paddy, or pleasure, like me, ye didna waste your time. If you look back in sorrow, then you know it's been wasted."

"I never mean to waste time."

"Oh, my, look at me, trying to put an old head on young shoulders, and I should know better at my age, too. I'm sorry, pet. I'm that used to Paddy being here to natter at that I went on without seeing who I was going on at. You're a bit wee for all that yet. Never you mind. Shall we have a nice big mug of cocoa? Then you must be off to bed."

They hugged one another and went into the kitchen to have their cocoa.

The children found comfort in the sameness of every day that followed the one before. The rhythm couldn't very well change as long as Pete and Bruce wanted to continue farming a mixed farm with butter supply cows, fat lambs, potatoes, corn and fruit. As long as the same animals needed the same attention at the same time each day certain things would always be the same.

The children buried themselves in the familiarity of it all taking all the comfort there was to be had from knowing what to expect of each minute. At the same time there were some things so new and different that the children found themselves almost unable to cope with them. The first of those shocks was when Paddy flew to be with Xantha after the funeral. She was gone for only two days, but it was unheard of for Paddy to go anywhere. Gahsie told them that was why she did it. She wanted to do something she hadn't been able to do. Besides, she wanted to see Xantha's house.

The second unbearable thing was the endless emptiness of the house. It seemed to have become enormous, old and draughty. Life there felt pointless, somehow. Jay didn't know why it was pointless or how it had lost its point. On the other hand, she couldn't remember why she had thought life had a point to it before.

She sat on the sofa, stroking Corker, staring at the tapestry that covered the cold, cleaned fire place. Paddy sat down beside her and gave her a hug. "Would you like to tell me what's gnawing at you, sweetie?"

"I like it better when the weather's cold."

"And why would that be?"

"I miss the fire when it's warm."

"I know what you mean. But this is a nice old house anyway, isn't it?"

"Is it true Inch Brae's 100 years old?"

"Well, this room, anyway, I gather. This room was the whole house when the first McLean built it in the 1850s. Each generation has added something. Before the front room was built those glass doors were the front doors. Mum put in the indoor plumbing. I think hers was the best addition, don't you?"

They laughed together.

"I love it here," Jay told Paddy. "I never want to leave."

Paddy smiled, full of pride and love for Inch Brae. "It's been a nice old house, this dear old house. There's been a lot of living here, you know. Babies have been born in the bedrooms, grown up, been married in the front room, seen their own babies born in the same bedrooms, grown old and died . . . "

". . . And had their coffins in the front room where they were married."

"That's exactly right. My father was born in my bedroom. How's that for something no one else can say?"

"Wasn't he born in a hospital like wee Davie and Jane?"

"No, they didn't have the hospital close enough in those days. Besides, there were no cars. The ladies took care of one another at home. Things are different now."

"Are you going to leave us now?"

"I didn't mean different in that way."

"But are you?"

"No, honeybun, I'd never do that to you. I'm going to go out a little bit, but I'll only be at the pictures, or an Ingleside, or up at Xantha's or over at McGregor's, I won't be far away. Don't worry, Gahsie and Pete will always be with you if I'm not and I'll never be gone long."

Jay was relieved to hear that. She felt as if everything was going to be alright after all, until she saw Paddy in the cowshed later that evening. Then the strangeness of Inch Brae without Poppa upset her all over again.

Carrots was lost without her Poppa. She sucked her fingers and cried a relentless muted whining cry, clinging to Gahsie's skirts when Paddy wasn't there.

"Might have to give this one a bit more time to get used to things before you gad about too much, Patsy lass," Gahsie said in her gentle voice.

After that Paddy took the children with her to McGregor's and to Macintyre's. They discovered she had more time to help them with their jobs and with their homework, which left them more time to go to the beach. Wheedling for all they were worth they convinced Pete to trust Paddy with his new car so that she could take them to the beach. With Leafless, but not with Fleabag. Fleabag was too brainless when he was at the beach. Then Jay had such a good time she was almost glad Poppa was gone and spent the night in secret tears of guilt because she didn't mean that at all.

But by that time the daily trip to school in Gertie was becoming fun again and Jay could nearly forgive the boys for ragging poor Reuben when Gertie conked out when they got off after school. Reuben couldn't give Gertie a running start when she was facing uphill, he had to crank her and she didn't want to be cranked. None of the boys offered to push uphill.

"Come on, Reuben, get her going. We'll be late for milking."

"Keep yuh hair on, Marshall. I'm not a ruddy mechanic."

"Ah, Reuben, if my great grandfather hadn't brought civilization to your great grandfather, you'd still be picking pipis for a living."

"And if my great grandfather hadn't of eaten your great grandfather you wouldn't be such a pain in the belly."

That time the boys howled with laughter on Reuben's side, cheering him and telling him, "Good one, Reub. That's telling him! He called your bluff, Frank Marshall. Come on, then, let's give her a push for old Reuben."

For once the boys piled out on the way home, clustering around the bus, telling Reuben to get in and steer. The girls got out, too, to lessen the weight.

"If I hadn't of hurt me hip I could push her too," Reuben lamented. "Mind you, if I hadn't of hurt me hip I could still be a fisherman and not need to drive this rattletrap every damned day."

"You don't like driving a bus, do you?" Jay asked him, sympathetically.

He looked down at Jay, watching him with sympathy. He put his enormous brown hand on her boney little shoulder and told her under his breath, "I cried for you last night, missy." Then he hauled himself into his seat, cursing his stiff hip and the boys who'd greased the steering wheel while he'd been out of the bus trying to get it started.

Jay stood, stunned, watching the huge effort to get Gertie restarted without seeing what she was looking at. Joe was bravely trying to help the bigger boys push, leaving Jay alone with her thoughts. Could a grown man cry? If so, would he cry for a little girl? Why would he? Was it because he knew how lost she was without Poppa? Jay herself had not cried for Poppa, she was still too numb, so why in the world would someone who wasn't even family say he'd cried?

Joe cried when they got in the house and were told that old Skip's time had run out, but still Jay didn't cry. She didn't even rage at Pete when she found out that Pete had shot old Skip. She knew how heartbroken Pete and Bruce were.

"Skip was Dad's dog," Paddy told the children. "He knew Daddy was gone. Dog's know these things. Ever since then he's found it too hard to get around. He lay down in the paddock and couldn't get up again. Pete thought it would embarrass the poor old dog to be carried home, so he helped him to go to Daddy, where he wanted to be. We buried him right where he lay down."

The children went out and looked at the square of freshly turned soil on the top of the hill where Skip had liked to stand to watch to other dogs work the cattle. Joe sobbed for the dog, but for Jay it was just another proof that nothing was the same any more. She wondered if Reuben had known and that's why he'd said such a strange thing to her.

Paddy drove the children to school the next morning. She was going to court again, the time was up for the judge to decide whether or not Mrs Easton had earned the right to have unsupervised visits with the children. It was the first time she hadn't needed to worry about how Poppa would fare without her. Gahsie was able to go with Paddy with no worries because they let Carrots spend the day with Sharon. No one talked about the court. Paddy and Gahsie were excited about meeting Xantha who was coming to give her opinion to the judge. They all planned to go to town and do some shopping once it was all over, the first time the three of them had gone out together since the war.

Jay and Joe didn't want to think about it. If it went wrong they would be alone with their mother on her visits. She might go off with them, try to make them go back to her house. They couldn't face one more thing. They sat silently in the car listening to the women plan their happy day together.

Mrs Hone was waiting for Jay and Joe when school was over, as she usually did on Wednesdays. They were just as happy to go with her. She usually bought them a treat of some sort while she tried to get them to tell her their secrets. They were pleased to see Carrots in the car already, since that meant she was getting over her clinginess. When they told Mrs Hone about poor old Skip both Joe and Carrots cried again, but Jay sat quietly, unable to shed a tear.

So it was Jay who realised they had driven past the place they usually had an ice cream when Mrs Hone picked them up from school. "Where are we going?" she demanded in sudden panic.

"Home, Jacqueline, I'm taking you home."

Jay sat in numbed, stunned silence.

"This isn't the way home," Joe called out, the tears freezing where they lay on his cheeks.

"Yes it is. Your home isn't with the McLeans anymore."

"Why? What did we do?"

"You didn't do anything. The judge has given custody back to your parents."

"But it wasn't for that. It was to see if Mr Potae was still going to be with us every time she came."

"You're too young to understand, Jacqueline. When you're older you'll understand. A lot of things have changed since the first decisions were made."

"You lied to us! You said we'd be at Inch Brae forever."

"I certainly said no such thing. No one should ever have said anything like that to you.

Jay couldn't speak. She stared out of the windows of the car, willing it to be a bad dream that she would wake up from. It couldn't possibly be true.

Joe sobbed, pleading with Mrs Hone to turn around so that he could say goodbye. "What will happen to Misty?" he wailed. "I have to take care of her."

Carrots buried her head in Jay's lap, weeping for Paddy. Mrs Hone drove on, telling them that a clean break was better in the long run and that they'd understand when they were older.

Chapter Fifteen:

You Can't Go Home Again.

Ursula and Harold Easton wouldn't let the children write to the McLeans or phone them. Most definitely there was to be no visiting back and forth. Although both parents were trying as hard as possible to make the homecoming pleasant for the children they wouldn't hear a word that the children had ever been anywhere but in the tiny, cramped weatherboard house on the seaside. The entire time at Inch Brae was to be erased as if it had never happened. Any memories the children had were nonsense, any thoughts of seeing the place again were tantamount to treason.

Christmas was upon them within a month. Day by day Jay saw in her mind the coming of Christmas at Inch Brae, pretending that each week of December had its own special treats. No matter how her parents bent over backwards to be kind she yearned for the Christmas season on the farm.

Jay thought often of the way Reuben had spoken to her the last time she saw him. Had he known something was going to happen to her? Was it just because she had been sympathetic towards him when all the other kids taunted him all the time? She wished she'd known him better and wondered whether or not she would ever see him again and if he was going to spend the rest of his life doing something he hated, driving a rural school bus instead of something he loved, shell-fish farming.

If he could do something he hated every day of his life and still be a nice man, then she, Jacqueline Amelia Easton could live somewhere she hated and still be a nice girl.

The first slaps and cuffs were brought on by the children's names. They were to be known as Jacqueline, Jonathan, Lucinda, and Alexander. No nick-names, no pet names, no abbreviations and definitely no vegetable names! Carrots didn't remember that Lucinda meant her at first, so she didn't answer when she was spoken to. Jay and Joe cringed for her, expecting the blows. What they didn't expect was that they were the ones who were hit for it.

"The poor little thing's not to blame," their mother shrieked at them. "You've led her astray."

Jay and Joe had forgotten how confusing life was at 'home'. For nearly two years they had lived under rules that stayed the same and made sense in the first place. Now they had returned to a world where the very thing that was praised one day earned the strap another day. Where what one child did got another punished, where guilty and innocent depended on Mother's mood at the time. Where truth was as changeable as the wind.

Jay sought solace in her mind. Joe wet his bed. Carrots sucked her fingers and didn't talk.

Ursula and Harold Easton told friends and family how they had rescued their children from the machinations of that barren McLean woman who had used trumped up charges to steal their children because she couldn't have any of her own. The children didn't dare speak out in Paddy's defence.

On Christmas morning the children wept that there was not a word, not a card, not a gift from the McLeans. "That shows how little they really cared about you," their mother explained, hugging them and baking their favourites to show how much she cared.

In between Christmas and New Year Mrs Phillips brought the children the gifts and greetings that the McLeans had sent through the welfare. Jay wondered if they had been sent by way of the workers because Paddy didn't trust the parents. She wrote a note to Paddy, Gahsie and Pete while Mrs Phillips was still there and asked her to see they got it. The three children all went into spasms of pleasure over their gifts. Carrots even said a few words.

The parents' efforts to act out their vision of little lost children restored to the bosom began to wear thin.

After Mrs Phillips left the children found out what names were allowed to be used instead of Jacqueline, Jonathan, and Lucinda. Aside from the 'darling' that they were known as in front of welfare workers, every other name that their parents called them would have had the children punished for using dirty language if they'd dared say such things.

Bit by bit the old ways were relearned. If a child dared to close a door there was an immediate scene – their mother had to know everything they did or said every minute. She was convinced they were talking about her behind her back, or at least that they were misbehaving any time she couldn't see and hear them.

Meals were served with the food already on their plates. Their parents knew better than they did how much they could eat and sat at the table with a strap beside them to make sure every scrap was eaten without a word said. That would have been bad enough if they had liked the food, but cooking was not one of their mother's talents. Pork chops were fried until they were an orangey colour and tough as an old boot. Boiled fish was plunked on the plate with potatoes boiled to mush and cauliflower without even a sauce to relieve its drabness.

When Jay did her best to point out that what they missed was the variety of the farm food, their father added cocoa powder to the oatmeal in the morning and then beat them in his fury that they weren't delighted by his effort. When he added raisins to the oatmeal Joe liked it more, but then their mother's feelings were hurt that they didn't appreciate a thing she did for them.

Jay remembered breakfasts of bacon wrapped around morsels of kidney in a brown gravy on toast with bowls fresh fruit and something else for anyone who didn't like kidney as if she had made up the whole thing. She began to doubt what she knew to be true and to believe her dreams.

She got used to eating her meals in silence, sitting up straight, no elbows on the table, not a scrap of conversation. She wondered if it was true that they had been spoiled and had to learn manners, which is what her mother told her when she tried to describe what it was like to chatter at the table, serving themselves from dishes in the middle, everyone having a good time.

Joe wet his bed every night, which led to rousing melodramatic scenes. "I suppose 'they' didn't care whether you were a filthy pig or not!" their mother screamed at him when he had wept at her that Paddy didn't take the stick to him for wet beds.

Jay had her face slapped for lying when she claimed Joe hadn't wet his bed at Inch Brae, but after that their mother mostly ranted that he, "Only do this to me, don't you? It's only to spite me that you piddle in the sheets, you little swine! You know how hard it is for me to wash bedding out by hand every day? You're trying to kill me with overwork, aren't you? You're just like your father, you inconsiderate, rotten bastard!"

Although Jay could hear him crying into his pillow at night, she didn't dare go to him. She never knew when something like that would bring him a smacking for 'keeping the whole damned family up all night'. Only if she was absolutely sure both parents were asleep would she creep over to his bed to stroke his hair, hug him and ask him if he wanted to tell her what it was the way Gahsie used to.

They held each other tight and whispered under the blankets how unhappy they were and how they missed their pets. Joe couldn't get over the loss of Misty. He worried constantly that no one would take proper care of her. No matter how Jay tried to convince him that no one at Inch Brae would let an animal starve, he insisted he could hear her calling him at night because her stake had never been moved and she'd eaten all the grass she could reach and no one had the time to give her a bottle. Night after night he wept for his lamb, wondering what had happened to her and if she thought he didn't love her anymore because he'd left without saying goodbye.

Jay managed to find a moment when her mother wasn't watching and quick as a wink she phoned Inch Brae to find out about Misty for Joe. Her knees buckled at the sound of Sharon's voice, nearly making it impossible for her to stay on her feet to reach up to the mouthpiece. That's how she found out that everyone at Inch Brae had written letters that the children had never received. All of their toys and clothes had been sent and not given to them, too. Their pets were all well and Misty was a grown up sheep perfectly well and happy.

Whispering under the blankets at night Jay and Joe wept tears of rage instead of sorrow. They didn't doubt that their parents had kept or thrown out anything sent to them from Inch Brae. It helped Jay to have her sadness turned to anger, but Joe still wept for Misty. He knew she wasn't starving, but he still worried that she'd never know why he left her.

Unfortunately it had been a toll call so when the bill arrived both Jay and Joe were strapped. No matter how Jay tried to say Joe hadn't known that she would call, no one would believe she had done it by herself. Since she couldn't have been in worse trouble, Jay accused her parents of stealing the mail. The fight they got into with one another over it and the way they kept on reminding her of the terrible thing she'd said to them, accusing them, her own parents, of stealing made all of the children sure it was the truth.

After that Jay learned about collect phone calls, which she found she could place from any phone she could find. In that way she discovered that Paddy had left Inch Brae to go to the university to become a welfare worker, hoping she could change things for children like the Eastons.

Jay and Joe were shattered. They had each harboured a secret dream that Paddy was fighting to get them back. They couldn't bear to picture her anywhere but waiting for them to come home. Inch Brae wouldn't be Inch Brae without Paddy. Hadn't she said she would never leave them?

The first chance he got Joe phoned, to prove that Jay had got it all wrong. By the time he was able to find a phone he could use without anyone stopping him, Pete and Margaret had married. But they weren't living in Inch Brae, either. They were living at McGregor's, Margaret's father's farm, the one with the duck pond that the school bus wanted to swim in.

How could Pete and Paddy have both left poor Gahsie alone? Was there no one with Gahsie?

Gahsie had left Inch Brae, too. She had gone to live with Xantha and Malcolm to take care of their girls so that Xantha could go back to work. Xantha wanted to see what she could do through the schools to help children like the Eastons.

"But there's no one there but you and Bruce?" Joe asked Sharon, his voice squeaky with shock. "How can you do everything by yourself? We have to come home and help. Tell that judge man we have to do our share. I'm really big now. I'm not scared of pigs anymore."

"We're modernizing the farm," Sharon explained. "It doesn't need as many people to run a town supply as it does to run a mixed farm. We manage and we have a share milker now."

Jay lay awake thinking about Inch Brae. The strap marks on her behind were burning, so she had to lie on her stomach. She sighed, remembering her bunk and the Shirley Temple books – sitting on her log in the morning – helping Pete clean the cow shed – scene after scene floated through her mind like a string of pearls, luminous and perfect. The whole twenty months was dreamlike, as if her parents' house was real and Inch Brae was fantasy.

It was hard to believe that there had been people who had thought she was brave or good, or who had called her funny pet names like 'puddin'.

To make things bearable she clung to memories like the time she Pete watched a sunrise after a rain that had lit the morning with gold first before the pink and the light. They stood together on the highest hill, watching the birth of the day in magnificent silence – it was too cold for crickets or frogs and the roosters were too cross and wet to crow. The few birds they could hear twittered unhappily about being rained on all night instead of welcoming the day.

Pete and Jay alone watched and admired, not a chirp, not a buzz, not a crow, just a silent unrolling of splendour. Each cloud kissed with pink and trimmed with gold, the freshly washed air crisp and clean on their faces, their breath making puffs that hung, suspended, in front of them.

In the hollows the cattle moved magically, their legs hidden in the mist. Not a rustle – not a leaf moved, but each bore its own water droplet lit with gold. Not a breath of wind to disturb the gold bead on every leaf and twig.

The grass was cold against Jay's legs, but she didn't move, she couldn't bear to disturb the beads of gold on the tip of each blade. They were all shimmery, trembling with life and promise. Pete called them beads of molten gold.

The whole time at Inch Brae felt like that to Jay. Still and shimmery and liquid and unreal, like one bead of molten gold surrounded by the chill dark of the rest of her life.

Jay's memory was blank about most of her life in her parent's house. Inside her head she had never left Inch Brae. When she dreamed, she dreamed she was there, or she dreamed she was the only person in the world who could sprout big, feathered wings from her shoulder blades and fly up to the rooftops out of danger. At first she was startled out of her day dreams by blows, but it took very little time before she regained her sixth sense so that she could give the appearance of being aware of her surroundings without actually needing to be there. Then she could sail the private, uncharted harbours of her mind without interruption.

She heard her daydreaming and sullenness explained away as the shock of experiencing a death at such a tender age and of being 'uprooted'. Obviously, Jay thought, none of the welfare workers were going to help her if that was what they thought. None of the children mentioned that they were beaten, called names and that their mail was stolen. They had no faith that it would help if they did and plenty of evidence that it was dangerous to talk.

No matter how much the welfare workers told the children that if anything was upsetting them everything possible would be done to help them, not one of them said a word. They had heard too many lollipop stories by then to believe that Mrs Phillips or any of her comrades were to be trusted.

One too many times Ursula Easton changed faces. She had given Mrs Phillips a cup of tea at the dining room table, serving slices of her excellent home-made coffee cake, smiling at the children and calling them 'darling' until the car was out of sight. Then she spun from the window yelling at Jay for something she had said when Mrs Phillips had asked her a question.

Joe sat frozen where he was at the table, trying to be invisible by not moving. As she stormed past him to get to Jay, she punched him in the back of the head, calling him a filthy swine. His head hit the table with a crack.

Alexander started to howl. Their mother shrieked, "Now look what you've done!" and laid into Joe with the strap. She dragged him to his feet, where he stood like a rag doll, making no effort to defend himself or move away while the strap thudded against his arms, his back, his legs.

Something snapped inside of Jay. Ever since Mrs Hone had picked them up from school and he'd sat limply in the car, that had been his expression. Limpness. He didn't argue with anyone, he didn't play, he showed no feelings except in the middle of the night when he cried about Misty. All he had done was sit on his bed with his stamp collection.

Jay flew at her mother, catching the swinging arm. "Leave him alone, you big bully!"

The shouting and hysterics from that went on for a long time. When it was finally over, their mother was locked in her bedroom, refusing to open the door or speak no matter how much the panic stricken Carrots knocked and pleaded. While Carrots cried herself to sleep at the base of the door, Jay did the best she could to soothe the strap cuts and bruises on Joe's back, arms and legs.

"You have to stick up for yourself," she told him.

"Doesn't make any dif," he said. "What d'you think'll happen to you when Pa gets home and finds out about this?"

"I'll be alright. He'll be too mad at her that his tea's not ready to bother with me."

Even as she said it, Jay knew she was just making a show. Fear trickled coldly down her back. She knew it would all be her fault. Not only would he take the strap to her, but their mother would complain about it every time any of them did anything wrong for months or longer. Jay would be punished for this one many times.

She would have been glad that for once their mother wasn't watching them, but the baby's nappies were in their parents' bedroom. He was soon wet.

"Mum, open the door, please. Please, Mum. Alexander has to be changed."

"Tell your 'Paddy' what a 'big bully' I am. Let her change him. She wants to take him from me too, anyway."

Jay looked at the phone, considering the chances of phoning Inch Brae while their mother wasn't watching them. No, it was too close to the bedroom. There was too much chance their mother would hear her and come angrily out of her room. Jay would rather enjoy the time of not being watched as best she could. Who knew when or if there would be another time the children could do or say anything they pleased without fear that their mother would appear behind them, angry about what they were doing or saying?

They didn't do anything special with their time. Jay found tea-towels to use as nappies for the baby, after which he crawled over to the door and went to sleep on the floor beside Carrots. Jay and Joe sat at the table looking at one another. They finished the cold tea and the cake, but they couldn't think of a thing to say.

Joe was aching. He went to his bed and dozed off over his stamps. Jay put a blanket over Carrots and Alexander. She listened at the door. She could hear the radio serial her mother usually listened to while she cooked their father's tea. That meant he'd be in the door, not at all pleased, in a few moments.

Hardly noticing what she was doing, Jay picked up her leather school satchel, tucked into it the cloth doll Gahsie had made eighteen months before, for her eighth birthday, then scoured the kitchen for food that wouldn't go bad or squishy too easily. Tip toeing so she wouldn't wake Joe, she took a change of clothes and three doll blankets. She thought people blankets would be too big to carry. Hoping to buy some time when her mother came out of her room or her father came home, whichever came first, Jay made a bed dummy, then tip toed through the house avoiding all the creaky floorboards. She forced two of the doll blankets into the top of the satchel, then folded the other one across her shoulders as padding, adjusted the satchel on her back and set out.

For all that she worked quickly and quietly without a glance at the others, Jay worried about what would happen to them when she was gone. They would have to shift for themselves since she couldn't see how to take one of them, not even Joe. Maybe they would learn how to stick up for themselves if she wasn't there to do it for them. She meant to come back and get them as soon as she had grown up.

She climbed out of the bathroom window so that the squeak of the door hinge wouldn't bring her mother. Besides, that way she could leave the doors locked from the inside and slow everyone down by getting them to hunt for her in the house.

Off into the comforting friendly darkness she sped.

The first chance she had she branched off from the main road and turned towards the forest, keeping to the grass so she wouldn't leave her foot prints in the dirt beside the road. She stopped at the crest of the hill to look back towards her parent's house. She was worried about Joe. What would happen to him when they found out she was gone? Would they accuse him of locking the doors behind her?

From the top of the hill Jay saw the lights of her father's car turning into the driveway. Whatever was going to happen about her was happening now and there was nothing she could do about it. All at once she felt warm and light, freedom lent wings to her feet, the chill of the damp grass on her toes sparked shivers of thrill up her back. It was April again, the month she'd first arrived at the farm two years ago. In the early evening it was nippy to be outside running in the grass in bare feet.

She turned her back on her parent's house and ran to the forest. It felt as if she were running a hundred miles an hour down the hill. The moon was ducking in and out behind the edge pieces of clouds, peeking and laughing with her. Stars started to flicker in the clear spaces between the clouds.

A perfect night for running away. Although it was autumn it was still warm enough to be comfortable, with a friendly, sea scented breeze, yet cool enough for her to run on and on without overheating. She settled into an even trot that she could keep up for hours.

When the weight of the satchel wore her down she slipped it off her back and carried it, switching it from hand to hand. By then she was in the forest where she knew no car could follow. The forest paths were darker than the road, but the earth of the path was drier and warmer than the grass.

Jay slowed her trot so that she could listen to the moreporks and frogs. Such a friendly night. Such comforting sounds. Her feet thud, thud, thudded on the hard packed path, her breath kept time.

The moon was high overhead when her knees threatened to buckle. She stumbled on, her calf muscles shuddering. She slowed to a walk, concentrating on the rhythm of her walk to keep it going. She managed one foot in front of the other for a while longer, but after that no amount of will would keep her legs straight enough to hold her up. She battled back to her feet a number of times.

When the path passed a small clearing she saw she was beside a heavy outgrowth of honeysuckle. Her breath coming in painful, uneven gasps, she rolled to the side of the path, hid in behind the honeysuckle vines and slept until the damp cold woke her.

Dragging herself onto her aching legs in the shivery half-light before dawn, cursing her satchel, she staggered off along the path again. Gradually the feeling came back to her calf muscles. As soon as she could walk properly again she experimented with a gentle trot, concentrating, forcing her breathing to keep time until the stiffness was worked out of her muscles and she was moving smoothly again.

She kept a steady pace until she came to a road. Dawn was pinking the sky, but there was no traffic that she could hear. Just the same, she checked carefully before she slid down the grassy slope to the roadside ditch. Jay was pleased to see the ditch was deep enough to keep her hidden from the road if she stayed down. She flattened herself when she heard a motor. Sure she hadn't been seen by a single person so far, she didn't want to make a mistake at that stage.

Cursing the weight and awkwardness of the satchel, she crawled along the ditch until she found a gorse bush overhanging the ditch so thickly that she was sure she would be completely hidden under it.

By picking handsful of the dry grass along the sides of the ditch, Jay was able to make a comfortable nest in the sand under the gorse. She had some nasty things to say about gorse thorns until she had her nest cleared of them. She brushed her tracks from the floor of the ditch as best she could, then crawled into her nest. The sun was fully up, the traffic was heavy and it was time to be out of sight.

She covered herself with the doll blankets, which only worked when she was curled up, wriggled until the nest was comfortable, ate a chunk of cold roast beef and an apple and slept for hours.

Jay woke in the middle of the day, her legs cramped and aching. She stretched them to ease them and looked around her little hidey-hole to see what she could do about the problem of relieving herself. It had been no problem in the forest, but beside the road she was afraid of leaving a trail and afraid of being seen.

When she was sure there were no cars around she scooped a hole in the sand on one side of the ditch, making sure she stayed low. When her foot prints had been swept from the sand with a gorse branch, her main problem was thirst. Not daring to climb out of the ditch in broad daylight, she curled back up in her nest, ate another apple and went back to sleep cuddling her doll, 'Shirley'.

Once it was dark she dared to leave her ditch, dash across the road and start crossing farms in an effort to reach the sea. She had no idea where Inch Brae was or how far away, but she knew from the position of White Island which direction it had to be in. She reckoned if she went along the coast eventually she had to come to the beach she had played on when she'd lived with the McLeans. She knew her way from there to Inch Brae.

Traveling at night and hiding during the day, she lost track of how many days she had been on the run. She bathed in cow troughs by moonlight, stole food from farms if she could get to it without setting dogs barking and slept in hay-sheds when it rained.

Built up areas frightened her. There were too many people in them and not enough places to hide. Just the same, it was in a township that she had her biggest laugh. She saw a newspaper when she was stealing milk from someone's doorstep before dawn. Crouching down behind their hedge so that she wouldn't be seen from the street she read by the light over their door about the search for herself. Knowing that the search was concentrated where her parents lived not only made her laugh, it put her mind at ease. They were nowhere near to catching her.

She put the paper back, laid the milk bottle down so that it looked as if a cat had got at it, then crept into their garden shed. She slept on sacking up in the rafters, though she hated being caught by the dawn before she could get away from the houses. The problem was that it was always nearly dawn before the milkmen delivered to the houses and milk was so filling it was impossible to resist.

The next night she trotted off back to the beach, making a meal of raw pipis when the tide went out and running unconcerned along the sand at low tide because she knew the returning tide would take her foot prints. All she had to do was make sure she didn't leave any footprints on the soft sand when she left the beach. As soon as she saw wheel tracks along the beach she ran along them. Although she didn't want to leave the ease of running along the hard packed sand so early, she didn't dare pass up the chance to hide her prints because she had no way of knowing how far she would have to run before she got another chance. If dawn came first she would be left with a choice of being caught out in the open or leaving footprints in the sand.

It turned out to be a good choice to follow the wheel tracks. They led past a school. Jay loved schools. Schoolyards were goldmines of discarded food. She found apples, oranges, sandwiches and, wonder of wonders! the truck had already left the school milk in the milk stand. Jay found enough food to put some in her satchel and to stuff herself right then. She didn't think she'd felt full since she'd first run away. She showered in the showers on the sports field, glad some careless person had dropped their soap. She also hadn't felt clean since she'd run away.

There was a foresty part beside the school, so she headed in there to be hidden by the time people arrived for school. The school was deserted early enough that she dared to go back to it to raid again and shower again before she set off through the woods. Because the trees hid her she dared to travel before it was fully dark, padding along paths listening carefully for any sound that didn't belong to the forest. The slightest thing sent her ducking out of sight.

She much preferred running along the beach when the tide was low at night, so off she headed to do just that. The beach looked familiar. She stalled, not sure in the darkness. It didn't matter as much if anyone saw her, she didn't think there was time for them to find her before she got to Inch Brae. She stretched out on the soft sand of the dunes until it was light enough for her to be sure of where she was.

Jay didn't bother to hide in the daylight, but ran excitedly along the roads until she came to the dirt road that ran along Inch Brae's fence. Unable to bear waiting until she got to the front gate to touch the soil of home again, she climbed the fence and rolled in the grass in sheer joy.

While she ran across familiar paddocks she half formed a vision of how pleased Bruce and Sharon would be to see her again. They would take her in and give her her old room back. Pete and Margaret would come over from McGregor's. Together they would find a way to get the other three children home with them.

'Wonder if Gahsie and Paddy would come home once everyone else was here? We'd all be so happy!'

A rather bedraggled Jay slowed to a rambling walk, drawing near the cottage on her way to the house. She drank in the sights and sounds of autumn. New mown hay in the next paddock. The one she was in all tall and sweet smelling and brown, ready to be mown as soon as they got to it. The big red balers huffing and chugging across the tedded lines of hay, spitting bales out their back ends to leave tidy rows of rectangles at attention behind them. The rolling countryside hid the machines from her now and then, but she could hear tractors tedding hay behind the pine windbreak.

'The pines are taller here than anywhere,' she thought, looking around in satisfaction. She saw black and white cows as she crested a hill. She stopped, puzzled, to make sure they were on Bruce's land, not McKenzie's. 'Friesians? Where're Pete's jerseys?' Try as she might, she could not see one small brown cow, only those great tall black and white ones.

Slightly uneasy, she set off for the cottage, sure it would be empty. It was obvious Bruce and Sharon would have taken over the farmhouse once they were the sole occupants of the farm. She planned to hide out in the empty cottage for a bit until she knew what was happening on the farm. If the water and electricity were still hooked up she planned to clean up before anyone saw her.

But the cottage was still occupied. Mown grass. Flower beds. Stack of firewood.

No one answered her knocks or calls. 'Maybe the share-milker lives in the cottage. Why wouldn't he live at Inch Brae with them? There'd be more than enough room. Maybe it's a married share-milker. Could even be cousin Gary, or Pete. Maybe Pete and Margaret live here and they swapped houses with Bruce and Sharon. Well, Pete and Margaret wouldn't mind if I used their bathroom.'

Jay wandered through the cottage. Bruce's and Sharon's things. Their wedding photo on the wall with Xantha and Malcolm's photo and Pete and Margaret's photo. Sally and Pam had been flower girls. Jay felt sick. If she'd still been at home she would have been a flower girl too.

Photo of Davie. Bigger than she'd seen him. Photo of all of Xantha's girls. They'd grown too. Oh, what Jay would give to see Sally Murphy again. Photo of the three Eastons. They hadn't grown. It was as if they had been frozen while life here went on without them. A hard lump filled Jay's throat. There was a photo of another baby. Sharon's? Xantha's?

Suddenly she felt alien. As if she didn't belong. What would Sharon say if she found Jay in her house uninvited? She looked out into the back garden. Vegetables. Pete's hammock. A sandpit with baby toys strewn around it.

Panicked, Jay ran out the front door, out the garden gate. She looked as far as she could in every direction for Sharon. Nothing. Just the rented baler and its crew relentlessly circling the paddock. She whistled Fleabag. A far off bark. Was it an answer or a different dog? Maybe McKenzie's dog.

She ran to the wheel track to look towards the cowshed and was thunderstruck to see the familiar, loved wooden shed half torn away into a pathetic heap of ancient timbers. Half built was one of those flashy new-style herring-bone milking sheds, all stainless steel and galvanized piping.

Jay backed away. Her Inch Brae was violated. She turned towards the house and trudged up the track she remembered so fondly. At least everything still looked the same there.

'If Bruce and Sharon still live in the cottage, who's in Inch Brae? It could only be Gahsie. And Pete and Margaret must have moved here from her Dad's. They couldn't stay away. McLeans have been in this old house too long to just leave it like that.'

She ran the rest of the way to the home paddock, climbed over the gate and ran to the kitchen door. The garden looked overgrown. The hen house seemed oddly quiet. The kitchen door was stuck, the nursery door shut. No cats. Odd.

She ran around to the front.

And stalled.

The grass was long, unkept. The flower beds untended.

Alphie's old stake still stood where it had been when they left for school on the last day. What had happened to Misty? She must have been put with the other sheep that very morning if the stake was never moved. They had told her over the phone that Misty was doing well, that's all. Jay stared at the stake, seeing Pete make it and put it in the ground for the first time when Alphie was tiny. Moving it each time the circle of grass was eaten down. Explaining to her that Alphie was too big to be a pet any more when he was strong enough to pull the stake out of the ground by himself.

With dragging feet Jay wandered over to the stake, wrapped her arms around it and sank to the ground.

She turned ever so slowly to look at Inch Brae.

'Why must the wind groan in empty houses? Aren't they lonely enough without that?'

There were boards across the glass doors from the veranda to the front room. Boards!

There were pine needles and twigs on the steps of the veranda. The bamboo shades were gone. Pete's hammock was gone. The rocking chairs were gone.

She couldn't bear to walk across the lawn onto the veranda to peek in the front room windows. She didn't want to know what the room would look like without its beautiful old things. The doilies. The cut glass. The piano. Poppa's armchair.

Poppa.

The tears that had kept themselves from her ever since the morning she had stood in the doorway and looked at his body finally stung her eyelids.

She tried to focus through a film of water.

There was Poppa's window. No curtains, it stared back at her unflinchingly, a lidless, hollow eye.

Quickly to the right, quickly. The window of Gahsie's room. The totara tree in front of it. The windows and boarded up front room doors behind the neglected veranda. Paddy's window. Her own window. The wide sill she used to sit on and dream. Her morning log under the tree line. It was covered in moss where once her rear had worn the moss off.

She was unable to get up and look at the back of the house. She knew there were no hens in the hen house.

She remembered the baby bunnies. The kitchen garden. Paddy working in the garden, her pants rolled up above her ankles, the kitchen window open and the radio on the window sill asking "How Much is that Doggie in the Window?" Paddy hoeing in time to the music.

The bushes she'd hidden sheets behind in a previous life, a thousand years ago at least. Now that she'd been jerked back to the cold, dark, endless stretches of time her life dragged her through, she could almost understand why she'd done that. She was different now, though. Even being back with her parents hadn't made her back into the way she was. She was glad of that.

The twenty months Jay had lived at Inch Brae glowed in her mind, shining with a deep lustre, with no brittleness or cheapness or impurities. But the memories of this place were utterly isolated from her real life like a bead; a single bead of gold, shimmering and glowing as if it had not hardened or cooled.

Remembering the evening that Jay had sat on the veranda while Gahsie told her about wasting time, she tried to find a way that Inch Brae would never be wasted. If she couldn't get it back or keep it going, she had to make sure it wasn't wasted. Somehow she had to be like Paddy and Gahsie, not like her parents.

She thought about the comfort of sitting in Gahsie's lap on the very first morning and rocked herself, wondering what had happened to the kitchen sofa. And the Shirley Temple books. She hoped Sally Murphy had them and that she loved them.

Jay turned back to the stake, tightened her hug of it, leaned her forehead against the weathered wood and wished she could cry.

The Inch Brae she loved didn't exist anymore.

Maybe it never had.

If she couldn't go back, what was forward?

Someone would find her.

They'd return her like a strayed dog.

The welfare workers would ask stupid questions.

Her parents would rage.

The welfare workers would make soothing noises.

The judge would leave her with her parents with no one to make her safe.

She wasn't safe anywhere in the world.

She rolled onto her back and looked up the height of the pines that had marched past the house for a hundred years. She would be safe if she really could fly up there. The birds wheeled around the tips. How free they looked, how uncaring for beings that lived only a year or so. How permanent the trees looked. They'd already been old when Gahsie was born.

Jay pretended she still lived here. She could climb those trees, they were hers. She and Joe could sit in them in a storm and ride them like bucking horses. The time she had gone to the tree tops when Pete and Bruce had shot the rabbit. The storm that broke that branch over there. Gahsie, panicked, ordering her down through flying twigs and needles.

Gahsie's gentle voice, her rocking, stroking, sewing, cooking.

Paddy who was stern and soft at the same time. Paddy, who cared for them all and for Poppa.

Oh, Poppa. Oh, Poppa.

Then she cried. Howled and sobbed and wailed and beat the ground with her fists.

Fleabag slunk through the grass, puzzled and worried. He lay close beside her, whining softly. Licked her face. She clung to him, buried her face in his rough, bristly neck and waited.

If You Wish

When Jay came of age, one of her high school girl-friends got a job in the records department of the offices of the court. At the risk of losing her job, Jay's friend got a copy of the court records so Jay could find out how the Easton children came to be taken from Inch Brae.

The records showed that the regular judge was on holiday, and the replacement, in his infinite wisdom, had decided that the young, unmarried, foster mother would in all likelihood lose interest in the children once the one thing that had kept her anchored, the care of her invalid father, no longer tied her down.

He felt the children would be adversely affected by being forced to live in a house wherein they had witnessed a death. He thought it was obvious that small children needed their mother at such a time. All those factors led him to believe there was good reason to reconsider the custody of the children, despite the fact that the current appearance before him had been intended merely to study whether or not the parents should still be denied unsupervised visits. The circumstances had changed enough that the whole situation needed reviewing.

To start with he could see no reason for the children to be so far from their parents. He couldn't imagine why the judge who had handled the case up to that point had put the children at such a distance that it caused the parents unnecessary difficulty to see them.

In his opinion Mrs Easton's devotion to her children had been amply proven by the fact that she did travel all that way to see her children every chance she got. She had also shown genuine concern for her children's well-being by bringing to the court's attention on two different occasions that the children's innocence was not respected and that they were used as free farm labour. They had been known to be kept out until after midnight in bitterly cold weather delivering calves at only seven years of age; they chopped wood; they were up to see the cows taken to milking at 4:30 am, yet expected to do a heavy load of work both before and after school. Ill health did not spare them their work; the boy was known to have been taken from his sick bed to tend the fire. When the youngest child was not yet three years of age she was tending the invalid father, who was known to be incontinent. From the age of six the children were carrying heavy pails of eggs and milk, being refused their meals until their work was done. They even protested that their parent's visits on weekends interrupted their work.

The welfare workers' objections didn't overcome the evidence the judge had that the Easton children had been removed too hastily from their parents twenty months before. Considering the parents had steadfastly demonstrated their real and deep concern for their children's wellbeing ever since, the courts felt that the children would benefit most by being returned to their parents immediately, while a study was carried out to see whether or not they should be left there.

The Mcleans.

Sally McLean, 'Gahsie,' took care of Xantha's four girls for some years, eventually returning to Inch Brae to live in the new, modern farm house Bruce and Sharon built. She died in her sleep in her eighties and was buried beside her husband in the gravesite high on the hill overlooking the Pacific Ocean.

Xantha Murphy worked in her capacity as a teacher to make changes in the way the schools dealt with children having problems at home, so that children like the Eastons could be helped by school counsellors. Before the 1950s what happened in a child's home was not the concern of the schools. Now schools do the best they can to help the children of malfunctioning families.

Bruce and Sharon modernized Inch Brae, running it as town milk supply with the help of share-milkers who lived in succession in the share-milker's cottage.

Pete and Margaret farmed McGregor's farm in the traditional way of mixed farming and butter supply, having it for their own when Mr McGregor died.

Paddy became a relentless lobbier for children's rights. She married an environmental activist in the sixties and they have two children, a boy and a girl. As an adult Jay saw Paddy again, met her husband and two children, but they didn't keep in touch.

The Eastens.

Ursula and Harold Easton divorced. He later died so alone and disliked that his body wasn't found for days. All of Mrs Easton's children ran away from her at least once as children, all of them changed their names and moved away as adults, and none of them kept in touch with her on a regular basis. Not only were her children not around her, they were in foreign countries and had children she never knew about.

When she was very old and dying, Jay and her son went to New Zealand, paid off her mortgage, and allowed her to move. Having alienated everyone around her, she finally took up Alexander's offer to move to Australia, though he wouldn't have her live with him. She died in a few months.

Jay and Joe ran away together when she was returned to her parents after her trek back to Inch Brae. They were not returned to their parents when they were found, but were placed together in another 'permanent' foster home. They were loved and happy there until Jay was fourteen, their mother continuing the same type of agitation in the courts against the foster parents that she had learned when the children were at Inch Brae. Aside from the times they were back with their mother they didn't live with their brother or sister again.

Jay married in her teens and had a mixed bag of adopted, fostered, and natural children. Though she and her husband later divorced, they continued to work together.

Now that they are grown, most of her foster children keep in touch, giving her a healthy crowd of foster grandchildren and great grandchildren. She keeps in touch with her ex-husband, who helped raise the crowds of kids, causing Christmases and birthdays to be massive affairs, with his children and grandchildren as well as theirs and spares. She was engaged to be married again, but the man died of a heart attack and she remained alone for some years. She has found a companion in her old age.

Joe was in trouble with the law in his teens and spent some time in a psychiatric centre, and some time in a juvenile detention centre. He spent time in a hippy commune in Western Australia in the early seventies and had a daughter. When the mother went to put the child up for adoption, he moved in and took her. They went to England where he met a lady and had a son, but they broke up. He met another lady and had another son, but she suffered from Post-Partum depression and the baby wasn't safe with her. Once again Joe moved in and took the child. He went back to Australia and raised his son and his daughter. He never married, but his daughter did and has a son.

Carrots left school at fourteen to have her first baby and has since had three more children and three marriages, not all to the fathers of her children. She has no recollection of the time at Inch Brae or the nick name. Her eldest son was taken from her and put up for adoption, later finding her when he'd turned 18. He eldest daughter was taken from her and fostered. The younger two children were raised by her, but she followed her mother's patterns and they have since cut their ties with her.

Alexander only ran away from home once, when he was fourteen. The next time his family heard from him he was 21 with a completely different name. He earned a good living in the music industry. He has a son, in New Zealand with his mother, and two daughters in Australia with their mother, who he married. They later divorced and he lived in England for some years, returning to Australia to be near his children. After his mother died he married again taking on step-children with his wife.